Finding Father Christmas | Engaging Father Christmas

Books by Robin Jones Gunn

Finding Father Christmas
Engaging Father Christmas
Kissing Father Christmas

TWO NOVELS IN ONE BOOK

ROBIN JONES GUNN

New York Boston Nashville

Cover design by JuLee Brand
Cover Illustration by Mark Stutzman

FaithWords
Hachette Book Group
1290 Avenue of the Americas
New York, NY 10104
www.faithwords.com
twitter.com/faithwords

First Omnibus Edition: September 2016

FaithWords is a division of Hachette Book Group, Inc.
The FaithWords name and logo are trademarks of Hachette Book Group, Inc.

Additional *Finding Father Christmas* credits:

With thanks to R. W. Crump and Louisiana State University Press for their work on *The Complete Poems of Christina Rossetti*, volume one of which includes the text of "A Christmas Carol," here quoted as "My Gift."

Print book interior design by Fearn Cutler de Vicq.

Additional *Engaging Father Christmas* credits:

Print book interior design by Fearn Cutler de Vicq.

LCCN: 2016946164

ISBNs: 978-1-4555-6594-8 (trade paperback), 978-1-4555-6595-5 (ebook)

Printed in the United States of America

RRD-C

10 9 8 7 6 5 4 3 2 1

Rachel and Stephanie, you made our research jaunt to London an absolute delight.

Trish and Libby, you saw the Hallmark Christmas movie story hidden on these pages and worked tirelessly for five years to make it happen. My heart is deeply grateful.

Janet, you are the best agent in the world. Peace and grace reside in you.

Acknowledgments

A round of warm thank-yous to my British friends: Penny and Anna Culliford, who showed me the Kent countryside and introduced me to English pudding; Marion Stroud, who opened to me her heart and home and gave valuable feedback for the story; and Heather Thomas, who recognized the Christina Rossetti Christmas poem when she read the first draft of this manuscript—and then sang the poem for me as she did when she was a child. A forever thank you to my husband, Ross Gunn III; to my agent, Janet Kobobel Grant; and to my blue-beach-chair sister, Anne deGraaf. Each of you infused this little book with your encouragement and support. Many thanks to Rolf Zettersten, Chip MacGregor, Christina Boys, and Becky Hughes.

Finding FATHER CHRISTMAS

ENGAGING *Father Christmas*

Finding Father Christmas

"Come in! Come in, and know me better."

—Spirit of Christmas Present
from *A Christmas Carol* by Charles Dickens

Chapter One

A string of merry silver bells jumped and jingled as the north wind shook the evergreen wreath on the heavy wooden door. Overhead a painted shingle swung from two metal arms, declaring this place of business to be the Tea Cosy.

As I peered inside through the thick-paned window, I could see a cheerful amber fire in the hearth. Tables were set for two with china cups neatly positioned on crimson tablecloths. Swags of green foliage trimmed the mantel. Dotted across the room, on the tables and on shelves, were a dozen red votive candles. Each tiny light flickered, sending out promises of warmth and cheer, inviting me to step inside.

Another more determined gust made a swoop down the lane, this time taking my breath with it into the darkness of the December night.

This trip was a mistake. A huge mistake. What was I thinking?

I knew the answer as it rode off on the mocking wind. The answer was, I wasn't thinking. I was feeling.

Pure emotion last Friday nudged me to book the round-trip ticket to London. Blind passion convinced me that the answer to my twenty-year question would be revealed once I reached the Carlton Photography Studio on Bexley Lane.

Sadly, I was wrong. I had come all this way only to hit a dead end.

I took another look inside the teahouse and told myself to keep walking, back to the train station, back to the hotel in London where I had left my luggage. This exercise in futility was over. I might as well change my ticket and fly back to San Francisco in the morning.

My chilled and weary feet refused to obey. They wanted to go inside and be warmed by the fire. I couldn't deny that my poor legs did deserve a little kindness after all I had put them through when I folded them into the last seat in coach class. The middle seat, by the lavatories, in the row that didn't recline. A cup of tea at a moment like this might be the only blissful memory I would take with me from this fiasco.

Reaching for the oddly shaped metal latch on the door, I stepped inside and set the silver bells jingling again.

"Come in, come in, and know me better, friend!" The unexpected greeting came from a kilt-wearing man with a valiant face. His profoundly wide sideburns had the look of white lamb's wool and softened the resoluteness in his jaw. "Have you brought the snowflakes with you, then?"

"The snowflakes?" I repeated.

"Aye! The snowflakes. It's cold enough for snow, wouldn't you say?"

I nodded my reluctant agreement, feeling my nose and cheeks going rosy in the small room's warmth. I assumed the gentleman who opened the door was the proprietor. Looking around, I asked, "Is it okay if I take the table by the fire? All I'd like is a cup of tea."

"I don't see why not. Katharine!" He waited for a response and then tried again. "Katharine!"

No answer came.

"She must have gone upstairs. She'll be back around." His grin was engaging, his eyes clear. "I would put the kettle on for you myself, if it weren't for the case of my being on my way out at the moment."

"That's okay. I don't mind waiting."

"Of course you don't mind waiting. A young woman such as yourself has the time to wait, do you not? Whereas, for a person such as myself . . ." He leaned closer and with a wink confided in me, "I'm Christmas Present, you see. I can't wait."

What sort of "present" he supposed himself to be and to whom, I wasn't sure.

With a nod, the man drew back the heavy door and strode into the frosty air.

From a set of narrow stairs a striking woman descended. She looked as surprised at my appearance as I was at hers. She wore a stunning red, floor-length evening dress. Around her neck hung a sparkling silver necklace, and dangling from under her dark hair were matching silver earrings. She stood tall with careful posture and tilted her head, waiting for me to speak.

"I wasn't sure if you were still open."

"Yes, on an ordinary day we would be open for another little while, until five thirty. . . ." Her voice drifted off.

"Five thirty," I repeated, checking my watch. The time read 11:58. The exact time I'd adjusted it to when I had deplaned at Heathrow Airport late that morning. I tapped on the face of my watch as if that would make it run again. "I can see you have plans for the evening and that you're ready to close. I'll just—"

"Che-che-che." The sound that came from her was the sort used to call a squirrel to come find the peanuts left for it on a park bench. It wasn't a real word from a real language, but I understood the meaning. I was being invited to stay and not to run off.

"Take any seat you want. Would you like a scone with your tea or perhaps some rum cake?"

"Just the tea, thank you."

I moved toward the fire and realized that a scone sounded pretty good. I hadn't eaten anything since the undercooked breakfast omelet served on the plane.

"Actually, I would like to have a scone, too. If it's not too much trouble."

"No trouble at all."

Her smile was tender, motherly. I guessed her to be in her midfifties or maybe older. She turned without any corners or edges to her motions. I soon heard the clinking of dishes as she prepared the necessary items in the kitchen.

Making my way to a steady looking table by the fire, I tried to tuck my large shoulder bag under the spindle leg of the chair. The stones along the front of the hearth were permanently blackened from what I imagined to be centuries of soot. The charm of the room increased as I sat down and felt the coziness of the close quarters. This was a place of serenity. A place where trust between friends had been established and kept for many years.

A sense of safety and comfort called to the deepest part of

my spirit and begged me to set free a fountain of tears. But I capped them off. It was that same wellspring of emotion that had instigated this journey.

Settling back, I blinked and let the steady heat from the fire warm me. Katharine returned carrying a tray. The steaming pot of tea took center stage, wearing a chintzquilted dressing gown, gathered at the top.

Even the china teapots are treated to coziness here.

"I've warmed two scones for you, and this, of course, is your clotted cream. I've given you raspberry jam, but if you would prefer strawberry, I do have some."

"No, this is fine. Perfect. Thank you."

Katharine lifted the festooned teapot and poured the steaming liquid into my waiting china cup. I felt for a moment as if I had stumbled into an odd sort of parallel world to Narnia.

As a young child I had read C. S. Lewis's Narnia tales a number of times. In the many hours alone, I had played out the fairy tales in my imagination, pretending I was Lucy, stepping through the wardrobe into an imaginary world.

Here, in the real country of Narnia's author, I considered how similar my surroundings were to Lewis's descriptions of that imaginary world. A warming fire welcomed me in from the cold. But instead of a fawn inviting me to tea, it had been a kilted clansman. Instead of Mrs. Beaver pouring a cup of cheer for me by the fire, it was a tall, unhurried woman in a red evening gown.

An unwelcome thought came and settled on me as clearly as if I had heard a whisper. *Miranda, how much longer will you believe it is "always winter and never Christmas"?*

Chapter Two

I ignored the mysterious whisper that had caught me off guard and quickly took a sip of the steaming tea.

"Very nice." I nodded to Katharine, who still stood near the table as if waiting for my next request.

"Did you come to Carlton Heath for Christmas?" Her voice was soothing.

"Yes. Well, no. Not for Christmas. I'm just . . . I was trying to find . . . I'm . . ."

"Just visiting?" she finished for me.

"Yes. Just visiting."

Now that I was inside the teahouse, I felt much less intimidated by the reason for my journey than I had when I stood alone outside. With my guard down, I looked up at gentle Katharine and said, "May I ask you a question?"

"Certainly."

"I was trying to find the Carlton Heath Photography Studio on Bexley Lane. I walked up and down both sides of the street as far as I could go, but I didn't find it. Do you know where it is?"

She shook her head.

"I have the name printed on the back of a photo." I lifted from my big purse the plastic sandwich bag in which I'd carefully placed the photograph. I handled it cautiously. That single photo was the precious piece of evidence that had driven me here to Carlton Heath on a whim after a very long time of indecision. Removing the wallet-sized photo from the clear bag, I turned the picture over, pointing to the name stamped on the paper: "Carlton Photography Studio, Bexley Lane, Carlton Heath." I handed the photo to Katharine carefully.

She looked mystified. "This is the only Bexley Lane in Carlton Heath. I don't know of any photography studios along the road. Perhaps they went out of business."

"That's what I was afraid of."

As she tilted her head, her silver earrings caught the light from the fire. "If they were in business here, I'm sure someone around town would know about them. I've only lived in Carlton Heath for a few years, so I'm not too helpful when it comes to the comings and goings of the past. My husband would know."

She paused before turning over the photo and asked, "Would you mind if I had a look at the picture?"

"No. Please do. And tell me if you recognize either of the people in the photo. I was hoping someone at the photo studio might have an idea who they were."

The image she gazed at was ingrained in my memory. I had stared at the photo so long in my adolescent years that every detail of the two people was familiar, including the nasty, faded green shade of the sweater the little boy was wearing. He appeared to be four or maybe five years old and was seated precariously on the lap of a man who was dressed in an odd-looking Santa suit. The boy was wailing, mouth open wide, head tipped back. His short arms were rigid at his side as if he was being a brave little soldier about the situation, but he wasn't too afraid to let his voice be heard.

I knew every line in the face of the man who was playing Santa Claus. His outfit resembled a Bohemian-style dressing robe rather than the usual red velvet Santa suit. Nor was his red cap typical Santa attire. Instead, it rose to a point before tipping to the side, and it was trimmed sparingly in black piping rather than the customary wide band of white fleece.

The whiteness in the photo was found in the man's long, flowing beard and in his thick eyebrows. He seemed to be trying to keep a straight face, yet his eyes merrily revealed his mirth as well as his age. The exposed laugh lines around his clear blue eyes put him past fifty, by my estimation. His large left hand, visible around the boy's middle, displayed a gold ring on the third finger and the edge of a gold watchband around his wrist.

"What a charmer," Katharine said as she looked at the photo. A smile grew on her lips.

I nodded. The photo couldn't help but bring a smile to any viewer.

"Curious," she said, tilting her head. "I believe I've seen this picture before."

My heart rose to meet the sip of hot tea I had just swallowed. I put the cup back in the saucer, not completely on target, and kept my eyes fixed on Katharine. "You have? Here in Carlton Heath? Do you remember where?"

"No. I'm not sure. I do remember the photo was in a frame, though. An ornate frame. It was lovely. I can't quite remember where I saw it."

I waited eagerly as she stared again at the photo and pursed her lips.

After a full minute she said, "I have a suggestion."

"Yes?"

"I'm not able to place where I've seen this photo, but someone in town might know. Others who have lived here longer than I have would also know about the photography studio. One of them might possibly recognize the man or the boy in the photo, as well."

"Whom should I ask?"

"Several residents, actually. My husband, for one. He and the others will be at the performance this evening. Why don't you come with me?"

"The performance?" I repeated.

"Yes, the Dickens play, *A Christmas Carol.* I should warn you, though, it's a rather wry version. But the resident thespians have kept up the tradition for more than forty years. Mind you, the play is an abbreviation of the original, and the adaptation of the characters is, shall we say, loose. But it is wonderfully entertaining."

I bit my lower lip and felt a sickening knot tighten in my stomach.

"Would you like to come, then?" Katharine asked. "As my guest, of course."

"I . . . I don't know."

"Ah." She handed back the photograph. "Perhaps you have plans. It is Christmas Eve, after all."

"No. I mean, yes. I do have plans. I need to get back to London. To my hotel room."

"Che-che-che. London is close enough. You won't have difficulty returning later in the evening."

I scrambled for an appropriate response while Katharine stood tall and graciously patient before me, hands folded across the front of her lovely evening dress, waiting for my reply.

"I don't have the right kind of outfit with me for the theater," I said.

She smiled. "I don't think anyone in attendance tonight would even lovingly refer to what you'll see as 'theater.' What you're wearing now is entirely appropriate. I'm dressed as I am because I've a part in the production. In the concessions, actually."

I stalled, looking down at the untouched scones on the china plate.

"Well, then," she said, easing my silence. "Perhaps I'll leave you to enjoy your tea, and you can take a moment to consider the invitation. If I can bring you anything, do ask."

As she turned to leave, I unexpectedly blurted out the reason for my indecision. "I don't go to plays."

Katharine's expression appeared unaffected by my strange declaration.

I added a little more information. "I stopped going to plays a long time ago and . . ."

The resolve that had fueled my boycott when I was nine years old now waned in the light of this room where all my logic and defenses seemed unnecessary considering my hostess's elegant grace.

". . . I don't go to plays," I finished lamely.

She stood still, a few feet away. After a pause, she spoke.

"What I have always loved about decisions is that you can make a new one whenever you like."

Then she slid behind the curtain that cordoned off the kitchen area from the half a dozen open tables covered in their crimson cloths and dotted with flickering votives. I sat alone by the comforting fire.

Yet I didn't feel entirely alone. A select convoy of early childhood memories gathered in the empty seat across from me. They rose to their full height, leaned closer, and stared at me, waiting to hear whether they still held power over my decisions.

Chapter Three

In the silence and safety of the Tea Cosy, the echo of my gloriously odd childhood bounced off the sooty hearth and returned to me.

All the memories began with my mother. She was an *actress.* Not an actor. Please. An *actress.* She introduced herself as "Eve Carson, the actress," and people responded with a hazy nod of vague familiarity. The truth was, none of them had ever heard of her.

Each summer Eve Carson, the actress, cavorted about the stage, embodying some immortal character or other at the Shakespearean theater in Ashland, Oregon. The rest of the year she packed our forest green Samsonite suitcases into the hatchback of our little blue car, and we traveled up and down the West Coast, calling on her string of theatrical connections.

In Santa Cruz, my mother went to work wearing a Renaissance costume that was sewn by a bald woman who had seven cats and no television. In San Diego, our hotel room was right next to the dinner theater where my mother sang and danced every night in a sailor suit. Performances were twice on Saturdays, and the food was plentiful, if I didn't mind eating at midnight, which, of course, I didn't.

I was a gypsy child. An only child. As such, I believed everything my mother said, including her embellished account of how, one moonlit night, she slept beside a lake on a feathery bed of moss.

"Silently, so silently, the Big Dipper tipped just enough to drop one small yet very twinkling star into the hollow of my belly. That tiny star sprouted and grew like a watermelon until . . ."

Her deep, midnight blue eyes would widen as she declared that one day, without warning, I popped right out and peacefully went to sleep in her arms.

"And that day, my darling," she would conclude in her winsome voice, as a plumpness rose in her high cheekbones, "was the happiest day of my life. You became to me the sun, the moon, the stars, and all my deepest dreams fulfilled. Never doubt the gifting of your being or the beauty of your light, my sweet Miranda."

Like a baby bird, I swallowed every juicy word that tumbled from my beautiful mother's mouth. We looked alike, with our dark hair, defined eyebrows, and slender legs. Her eyes were the deepest shade of blue before the color could be called black. My eyes, however, were the fairest shade of blue with the sort of transparency seen in a marble when held up to the sun. The lightness in my eyes and skin transferred to the feathery lightness of my logic, as well.

Until I was almost nine, I had no formed sense of reason. I was a child with delayed rational development. I didn't understand the peril of such an existence with such a woman. I didn't know a fine line existed between art and deceit. I couldn't tell when she was performing and when she was telling the truth. All of it was real to me. Every word, every smile, every tear.

My strongest memories begin with the day we drove into Ashland. The hillsides of southern Oregon were paling from green to yellow, and the hot scent of the drying grass came through the car window like a faint sweetness riding over the sticky smell of the eternal 5 Freeway's tar and asphalt.

We checked into our room at the Swan Motel on a Tuesday afternoon and ate pizza, sitting cross-legged on our bed. After that, we were living in the rhythm of her performance schedule. Every day seemed to be a Wednesday or a Thursday. It didn't matter. My mother only came back to our room to sleep for a few hours during the darkest part of the night.

Most days I would go with her to the theater, where I would find new ways to make myself invisible. For a nine-year-old I was fairly successful at my career as a phantom. When I wasn't so successful, the next day I always had a babysitter named Carlita, who brought me cookies made with pink coconut.

A few times I stayed by myself in the motel with the door bolted and the television turned up as loud as it would go. I never told anyone that my mother left me alone.

The best mornings were the ones when I would wake to the sound of water running in the shower. That meant she wasn't going to sleep for hours while I tried to stay quiet. On those mornings I would stay in bed, pretending to be asleep, and soon my mother would lean close with her long, black hair dripping tiny kisses on my face. She would say, "Awaken, my little bird! Let us fly away and dine on golden sunbeams."

Those were the mornings we crossed the street holding

hands and ate breakfast at the small café with the purple flowers by the front door. We always sat next to each other, nice and close, in the red vinyl booth. I always ordered waffles. Waffles with strawberries that came cold and mushy and tasting of freezer burn. Over the waffles and strawberries I would hold up the small jug of maple syrup and pour a spinning circle of liquid gold. The first touch of golden syrup on my tongue tasted like joy.

Eve Carson, the actress, always ordered scrambled eggs, with tomatoes instead of hash browns, and a small grapefruit juice. As the waitress walked away, I would watch my mother slip six or eight packets of sugar into her purse. She nabbed them in one smooth motion without taking her deeper-than-the-Pacific blue eyes off of me. One time she took a spoon. My mother was very good at the small things.

Whenever we were cozied up to each other like that, I didn't feel neglected or jealous of the hours she spent doting on her other love, the theater. When I felt her close, I found it easy to believe that I was to her the sun and moon and stars. I believed everything she said.

Until the day I found the blue velvet purse with the golden tassels.

Chapter Four

Before I found the purse, I found the one-eyed dragon.

If I had believed in an ordered universe at that time, I would have understood why the one came before the other. But as I mentioned before, I was young in my logic and naive in all areas of theology.

The discoveries came close to each other while we lived in Ashland. On a beastly night during the second month of our stay at the Swan Motel, our air conditioner stopped working. It was too late to ask the front desk to call a repairman. And it was too hot to sleep.

My mother told me to lie still and imagine I was a snowflake, floating on an iceberg in Alaska. I tried, but it didn't work. My Method acting skills were sadly lacking.

"Then come with me, my little fish," she said. "We shall go for a swim."

"Now?"

"Yes, now."

I followed my mother down the stairs, both of us in our thin, cotton pajamas. The motel pool was small and separated from the parking lot by a chain-link fence lined with sheets of hard green plastic. All the outside lights of the Swan Motel glowed with a pale weariness as if they were too hot to shine their brightest and had turned themselves to dim.

"It's still hot out here," I whispered.

"Yes, it is," she murmured in the stillness. "Hot as dragons' breath."

My mother lifted the latch on the gate that led into the pool area. She walked right in as if the "Pool Closed After 9 PM" sign applied to everyone but us.

"They'll be looking for a cool watering hole this night." She dipped her foot into the shallow end. "When they come, you will allow the dragons to drink as much as they like, undisturbed, won't you?"

I nodded.

"Your movements in the water must produce only the tiniest of ripples."

I nodded again and lowered my thin legs into the water.

That's when I saw him. The one-eyed dragon.

In the darkness of the still waters, the smoldering light under the diving board appeared to be the half-opened yellow eye of a camouflaged dragon gazing back at us.

A shiver raced up my torso.

Ignoring the dragon, my mother demurely slipped her slender frame all the way under the water, submerging with barely a sound. I watched as her oversized pajama top billowed around her like a jellyfish.

Bravely lowering myself into the water only up to my neck, I kept a watchful eye on the dragon in the deep end of the pool.

He did not move. Neither did I.

The gap between us remained a flat distance of undisturbed, watery space.

My mother swam about freely, silently. I bobbed and blinked only when I had to. Then she motioned for me to follow as she slipped out of the pool.

We trotted as quickly as we could back to our room.

With a finger to her lips, she said, "We must hurry before one of them follows us into our room. Dragons are drawn in by the scent of chlorine."

She silently slid the key into the door and jiggled it once, twice, three times.

"Hurry!" my tiny voice begged. The legs of my cotton pajamas clung to me as the dripping pool water puddled at our doorstep, leaving more traceable chlorine with every drop.

"Open!" my mother commanded the doorknob. Suddenly the key worked. We pressed through together as I stifled my squeals.

My mother quickly shut the door, locked it, bolted it with the chain, and motioned for me to cautiously peek out the front window behind the closed curtain. I squinted at the submerged yellow eye that hadn't moved from the pool's deep end. We stood together, barely breathing in the darkness, reeking of chlorine. My heart raced deliciously.

A few days later I was in our motel room alone, waiting for Carlita to arrive. I had planted myself in a chair beside the window and was watching a girl in a flowered bathing suit as she squealed and splashed in the pool.

I wasn't on a vacation like she was. I lived there at the Swan Motel, and I knew all about the yellow-eyed dragon that came out on sweltering nights and breathed his fiery breath across the pool water. I wondered if I should tell her.

The blithe girl scrambled up on her father's shoulders, plugged her nose, and did a clumsy free-fall dive into the deep end. She did it again. And again. She had no fear.

I wanted to do that. I wanted to gallop down to the pool and join them. I wanted to be the next one to dive off the shoulders of the laughing girl's strong father into the pool. I wanted what she had.

Hurrying to put on my bathing suit, I returned to the chair by the window. As soon as Carlita arrived, I would convince her to take me down to the pool. I would finagle my way into the father-daughter diving contest somehow. Once I did, I would be the best diver of all. The girl's father would cheer the loudest for me.

Then something inside me said no. That would never be so.

The man in the pool was her father. He was not my father. He would always cheer the loudest for her. No father would ever cheer the loudest for me.

That was the first time I realized what a gift a father was. And I hadn't been given such a gift.

Carlita came puffing up the motel steps and bustled into the room, wheezing with apologies for her delay.

"I want a father," I said.

Carlita chuckled. "Most girls your age want a pony."

"Well, I don't want a pony. I want a father." I stood up and put my hands on my hips, imitating my mother's extended chin gesture just so Carlita would know I wasn't making a childish request.

"You have a father." She set down her small bag of groceries.

"I do not."

"Yes, you do. Everyone has a father. Every person who has ever been born has a father. A father and a mother. It takes the two for you to be born."

I scowled at her. Carlita had no magic in her words the way my mother did.

In a more instructive tone she said, "This does not mean that every child gets to live with both her father and her mother. But you do have both. Everyone has both. You have a father, Miranda."

"Then where is he?" My voice was still defiant but diminished.

"Your father is somewhere. I don't know. Maybe he is dead. It does not matter. You have a mother who loves you and cares enough for you. You should be grateful. Now sit down. I have brought you some cookies."

That night, when my mother slid into bed next to me, I pretended to be asleep. When she was making the soft, sighing sounds of sleep, I rolled over and whispered to her, "Do I have a father?"

"Hmmm?"

I had often heard her carry on conversations in her sleep. Sometimes the half sentences were lines from one of her performances. Other times she twisted her neck and yelled at people with a muffled fierceness I never heard in her waking hours. My plan was to make her respond to me while those mesmerizing eyes of hers were shut.

I wanted to know the truth, so I tried to sound like an adult. "Eve Carson, the actress, does your daughter, Miranda, have a father?"

What proceeded to roll off my mother's naked lips was

the familiar litany of the moonlight and the moss and me, the watermelon that popped out.

Her answer was acceptable to me. Under careful examination she hadn't changed her story. Clearly, I didn't have a father. Carlita was wrong. She didn't know everything the way my mother did, and I would tell Carlita that the next time she came.

But Carlita didn't come the next time.

Instead, her teenage daughter, Angela, came. When Angela arrived, I had discovered a splinter in the palm of my hand, but all the pinching and biting I tried did nothing to bring it to the surface. Angela made me go look for a sewing kit so she could use the needle to remove the splinter.

"Your mother must have a little sewing kit somewhere," she prodded. "Every mother does. Look in all the drawers."

I dutifully scoured our sparse belongings and made a discovery. The bottom lining of my mother's green Samsonite suitcase was loose. It could be removed. Under the flat panel I saw for the first time the blue velvet purse with the golden tassels.

"Is that a sewing kit?" Angela asked.

"I don't know."

"Well, open it!"

I lifted the top flap of the purse. The smooth fabric was folded over like an envelope. I carefully shook the contents onto the bed. The inventory included a folded-up playbill of a production of Shakespeare's *The Tempest* with my mother's name next to the character "Miranda." Also inside was a certificate with a raised emblem in the corner and a wallet-sized photograph of a wailing young boy in an awful green sweater sitting on the lap of a bemused, wizard-looking Santa Claus.

Without a blink, Angela picked up the paper with the raised emblem. She took one look at it and repeated the same truth her mother had told me. The truth that my own mother had successfully kept hidden from me.

I did indeed have a father.

I had a birth certificate that came from a hospital, and even I knew that papers with raised seals on them had to tell the truth. The paper had a name written in on the line above the word "Father." The name was Jay Ames. He was real, my father. And my mother had kept him from me.

That day I vowed I would never go to another play. It was the only way I could think of to get back at Eve Carson, the actress, for all her lies, all her grand performances, all her many worlds of make-believe.

I denounced fables and fairy tales. Every mythical creature she had ever introduced me to ceased to exist. The tooth fairy, the Easter bunny, and especially Santa Claus.

The only fable I still believed in was the yellow-eyed dragon that drank from our motel pool on scorching nights. I had *seen* him.

In place of my imaginary friends, I secretly began to believe in my father. I believed he must be somewhere on this earth, lying in wait, with one eye open, wondering about me the way I wondered about him.

Chapter Five

"More tea?"

The question from Katharine reached into the depths where I had gone in my memories and carried me back up to the present and to England and to this place of comfort and serenity.

"I've brought some hot water." Katharine placed a white ceramic teapot on the table. "I can bring fresh tea, if you like. If you wish only to warm up the pot you have, you can add the hot water. The tea leaves might have made the tea too strong by now."

"Okay. Thank you."

She didn't step away.

"The scones are very good, by the way."

"Would you like another?"

"No. I will take the bill, though. How much do I owe you?"

"Nothing." She waved her hand. "Let this be my small Christmas gift to you."

"No, really, I would like to pay." I reached for my wallet.

"Not this time," she said with a calm firmness. "This time I would like to give to you. Next time you can give to me."

It seemed strange that her hospitality-clad services alluded to a "next time." I thought I had made it clear that I was passing through and had no plans to stay or to return.

"Have you decided then about the performance this evening?"

I paused. All my self-preservation instincts told me to be on my way. Ignore the possibility that someone else in town might be able to identify the man and the boy in the photograph. I didn't need to know. The mystery of my father's identity could die with me the way it had died with my mother eighteen years ago. If my mother were here today, she would be thrilled to go to the performance. I was not.

"Would your mother like to come, then?" Katharine asked.

I looked at her hard. Had I said something aloud about my mother? I thought my reminiscences had been only in my mind.

Several friends and roommates had told me over the years that I talked in my sleep as well as in my waking. They told me when I was deep in thought I would carry out the process half in silence and half in mutterings. I must have mentioned my mother, thus prompting Katharine's question about her.

"My mother passed away quite some time ago."

Surprisingly, I felt secure enough to add my simple, well-rehearsed paragraph. It was a disclosure that evoked sympathy while at the same time closing the door on the topic.

"She fell from a scaffold at an outdoor theater in Salinas when I was eleven. It was a dress rehearsal for *The Merchant of Venice.* She died from internal injuries two days later. However, the show did go on."

I realized that what I had just revealed to Katharine sufficiently explained why I wasn't on speaking terms with the theater. Even without my boycott of all things make-believe, this information was enough. Katharine certainly would withdraw her invitation to the Dickens performance.

She seemed unruffled, though. "I'm quite sad for your loss."

I nodded my appreciation for the care in her voice. Now that we had that piece out of the way, as often happened in my relationships, I felt we could go on to the business at hand. My business, as I saw it, was to be on my way to the train station.

Katharine's business seemed to be waiting for an answer about the play.

"I need to go back to London." I pushed the chair away from the table and slung my big purse over my shoulder. "Thank you again for the tea and the scones. They were delicious." I paused at the front door. "Are you sure I can't pay you, though?"

"Next time," she said with a smile. A silver earring peeking out from under her dark hair caught the light of the candle on the table and gave me a silvery goodbye twinkle.

I stepped out into the cold with much less gusto than the kilt-clad "Christmas Present" had earlier. Immediately, the chill went through me, and I wished for a longer coat.

"That's what I'll give myself for Christmas," I said as I headed downhill on Bexley Lane.

This time I knew I was expressing my thoughts aloud. It didn't matter. No one was around to hear me. I decided I would spend tomorrow, Christmas Day, in my London hotel room. Understandably, I felt most nostalgically at home whenever I was in a hotel room.

Then the day after Christmas I would go out shopping for a new coat. Surely London had after-Christmas sales that rivaled the ones in San Francisco.

That way, when I returned to the office next week, I would have something to show for my on-a-whim spree to London.

My legs stretched to their full length as I picked up my pace and retraced the path to the train station. Windows on either side of the lane were lined with festive decorations that jived in the gale that accompanied me, whistling down the lane. One of the two-story brick buildings was adorned with a single lit candle on each windowsill of the four symmetrical windows. Another place of residence had a large pot by the front door in which a four-feet-tall evergreen was strung with twinkling white lights and red bows tied to the ends of the branches.

I turned the corner toward the train station and pulled the collar of my peacoat closer to my ears. The charm of the Tea Cosy pervaded the village of Carlton Heath. If I ever decided to believe in fairy tales again, this would be the setting in my mind's eye.

Long, slender branches on the tall trees spread their protective embrace over glowing streetlights and stone cottages. The trees didn't seem to notice that they had lost all their foliage. Their role hadn't changed with the fierceness of the seasons; they still sheltered the people and the dwelling places on Bexley Lane.

I kept walking. Down the hill, around the corner, and past the ivy-covered chapel. I paused only a moment to have a look at the softly lit church with the arched entryway. It seemed to me as if the church were wearing her rambling cemetery like an appliquéd blanket. The blanket tumbled from the foot of the rose bed and fell haphazardly over a hundred sleeping kernels of life, lives that had built the chapel, paved the roads, and taken tea beside many a soot-covered hearth.

Now they were all silent.

One life. That's all we get. When will mine be silenced? Or should I be asking when will it truly begin?

I crossed the street and tried not to think of anything but my numb feet all the way to the train station. The station had a covered platform and a little station house. A single bench rested against the waiting area's back wall. A newspaper kiosk was positioned in one corner, and the ticket booth filled the opposite corner next to the blinking cash machine.

Aside from the ATM, everything else about the room I sat in to be away from the cold looked and felt as if it hadn't changed in fifty years. I noticed one modern addition. An electronic sign was positioned over the door listing the trains' times and destinations in a trailing news flash. To the right of the contemporary timetable was an old-fashioned, round-faced clock. I consulted the clock and then the sign with the trailing, red-dotted letters. The next train to London was scheduled to leave in twenty minutes.

My watch still gave the time as 11:58. I tapped it again and held it up to my ear. No sign of life could be heard.

Maybe I'll buy myself a coat and *a new watch for Christmas. Or at least a new battery.*

I sighed and leaned back. I was the sole traveler at the station. The only other person in the building was a dozing gentleman who sat on a stool, manning the newspaper kiosk.

Glancing again at the wall clock I wondered, *What time is it in San Francisco?*

Not that it mattered. I didn't have anyone back in the City by the Bay waiting for me to call him or her. No one would wonder why I wasn't coming to dinner on Christmas Day. I had covered all the bases at the office. I was a holiday nonentity.

That thought wasn't a comforting one. I could leave the country—or this planet, for that matter—and very few people would realize I was gone.

How did my life come to this?

Apparently the career I had begun at such an early age as a backstage apparition was still in effect. I was invisible.

Discontentment over my invisibility had fueled my passion-fire last week when I decided to book a ticket to London. I had been lying alone in bed, wide awake in the middle of the night, when I concluded that I had lingered too long at the shallow end of my life, staring across the divide at the unblinking father I had chosen to believe in. If he did exist, I needed to know. If for some reason he wasn't ready, willing, or able to come to me, then I would make the first move. I would float toward him and see what happened.

Hence, here I was in England. And nothing had happened.

"Well, I tried," I muttered defensively. I had followed the few clues and had tracked down the village of Carlton Heath only to find that the photography studio no longer existed. What more could I do?

There was Katharine's statement that she thought she recognized the photo. Someone in Carlton Heath quite possibly had a copy of the same photo I had. Someone who might know something.

Could I really leave now and have no regrets? Would I be content returning to San Francisco with nothing more than a new coat or other after-Christmas-sale merchandise? What about the answers I had come in search of?

No one else knew the purpose of my trip. But I knew. And I knew that a week from now, when I lay awake in the middle of the night, I would ask myself why I had given up so easily. Especially when one small lead still dangled in front of me.

I thought of what Katharine said about decisions.

You can make a new one whenever you like.

For several long minutes I didn't move. I thought briefly—only briefly—about what it would be like for the kernel of my short life to be tucked under a blanket of cold earth. Could I die knowing I had not exhausted all possible leads to finding my father?

Rising and pressing back my shoulders, I stepped away from the waiting room bench, drew in a deep breath, and made a new decision. I decided to go to the theater.

"Merry Christmas, Mother," I muttered. "I am going to see a play."

Chapter Six

Grey Hall, where the Dickens performance was being held, was easy enough to find. I had roused the dozing clerk at the newspaper kiosk inside the station, and he had given me clear directions in the most charming accent I had heard yet during my nearly seven hours on English soil.

The walk from the train station was uphill, and the temperature had dropped another few degrees. At least the wind had died down. The exertion of heading uphill warmed me as I walked. The distance was farther than I had estimated, and I hesitated at the second crossroad.

It's not too late to go back to the train station. You don't have to do this.

"Yes I do."

The abiding thought that kept me walking was that I needed to know. I needed to know who my father was, and I needed to know him. The only clues I had to his existence had led me to Carlton Heath. Although I didn't understand my trailing thought, I sensed that as much as I needed to know, I also needed to be known.

One determined foot in front of the other brought me into Brumpton Square and there, set a short distance off the main road, stood the Victorian-style meeting hall. Eight metal shepherd's hooks lined the walkway, and from each hook hung a lantern, illuminating the path in the crystalline air. Ropes of evergreen garlands draped the entrance, and magnificent curls of gingerbread façade on the building's face disguised its true age. The name, Grey Hall, appeared across the front of the theater in raised letters.

A large dedication plaque beside the entrance read, "Dedicated May 19, 1987, The Society of Grey Hall Community Theatre." The building had been constructed over a century too late for a Dickens appearance, yet it felt easy to believe that the author himself might be in attendance this evening where past and present seemed to have merged.

No other theatergoers were in view as I stood in front of the closed doors. My guess was that I had missed the opening curtain. I reached for the long handles on the double doors and slowly opened the right side just enough to slip into the foyer.

A short woman in a flowing pink evening dress came to my side. With a gloved finger held to her lips, she motioned for me to follow her to the far left of the reception area where a thick, blue velvet curtain separated us from the theater seating.

The woman's short, tousled hair was as pink as her dress and dotted with sparkles. Her perfectly shaped lips were painted the same cotton candy shade and dotted with a jewel above her top lip on the right side, a distinguishing beauty mark. She appeared to be in her early forties; yet, dressed up as she was, her heart seemed much younger.

Without a word, she drew back the curtain and nodded for me to step inside the dark arena. I entered and stood to the side, waiting for my eyes to adjust.

A booming voice called out, "Come in, come in!"

It was the merry Scotsman. For a moment I froze, thinking he was extending the invitation to me.

In actuality he was delivering the line onstage to a very short Scrooge who stood trembling before the ominous presence of the kilted greeter. Behind the Scotsman was an open door.

The invitation was repeated by the man with the wide, wooly-white sideburns. "Come in, come in, and know me better, friend!"

"Who are you and what is this place?" Scrooge cried in a pipsqueak voice. Under a long nightshirt and floppy cap, the leading actor was obviously a child.

My spirit softened to all things theatrical. Some images of make-believe had never truly left me, no matter how belligerent I had been about them. Just as I had earlier remembered wanting to be Lucy walking through the wardrobe into Narnia, I now found myself disarmed by this classic Dickens character, who brought an Oliver Twist feel to the role of the miserly Scrooge. I could see myself in the pint-sized presence who now held center stage.

The Scotsman wore a trim jacket atop his kilt and finished the look with a flat sort of hat perched slightly to the side and sporting a feather. From under the hat flowed a cascade of wavy white hair. I'd seen his balding head uncovered at the tea cottage and knew the tresses were part of his costume, but the tumble of hair was convincing.

Taking his cue, the Scotsman declared, "I am the Spirit of Christmas Present."

I smiled. *So he really was a Christmas Present, just as he said.*

"What will you do to me, Oh Spirit of Christmas Present?" Young Scrooge asked.

"Enter, and you shall see." Christmas Present stepped to the side, and the sliding prop door was moved off-center by unseen stagehands. Where a dark closure had been, a wonderful spread of Christmas cheer was revealed, with a flickering fireplace, a tree trimmed in lights, a stack of gifts, and a table spread with a feast.

"All has been made ready for you," the Spirit of Christmas Present declared. "Come."

Scrooge hesitated.

In that moment, I felt my defenses slide off me like pool water. All had been made ready for Scrooge, and yet he hesitated. I saw how I had been in that same Bah Humbug role for many years. I understood the hesitation. The standing back and not trusting. But no one had ever made a celebration ready for me and invited me to come in.

An old fountain of tears I had kept capped for ages began to leak. Instead of looking for a seat in the back of the hall where I could watch the rest of the play anonymously, I slid through the velvet curtains and returned to the reception area.

Feeling around in my large shoulder bag for a tissue, I didn't notice the woman in pink as she came to my side.

"Here," she whispered. She held out to me a handkerchief with a pink rosebud embroidered in the corner. Once I'd dried my eyes and curbed my tears, I held onto the handkerchief and stared at the crumpled cotton in my hands as the woman patted my arm.

I told her in a mumble that it had been a long day, hoping

that would explain my breakdown. But I wasn't sure I could even explain to myself why the image of a feast and gifts accompanied by a warm invitation to Scrooge had struck such a chord of longing inside me. I sensed that Young Scrooge was being offered everything I wanted but didn't know how to find.

Taking a deep breath and summoning another round of fortitude, I whispered that I was fine. Really.

With a nod of understanding, she continued with the gentle pats on my arm. All the while she seemed to be trying to fix her gaze on my eyes. Even in the dimmed lobby lights, I was sure the weariness of jet lag showed. No doubt she was checking for more tears. I had successfully repressed them and my eyelids were now puffing up with the reserves. Dabbing my nose, I continued to look away. She continued trying to look me in the eye.

"Well, thank you." I awkwardly held out the used handkerchief. I wasn't sure if I should offer to have it laundered before returning it. I had never been given a handkerchief before.

"Keep it," she said softly.

I hadn't decided if I was ready to go back for the rest of the performance. But she made the decision for me by ushering me through the velvet curtain and pointing to an empty chair in the second row from the back. I had just enough time to settle in and refocus before Scrooge began to argue with the Spirit of Christmas Present over his discomfort at the revelations he had faced during his waking dream.

With his skinny arm dramatically shading his gaze, Scrooge cried out, "Take me from this place, I beg of you, oh, Spirit of Christmas Present. Do not force me to look any longer at what I have become. Tell me instead what is to come."

"And so it shall be." The Spirit of Christmas Present turned, and his kilt's pleats kicked up. Scrooge stood alone on the stage. The lights dimmed as Scrooge drew both fists to his mouth, frightened as a mouse.

"Please! I beg of you! Do not leave me like this!"

All the lights extinguished, and silence covered us all. Then a shuffling of feet and clicking of theater seats rolled across the room as the curtain closed and the lights came up slowly.

While the rest of the audience rose and made their way to the lobby for intermission, I stayed in my seat, taking in my surroundings. The auditorium was smaller and narrower than I had pictured in the dark when I entered. Fresh boughs of evergreen had been shaped into huge Christmas wreaths that hung from Victorian-style lighting sconces. The ceiling was inlaid with plaster frescos that had a repeating pattern of mellow golden white on purer white. The padded seats were covered in deep blue velvet and matched the dark blue velvet of the stage curtains that were trimmed across the top with golden tassels.

The deep blues reminded me of my mother's eyes. She would have liked this theater. She liked small, intimate settings where she felt she could wrap her arms around the audience and keep it in her embrace.

I settled into the comfortable seat and took in the whole "envelope"—the size and shape of the theater and the deep blue velvet stage curtains with the golden tassels. In a strange way, I felt as if I were sitting inside an enlarged version of my mother's secret blue silk purse. Now I had become one of the curious clues hidden under the tasseled flap.

Chapter Seven

The blue velvet purse had been given to me along with the rest of my mother's meager possessions after her death. She had no other surprises in her green Samsonite suitcase nor in any previously unrevealed secret places such as a safe-deposit box. She left this earth without providing a clue as to how to find another living relative such as a grandparent or aunt.

In light of my true orphan status, Doralee, the bald woman in Santa Cruz with the seven cats and no television, gathered me up.

When I first went to live with Doralee, she was determined to track down my father and do the right thing—give him the option of claiming me. All we had to go on was the name listed on my birth certificate, Jay Ames.

Doralee checked all the "Ameses" she could find. Nothing matched up. After weeks of diligent searching, we came to the conclusion that, true to form, my mother had invented my father's name on the birth certificate.

I then became Doralee's "niece." My new aunt proved to be as skilled as my mother had been at fabricating information to fit comfortably into what people wanted to hear. Documents were created as needed to enroll me in public school for the first time in my life. Stories of my genealogical history were embellished to satisfy probing principals, and Doralee made sure that I was well clothed with her own sewing-machine creations.

Whenever I started to sink into myself, she would do this funny little wiggle of a dance and sing, "Everybody doesn't like something, but nobody doesn't like Doralee." I trusted myself to her.

One day at school a girl I didn't like was singing Doralee's song.

"Where did you hear that?" I demanded.

The girl and her friends stared at me as if I were a freak, which in some ways I'm sure I must have been, even in Santa Cruz. They all sang the song together and then told me it came from a commercial for frozen pastries on TV.

I had never heard the commercial because we didn't have a TV, and we never, ever ate frozen pastries. We ate only organic foods and socialized with an eclectic group of all-natural free thinkers. Birthdays and holidays weren't celebrated, but journeys to enlightenment were encouraged with gatherings and music and dance.

I told those three girls to "buzz off," only I used a more earthy term than that. Afterward I never belonged to anyone or any group the rest of my time in school.

Four years into our make-believe family affair, Doralee's cancer returned, and two things happened. Actually, three.

The first pivotal event was Doralee's reading a book that prompted her to spurn all her earthy rituals, burn down a shrine in the backyard, and embrace an oddly traditional form of Christianity. She prayed regularly in the name of Jesus Christ and read entire chapters of the Bible every day.

"The true return to Eden is found in Christ," she told all her friends. "Not in this lifetime, in these fallen and broken bodies. It's all yet to come, in eternity. Everything we've longed for can and will be fulfilled in Christ. He is coming back to claim all that is rightfully his, including the souls of all who have been adopted into his kingdom."

Doralee lost a lot of friends, especially toward the end, when her passion for God, heaven, and her new, resurrected body were the only things she wanted to talk about. Even up to the hour of her passing, she didn't waver from her claim that she had received a new life—an eternal life—when she trusted in Christ. She kept talking about "the Lamb" redeeming her.

I was with her that afternoon. I watched death come and take her, and it was astonishingly beautiful. Her expression transformed from the constant pinch of agonizing pain to a smoothness and a very real absence of fear. Her aura was the closest thing I had ever seen to genuine peace. And then, as I watched, she left her body.

The second significant event with Doralee was that, before her pain became unbearable, she revived the search for my father. She made a list of all the names of actors who appeared on the playbill of *The Tempest* and set about trying to track down any one of them. The dates of the performances listed on the playbill were nine months before my birth date. Doralee made the connection one day and concluded that one of the participants in the theatrical company might know something or someone. Or one of the actors might be someone. Someone such as my father.

Fifteen years is a long time when it comes to picking up a trail on a troop of gypsies. None of the leads went anywhere. However, Doralee's realization that the performance dates of *The Tempest* connected to my birth played on me for years.

The third turning point occurred after Doralee's death. As an unusually savvy fifteen-year-old, I chose to emulate the lifestyle of deceit that had been so professionally demonstrated to me over the years. I left school, and since I looked older than I was, I fabricated the few necessary documents to appear eighteen. Then I moved to San Francisco.

Within a week I had effortlessly landed a job as a waitress at a large hotel and had enrolled in a bookkeeping class. I wanted a career in numbers and not words because even I knew that numbers couldn't lie.

For the next thirteen years I remained steadily employed at an accounting firm in the Transcontinental Building. I had a nice studio loft with an excellent view of the Bay Bridge, a loosely held circle of friends, no cats, and two ex-boyfriends. Josh, the longest running boyfriend, was the one who had unknowingly prompted me to make my journey to England.

I should have realized why a graduate psych student who wanted to work with abused children was keenly interested in me. Josh was convinced I was hiding something.

My clear-eyed response to him had been, "I had a wonderfully unusual mother, and she was very protective of me. I was not abused."

Josh went with my answer but always seemed to be looking for more. "Not all abuse is physical," he claimed.

I had become such an expert at making my history invisible that the only details I willingly handed over to Josh were airy and unsatisfying to someone who wanted to one day make his living analyzing the human psyche.

Up until Josh, everyone who sincerely asked about my life before San Francisco was given the sparse yet dramatically satisfying account of how my mother had died in the arms of her other love, the stage. Orphaned, I'd gone to live with an "aunt" who later died of cancer. If the interviewer probed further, I easily sidetracked him with details about Doralee's seven cats, all named after Egyptian pharaohs.

Josh was the only person, aside from Doralee, who didn't stop probing about my father.

Early in our relationship I told Josh, "My father is dead. He died before I was born."

Then one night, in an uncharacteristic blip of vulnerability, I showed Josh the blue velvet purse. I showed him the playbill for *The Tempest* and the photograph. I did not show him my birth certificate. He thought I was twenty-seven. This wasn't the time to reveal that I was twenty-four.

Josh took the photograph and held it like a forensics expert would. "What if your father is alive, and these two clues are your trail to find him?"

I shrugged. All I had experienced in the past were dead ends.

"The photo looks old enough that this screaming boy could possibly be your father."

"Maybe."

"One thing we know is that the man in the photo is dressed as Father Christmas. There's no doubt. He's a British version of St. Nick, if I ever saw one."

Josh studied the stamped wording on the back of the photo. "The Carlton Photography Studio must be located in England then. Or somewhere in the UK. It shouldn't be too difficult to track down a lead on 'Carlton Heath.' It could be a town or a family name. And then you've got Bexley Lane, which is going to narrow it down for you. You have some key pieces here."

Josh speculated that my father might still be in the UK, but I told him my mother had never been abroad. At least she never had told me about being out of the US. If my father was from England, how and where did my mother meet him?

Josh didn't yet have a theory for that piece of the puzzle. He turned the photo over and over, deep in contemplation. Looking up at me with a lightbulb-over-the-head expression, he said, "It's a wallet-sized photo."

"Right." That fact was obvious.

"What if this picture was kept in a wallet?"

Now I was getting impatient with Josh, the amateur analyst.

"Don't you see? Your mother had a relationship with this man, and when she realized the relationship couldn't last, she stole what she could—a photo. She took it from his wallet."

Josh had no idea how close he was getting to the truth of how my mother would operate. I alone knew how smooth my mother could be at performing such a sleight of hand. But when? Where?

I took the photo back from Josh and noticed for the first

time how pointy Josh's ears were. He wore his hair too short for a person with such ears. On that night of my vulnerability, I stared far too long at his ears.

Two weeks later I used his ears as a frivolous excuse when a girlfriend at work asked why I broke up with Josh. "It's because of his ears," I told her. "I looked at him one night and realized I could never stay in a serious relationship with a man with such pointed ears."

She stared at me in amused disbelief.

"Think about it. If we had children, they would all come out looking like elves!"

A week later she asked Josh out to coffee on the premise of consoling him over our breakup. I think the two of them are still together. I'm glad. Josh deserved someone sincere. I had not yet learned how to fully develop that quality. But to my credit, I was trying.

I will always be grateful to Josh for his analysis of my mother's treasured pieces of evidence. It took me several years to move forward with Josh's leads and to allow myself to believe my father might be findable. Once I tracked down the village of Carlton Heath, a half-hour train ride southeast of London, it only took a few more clicks on the computer to find Bexley Lane.

And here I was.

I glanced around the auditorium and thought of Josh. He would have been happy to know I had taken this risk. He also would have been surprised that I set foot inside a performance hall.

The theater lights flickered the universal cue for the audience to return to their seats. I stood to let a trail of people pass me. Settling back, I gazed around the theater and realized I was sitting in the presence of my former competition—my mother's old love, the theater.

The lights dimmed. With a sigh, I nodded my acceptance.

Merry Christmas, Eve Carson, the actress. This is my gift to you. It's the only gift you ever asked of me. The gift I resisted giving you for so many years. Tonight I have made peace with your beloved theater.

Chapter Eight

Just before the curtain went up, I involuntarily glanced at my watch. The hands had moved one minute, now reading 11:59. Odd. I liked it when numbers were dependable. Having a broken watch was getting to me.

Wee Scrooge in his flapping nightshirt rose from the center of the stage on a belt and pulley and flew out of his bed crying, "Oh, Spirit of Christmas Present, speak kindness to me that I might not faint from lack of hope."

Offstage the Scotsman's booming voice replied, "You have yet a few more images to view before this night is passed."

I smiled at the sight of flailing Scrooge being whisked back and forth across the stage on the sophisticated rigging. One of his slippers fell off, prompting a ruffle of chuckles from the audience. The Peter Pan touch was endearing.

Just then I felt a soft tap on my shoulder. Katharine stood in the aisle, motioning for me to follow her out into the lobby. I slipped out as quietly as I could.

"I see you came," she said. "I'm glad. What do you think of our liberal adaptation?"

"It's clever. The young actor playing Scrooge is doing a great job."

"Yes, he is. Listen, I won't keep you from the last half. I wanted to speak with you before you left. Ellie was the one who told me you were here."

I remembered the rosebud-embroidered handkerchief in my pocket. "Is Ellie the Sugarplum Fairy?"

Katharine chuckled softly. "Yes, and she'll appreciate that you recognized her costume. I'm afraid I asked if she had come as a pink snowflake."

"I heard that." Ellie moved across the lobby to join us.

"I was just about to extend the invitation to the cast party at your home."

"Yes, do join us. We would be delighted." Ellie stepped up with a metal cash box in her arms. "I have to run this out to the car. Katharine, you and Andrew would be able to fit one more guest in your car, wouldn't you? Oh, and I'm Ellie, by the way."

"I'm Miranda."

"Miranda, you will come, won't you?"

Katharine added, "It would be the simplest way for you to connect with someone who might know about the photo. All the insiders from around Carlton Heath will be at the party. Please say you'll come."

I hesitated, concerned about catching a train back to London afterward.

Katharine and Ellie assured me I could find a ride to the train station whenever I was ready to leave the party. They both appeared eager for me to join them, so I took a small risk and said yes.

I returned to my seat, settled in, and enjoyed the entertainment. The local actors seemed to be giving the performance their all. Tiny Tim closed the night with one final "God bless us, everyone!" and the applause rose as the curtain fell. Cheers, chuckles, and more applause continued until the entire cast appeared onstage for a bow. I had forgotten how radiant some actors were when they stepped out of their characters and stood under the shower of streaming applause.

Those were the times my mother glowed.

Katharine was waiting for me in the lobby. She and her husband, Andrew the Scotsman, offered me a ride to Ellie's home.

We climbed into their compact car and were barely out of the parking area when Andrew said, "Did my wife tell you we've been married fourteen months come this Saturday?" He was still wearing the hat with the flowing white hair and was driving on what my brain kept thinking of as the "wrong" side of the road. I was seated in the front, at Katharine's insistence. The place I occupied should have been the side fitted with the steering wheel and brake pedal, were this an American car.

"And what about you? Are you married then, Miranda?" Andrew looked at me, but I wished he would look instead at the dark and narrow road we were rolling down at a precarious speed.

We seemed to be heading out of town. For a moment I wondered why I had entrusted myself to these strangers. At home I would never blithely jump into a car with people I had just met. Nor would I go to any sort of party held at the home of people I didn't know.

A voice in my heart was telling me what I hadn't expected to hear on this trip. This journey was changing me. Change had not been my goal.

"Are you then?" Andrew asked, looking at me expectantly.

"I'm sorry. What did you just ask?"

"I asked if you're married?"

"No, I'm not."

Andrew looked over his shoulder at Katherine. "Are you thinking what I'm thinking?"

Katharine didn't answer, but I nearly did. I was thinking: *You'd better keep your eyes on the road!*

Andrew glanced forward and then back at me. "I'm thinking you should meet my son, Ian. Will you be staying over the Christmas holidays?"

"Yes. I mean, no. Not here in Carlton Heath. I'm staying in London."

"Are you now? Have you got family in London, then?"

"No. I—"

"Andrew, my love," Katharine interrupted, "you've missed the entrance."

"Awk! I have indeed." With a quick turn, he set the small car in the opposite direction and steered through an open-gated entry to a large home lit up with tiny white lights around the eaves.

The home wasn't a manor per se. Not that I had ever been to a manor to compare it with Ellie's home. But it was grand, distinct, and impressive.

The large two-story house, composed of dull red brick, was dressed up with a grand arched entrance, tall rounded windows, and a fairy-tale-like turret in the south corner. Nothing about the picturesque structure looked standard or mass-produced. It seemed like a one-of-a-kind creation sprung from an artistic mind. The closer we drove, the more beautiful each curve of the house appeared in the headlights of Andrew's car.

"What a beautiful place," I said, wishing I could find better words to describe how the house made me feel.

"The house was built by Edward's grandfather, wasn't it, Andrew? Or was it his great-grandfather?"

"It was his great-great-grandfather. He was an artist of some fame. Have you heard of the Pre-Raphaelite Brotherhood, Miranda?"

I shook my head.

"Aye, well then, I don't imagine it would much matter to you who the builder was or why it was built in such a fashion, nor why Edward is so keen to keep the place as it is."

"And who is Edward?" I asked, lost in the conversation.

"Edward Whitcombe. Ellie's husband. Son of Sir James Whitcombe." He looked at me as if waiting for a response. "Have you not heard that name before? Sir James Whitcombe?"

I nodded slightly. I thought I had heard the name, but I wasn't sure where.

"We consider Edward and Ellie Whitcombe our resident touch of royalty, I suppose."

"Royalty?"

"Are you stretching the matter a bit, Andrew?"

Andrew cut the car engine and ignored his wife's admonition. "You see, when Edward's father was knighted by Her Majesty a number of years ago, it gave a certain rise to the village status. Katharine and Ellie have been friends for a long stretch. That's how Katharine came to settle here in Carlton Heath, not long after the passing of her first husband."

"Andrew, I'm not sure all of this family history is going to be useful to Miranda."

"Right. Well, to finish what I had to say about Edward and Ellie, I call them our resident Lord and Lady, just to get a rise out of them. They're nearly like family to us, wouldn't you say, Katharine?" Andrew slid out of the car and held out his hand to help Katharine disembark.

"Yes. Almost like family to us." Katharine slid her hand through Andrew's arm. He offered his other arm to me, and I played along with being escorted by Christmas Present across the gravel driveway. A dozen other cars were parked in the expansive area between Andrew's car and the house. We could hear sounds of laughter from inside as we traipsed through the cold air up to the well-lit front door.

Pausing under the arched entry, Andrew knocked soundly on the massive oak door. I noticed a banner of words painted over the doorway in a Victorian script: "Grace and Peace Reside Here."

The door swung open, and Lady Sugarplum Fairy welcomed us with her rendition of Andrew's line from the performance: "Come in, come in, and know me better, friends!"

"Well, there you have it," said Andrew. "Next year you're the one to play the role of Christmas Present, Lady Ellie. You have the lines already."

"Lovely! I was thinking an all-female cast would be a clever twist next year. What do you girls think?" Ellie's hair swished as she turned her head to look at Katharine and me. The motion invited a shower of pixie dust to leave her pink hair and rest in sparkles on the threshold.

"Do come in out of the cold before you answer that," she added.

"The answer is simple." Andrew motioned with a half bow for Katharine and me to enter first. "Have we not caused the poor man enough reason to turn over in his grave each Christmas when we take such liberties with his story?"

"Undoubtedly," Katharine stated.

Andrew removed his hat, hair and all, and handed it to our hostess as she collected our coats. "Then I propose we try something radical next year. We perform the blessed script the way it was written originally!"

"Bravo!" Ellie laughed. "Wouldn't that take the town by surprise!" Looking at me she added, "I'm so glad you've come, Miranda."

"Thanks for letting me crash your party."

Ellie looked at Katharine as if she wasn't sure why I would say such a thing.

"You're not crashing into anything. It was my idea for you to come. Katharine tells me you have a mystery to solve. I'm eager to hear about that, but first I must put away these coats. Katharine? Andrew? You will pick up my duties as hostess, won't you? Please make sure Miranda meets all the right sorts of people."

Ellie whooshed away in her pink gown, and I had a feeling my peacoat would forever carry sugarplum sparkles on it.

Ellie added a final thought over her shoulder. "And do avoid introducing her to the seedy characters, won't you?"

"Not a chance," Andrew said. "We're taking her directly to all the questionable guests to give her a true impression of the sort of individuals you associate with."

"That would include you, Andrew," Ellie called as she exited down a hallway.

With a wink and an aside to me, he added, "The only person I want to introduce you to is my son, but he's not here. So how about if I let Katharine carry on the introductions? If either of you needs me, you know where you can find me."

I glanced at Katharine, and she interpreted. "He'll be wherever the food and drinks are. Come. I suppose we should start with an introduction to our host, Edward. Do you have the photo with you? Perhaps you might show it to him."

I realized I had blindly handed my coat and purse over to Ellie. "No, I left it in my purse. Which way did Ellie go?"

Katharine pointed down the hall to the left. "She's probably put all the coats in the study. It's the second door on the left. Would you like me to go with you?"

"No, I'll be right back." A small and probably childish part of me wanted to roam about the poetic home by myself. In front of me was a polished staircase just begging to be climbed the way an unattended piano on an empty stage begs to be played.

I reluctantly turned from the stairs and went down the left hall of the L-shaped floor plan. The second door on the left led into a large study with built-in bookshelves on either side. In the air lingered a hint of worn leather and cherry almond pipe tobacco. In the center of the room sat a great desk made of a dark wood that had been polished until it reflected the amber light of the standing floor lamp.

Wow. One could rule a small country in a room like this and with a desk like that.

I spotted my coat, hanging from a standing coatrack near

the door. My purse shared the same hanger. As I lifted off the purse, I noticed the collection of photographs on the wall. All the pictures were framed in black. The center one caught my eye, and I stepped closer. Her Majesty, Queen Elizabeth, was standing beside a well-dressed man, whom I guessed to be Sir James Whitcombe. His stately appearance and perfectly groomed dark hair gave him a sophisticated air of royalty.

The framed photo directly under the knighting of Sir James was a contrasting image of the debonair figure. He was stretched out on a picnic blanket, eyes closed, as if trying to take a summer nap. Over him stood a little girl with ringlet curls and a mischievous grin. She was dropping rose petals on his face one by one.

I cast a sweeping glance over the other three pictures. One of them showed an informal family gathering around an outdoor table. Another was of Sir James and a lovely blond woman, whom I supposed to be his wife. The two of them stood with their arms around each other in front of the Taj Mahal. The third photograph was of Sir James sitting atop a camel with a hazy view of the great pyramids of Egypt in the background.

Leaving the study with my purse, I told myself to be on my best behavior. I had never been in such a home before nor in the company of people who possessed such wealth.

I realized I should have felt nervous or at least a little uncomfortable about being around all these people I didn't know. Strangely, I felt calm. Welcomed. Warmed. Ready to welcome Christmas Present with this glad company.

Chapter Nine

The largest room in the Whitcombes' luxurious home was referred to as the drawing room. When Katharine and I entered, I stopped and tried to take in the architectural features as well as the gorgeous decorations. Ellie had made use of her sugarplum theme by incorporating pink touches throughout the elegant room. Swags of greenery looped around the room at ceiling level. Tiny white lights and clumps of holly berries were woven into the garlands, which also were dotted with pink sugarplums.

The ceilings were high, and the voices of the thirty or so lively guests echoed in the large open area. Even though the room provided enough space for everyone to be comfortably seated, most of the visitors were standing, chatting in small groups. At the far end of the room a bushy Christmas tree was lit up with pink lights. At the other end, closer to the door where Katharine and I stood, was a long table covered with a smorgasbord of food.

"Be sure to try the crab puffs." Katharine handed me a china plate. "Ellie serves them with a fabulous sweet-and-sour dipping sauce."

I made my way down the line, filling my plate with

petite appetizers of all shapes and adding a spoonful of each scrumptious-looking salad. We stood as we ate, balancing our plates and being careful not to bump into anyone or spill our cuisine.

Katharine introduced me to a stout woman who had lived in Carlton Heath her entire life.

"Miranda is curious about a photography studio on Bexley Lane," Katharine said. "Do you know anything about the Carlton Studio?"

"Well, yes, of course. Wonderful people, the Halversons, weren't they? They were in business there on Bexley Lane for years. Such a pity when they moved, wasn't it? We had our family photos taken at their studio when the children were young. Such a loss when they went out of business, don't you think? One can only assume the failure of the enterprise was the result of the computer industry. All the digital cameras for sale these days. People are too impatient to wait and have something done right or to go to a specialist to have it done. They would rather take care of everything themselves at home on their computers. I don't have a computer. I don't plan to get a computer. This is all leading to terrible destruction, really. Don't you think? I tried to get my grandson to go one entire day without using any of his computer gadgets, and do you know, he would not do it. He would not. It's not only the computers, is it? It's all the other machines they carry with them to listen to their music and make all their unnecessary phone calls. Quite irritating, really. Have you seen them on the trains these days? All wired up as if they belonged in a hospital bed in the cardiac ward. They have this wire that goes to this ear and this wire that goes to that ear. Somehow they talk through something and carry on conversations that are entirely too private while out in public. It's deplorable, really."

As the stout woman paused for air, I glanced at Katharine, and she attempted a polite escape for us. "Yes, deplorable. If you don't mind, I've a few others to introduce Miranda to before she slips out to catch the train to London."

"You'd best check the schedule for the times. This being Christmas Eve, you know. I'm sure you've considered that. Tomorrow, of course, being Christmas Day, well, it goes without saying that when it comes to National Rail, I'm of the opinion that it, such as it is, is not accommodating the travelers trying to be with family for the day. No, I would think it's more along the lines of National Rail trying to accommodate all the employees who would doubtless ask for outlandish additional wages on the holidays. Not that anyone—"

Katharine interjected, "Oh, I see someone I need to introduce Miranda to. You will excuse us, won't you?"

Before the woman could answer, Katharine nudged me across the room through the maze of people. Some of them were still in costume, which made the gathering a familiar setting and awoke childhood feelings in my heart. Doralee had a lot of opinionated friends like the woman we had just listened to. I was much more comfortable around that sort of party guest than the ones who might ask me questions. It was all part of my preference to blend into the background when in a crowd.

We came through the human obstacle course with our plates of food intact and only a few bumps. A tall, dark-haired man stood in front of us, holding in one hand a small plate emptied of appetizers and in the other hand a piece of fluted stemware with some sort of pink beverage.

He wore rectangular-shaped glasses that gave him an English professor aura in a cool retro sort of way. He looked like the young teacher-of-the-year sort of professor who could be living on a sailboat near Belize if he chose to but instead spent his days shaping impressionable minds with the classics.

The person with whom he was chatting had just stepped away, making a natural opening for Katharine to move closer and make the introductions.

"Edward, I would like you to meet someone. Miranda, this is our host, Edward Whitcombe."

"Son of Sir James Whitcombe," I added, without realizing I was drawing from my earlier conversation with Andrew in the car.

Edward tilted his head with a vague weariness. "Were you a fan, then?"

"A fan?"

"Of my father. Were you a fan of his work?"

I glanced out of the corner of my eye at Katharine, hoping for some sort of clue as to what Sir James did or why I should be a fan. But she had turned to greet another guest, leaving me alone with my bumbling mess.

"I . . . I don't know."

Edward looked oddly humored by my response. "I believe that's the first time I've heard that answer."

I looked down at the uneaten crab puff on my plate and considered popping the whole thing in my mouth so I would be assured of not speaking for at least thirty seconds.

Instead, I chose an unusual path for me, especially with strangers. I spoke the truth. Rather involuntarily, I might add.

"I'm from the US and . . ." If my lack of British party manners hadn't already given away that I was an outsider, I was sure my American accent had. I tried another approach. "What I meant to say is that I'm not familiar with your father or his work. So I don't know if I'm a fan or not."

"Is that right?"

I nodded. "I am familiar with his name only because of a few details Andrew and Katharine told me as we drove over here tonight."

"And they didn't tell you what my father did?"

I shook my head and offered a tiny smile, hoping my faux pas would be dismissed.

He nodded slowly. It was the kind of nodding motion one makes when thinking. He kept looking at my eyes the same way his wife, Ellie, had tried to make eye contact with me at the theater.

I realized how jet-lagged I was and how much I could use a little freshening up before I tried to carry on a serious conversation with anyone else in the room. At least if I wanted them to take me seriously. I reminded myself that my objective was to see if any of these guests had a lead for me on the photograph.

For a fleeting second I considered asking Edward if I might show him the photo and ask for his input. But I felt off balance and didn't want to risk offending the "Founder of the Feast" by letting him know the only reason I was there was to carry out some amateurish detective work.

Instead of continuing the conversation in any direction, normal or abnormal, I looked away from his questioning gaze. "Would it be all right if I used your restroom?"

"Our restroom? Do you intend to have a rest?"

"Excuse me?"

"Were you asking if you might lie down to take a nap?"

"No. I would like to use the restroom . . . the bathroom . . . I want to wash up."

"Oh, of course. The WC. It's in the hallway, to the right of the stairs."

"The what?"

"WC. Short for water closet, of course."

"Oh. Thank you." I turned to go, wondering how it could be that though we were both speaking English, neither of us understood the other.

"Aren't you going to ask me what my father did?" he asked.

I stopped and looked at him over my shoulder. I wasn't sure of the proper way to respond, so I simply took the cue as if it were a riddle. "What did your father do?"

With a hint of grin he said, "My father was a famous actor."

Without a feather of a thought, I said what came immediately to my mind, borne of my life experience. "Then I'm very sorry for you."

A smile burst onto his face. He gave me an appreciative nod and raised his nearly empty glass in a toast.

I tried to inconspicuously slide out of the room.

Chapter Ten

I gave myself a stern lecture in the bathroom mirror. Or the "WC" mirror. Or was it a "looking glass" like in *Alice in Wonderland?*

Whatever it was I was looking into and whatever tiny room I was in with the itty-bitty sink and pull-chain toilet, I gazed at my pale expression and reminded my sorry self that I had never been particularly good in social settings and that this evening was further proof.

"Try to be polite, Miranda. Get some information, and then get out of here. Don't make these people remember you for all the wrong reasons."

Taking a minute to comb back my dark hair, I gathered my shoulder-length mane up in a clip and found some lip gloss for my dry lips in the side pocket of my shoulder bag.

Slightly freshened, I returned to the drawing room. The guests had gathered in an organized circle, and a game of some sort had begun. I stood at the back, observing. It took me only a moment to realize what type of game had been initiated. This was a company of actors and other theater aficionados. They were playing a form of charades, of course.

The guest who stood in the center of the room recited a line from a play, and everyone else tried to come up with either the play's name or the line that followed.

I hung back as a large man took to the center of the room and called out, "'What light through yonder window breaks?'"

The group laughed at his attempted falsetto.

Young Scrooge was the quickest to shout out, "*Romeo and Juliet!*"

Hearty pats on the back were in order for nimble Scrooge, who then moved to the center and recited one of his lines from the performance that evening.

"'Do not force me to look any longer at what I have become. Tell me instead what is to come.'"

The immediate response came from Andrew, as he delivered the following line in his Spirit of Christmas Present stage voice: "'And so it shall be!' That would be from *A Christmas Carol*, of course."

The group rumbled with comments on how, from then on, the lines should be from plays other than *A Christmas Carol*, especially because the Carlton Heath adaptation had so mercilessly slaughtered the original lines, making the quotes less than authentic. Everyone gave Scrooge a kind word or two, saying he'd done just fine.

Andrew moved right along with, "'Does it occur to you, Higgins, that the girl has some feelings?'"

"*My Fair Lady*," someone called out.

"Also known as . . ." Andrew prompted the group, as if this were a trick question. To add to the clues, he continued with the next line, "'Oh no, I don't think so. Not any feelings that we need bother about. Have you, Eliza?'"

"'I got my feelings same as anyone else,'" I said, filling in the next line under my breath. Only one person heard me. That person was Ellie.

"Well done, Miranda! You should receive extra points for coming up with the next line." To the group she said, "The play is *My Fair Lady*. Why are you stalling, Andrew?"

"Ah!" Edward stepped forward and said with a triumphant flash, "*My Fair Lady*, originally entitled *Pygmalion*."

A collective "of course" sigh rippled across the room.

"Miranda, were you in a performance of *My Fair Lady* at one time?" Ellie asked.

"No, I've never been in a play."

"Really? Neither have I. I like you better by the moment. Here I thought I was the only one in this group who was inexperienced on the stage."

I didn't respond to her comment because I couldn't say I was inexperienced on the stage. I just had never officially been in a performance. My mother had played the role of Eliza Doolittle on a stage somewhere when I was around six. She taught me how to read with that script.

Edward was in the circle now. He paused, thinking, glancing around the room. He looked at Ellie, as if seeking some bolstering of his courage. She glittered and glowed and blew her dashing husband a kiss. The charming moment led me to believe that Edward was much more humble than his circumstances would have suggested. I felt a fondness for both of them, which surprised me because I barely knew them.

Edward kept looking at Ellie, and then his sweeping gaze turned to me. In that moment, he seemed to have found his line.

I told myself I could be imagining the connection, but when I heard his line, I knew I had inadvertently inspired him. It was my name. He delivered Miranda's final line in *The Tempest*:

"'O wonder! How many goodly creatures are there here! How beauteous mankind is! O brave new world that has such people in't!'"

No one in the room responded. They looked at each other with shrugs and mumbles.

"Where did he come up with that one?" Ellie shook her head at her husband and showered my arm with her fairy dust.

"It's from *The Tempest,*" I said, being sure to keep my voice low.

"*The Tempest?*" she asked. "Shakespeare, right? How do you know all these lines?"

I shrugged, hoping to appear naive. I hadn't seen a production of *The Tempest.* I knew the line because I had read the script many times. During my years with the television-less Doralee, I read. I didn't go to plays, but I read dozens of them, many times over.

Edward repeated his line with an eyebrow partly raised in anticipation of victory at the parlor game. "Anyone? Anyone at all? Even a guess?"

I felt fairly certain it wasn't polite to one-up a host. Ellie didn't seem to think the same way.

"She knows it," Ellie said, pointing at me. "Go ahead, Miranda."

All eyes turned toward me.

I froze and then realized the best way to get all eyes off me was to say the answer. "*The Tempest.*"

Edward looked impressed, or maybe the better way to

describe his reaction was "intrigued." He bowed and made a sweep of his hand to show that the floor was mine. I had forgotten about that part of the game. It was my turn to stump the experts. I didn't want to be in the center of this group.

"That's okay." I raised my hand and stepped back, closer to the fireplace. "You can go again. I don't have any ideas. Just, please, go again."

"But it's your turn," Ellie said.

"Really, I can't . . . I don't have . . ."

My expression must have reflected my discomfort because Ellie, the perfect pink hostess, stepped forward. "Miranda gave her turn to me. And I have a good one. Are you ready?"

I appreciated Ellie more in that moment than she could ever know.

To avoid further embarrassment, I backed up a few feet from the rest of the group and stood beside the leather chairs by the hearth.

Ellie dove in with a line I didn't recognize. Another woman knew the play, shouted the answer, and gleefully took the spotlight.

I noticed Katharine across the room and remembered why I had been invited to this party in the first place. Glancing around for a clock to see what time it was, I wondered when I needed to leave for the train station. I spotted an antique clock tucked in among the decorations on the mantel. Taking two steps closer to the fire to see the correct time on the small face, my eye caught a lineup of family photos in an assortment of frames. In the first photo, a little girl stood beside an elaborately decorated Christmas tree. She wore a frilly dress with a wide sash around the middle and shiny black Mary Janes with white, cuffed ankle socks. She stood up straight, sporting a great big cheesy smile. Her arms were so closely pressed to her sides that her very full skirt was flat on either side while swooping out in the front and back like a canoe with a ruffly petticoat.

Next to that sweet picture was a larger photo. This one was of a little boy wearing pajamas and a pair of brown felt reindeer antlers. His expression was pure eight-year-old glee as he peered inside the partially unwrapped Christmas gift on his lap.

Moving on to the most ornate frame next to the clock, I drew closer, and my breath caught in the back of my throat.

It was the picture. *The* photograph. Father Christmas and the wailing boy. The exact photo I was carrying in my purse, only the picture on the mantel was larger and less faded. And in an ornate frame, just as Katharine had said she remembered. The picture was here. In this home.

I sank into the leather chair beside the fire and felt the room fold in on me.

How can this be? Who are these people?

The truth I had been seeking all these years was so close I could touch it. Only I couldn't move. I could barely breathe.

Chapter Eleven

My thoughts scurried around, trying to form some sort of order.

Who is the man in the photo? Who is the boy? What is the photo doing in this house? Why did my mother have a copy of that picture? Was Josh right? Did my mother know one of the people in the photo? Is one of them possibly . . . my father?

The game was beginning to wind down. Ellie floated through the circle of guests, urging them to have more food. I leaned forward, hoping to catch her eye. My unspoken request worked, and she came toward me.

"Would you like something to drink, Miranda?"

"No, I . . ."

"Have you tried the sugarplum punch yet? It's not spiked. At least I don't think it is. Trouble is, I haven't managed to keep my eye on Andrew all evening so I can't guarantee he hasn't instigated his usual shenanigans. Would you like something else to eat?"

"No, I . . ." I glanced at the mantel, feeling my heart pressing against my chest with firm thumps. "I . . . I wondered . . . is that . . ."

Ellie looked at the clock on the mantel. "Are you looking for the correct time? Because if you are, that clock is notoriously slow. You need to leave here in time to catch the train back to London, isn't that right?"

"Yes, but . . ." I instinctively glanced at my watch. Regardless of the actual time, the hands had moved another minute. They were now pointed straight up. Midnight. My journey through Christmas past and Christmas present had brought me here, to this "midnight moment." The photo in my purse matched the photo on the mantel; the past, present, and future had intersected.

"You would have no trouble catching the 10:42 to London, if you left here in about ten minutes," Ellie said. "Or fifteen, if you like. I would be happy to give you a ride to the station. How does that sound to you?"

I couldn't leave yet. Not until I knew . . .

"Ellie, I . . . I . . . The photo on the mantel. Who are those people?"

"Our children. They were downstairs at the beginning of the party, but they have both gone off to bed. Perhaps you didn't see them. That's our daughter, Julia. She's five now. And our son, Mark, is twelve."

"And the other photo? The one by the clock?"

"Isn't that the best? I love that picture! Everyone loves that photo. Everyone but my husband. I had to fight with Edward to put it out this year. His mother always had the picture there on the mantel at Christmas. You would think after more than thirty-five years my husband would give in to displaying it every year. Doesn't it capture a four-year-old's tantrum perfectly?"

"So that's Edward? The boy in the photo is your husband?"

Ellie nodded, smiling fondly at the photo.

I estimated Edward and Ellie to be in their late thirties or early forties. Edward wasn't old enough to be my father. That meant . . .

"The man in the photo?" I ventured, rising to my feet and standing next to Ellie for a closer look.

Ellie looked surprised that I didn't know. "That's James, of course."

My ears seemed to have opened to hear what Doralee and I had missed all those years ago. "Jay Ames," I repeated.

"That's right, Sir James. Edward's father."

I felt my legs wobble and lowered myself back into the leather chair.

"Sir James played the perfect Father Christmas for years. I remember sitting on his lap when I was five and having my picture taken. He gave me two lollies for being such a good girl that year. I really thought he was *the* Father Christmas."

"Sir James Whitcombe," I repeated, feeling the weight of his name on my tongue. Sweeping the room with my gaze I asked, "Is he here?"

Ellie looked at me oddly. "Do you mean, is he still alive?"

I nodded only once, not sure I could bear the answer either way.

"No. He passed away a year ago September. Perhaps the news wasn't as publicized in the US. I can tell you this: he was a wonderful man, regardless of what you may have read in the rags. He deserved to be knighted as he was. The lies that were said about him over the years were terrible. Just terrible. Sir James had so much dignity, so much integrity, that he never fought against the slander. He let people have their say and never went up against them to prove them wrong. I remember one time after Edward and I were first married when . . ."

Another wellspring of long-suppressed tears bubbled over my lower lids.

"Oh, you poor dear. You must be exhausted, and here I am, blathering on." Ellie perched on the side of the chair and patted my arm. "Katharine said you only arrived today. I'll get your coat, and we can be on our way to the station now, if you like."

With another pat on my arm, she added, "You know, it's such a pity you're not staying on in Carlton Heath. We do have a guest room, if I could at all persuade you to stay. We would be delighted to have you join us for Christmas dinner."

Before I could process the idea of staying, Andrew strode into the center of our conversation. "You've done it then, Miranda, haven't you?"

"Pardon?"

"The snow."

"Snow?" Ellie repeated.

"Have you not looked out the window since we arrived?" With a nod toward me Andrew said, "I asked if you had brought the snowflakes with you, did I not? What I should have asked was how much snow you planned to be leaving with us."

A number of the guests gathered by the front window, peering out into the twinkle-lit darkness. Several already were leaving the party, and the headlights of their cars spotlighted the slanting flurry of snowflakes.

Two of the older guests stepped up to Ellie, saying they had decided to be on their way before the roads became disagreeable. She hurried off to gather their coats and mine, promising to be right back.

I tried to think. It had all come at me so quickly.

What should I do? Should I show Ellie and Edward the photo? Then what would I tell them? That I have reason to believe Sir James might be—no, could *be—my father?*

"I can't do that," I mumbled.

"Can't do what? Stay on for the night? Of course you can." Andrew was still standing close by with a glass in his large hand. "I heard the invitation with my own ears. If you stay on, there's a good chance I can introduce you to my son."

Finding an easy smile for the endearing man in the midst of all my pulsing thoughts, I realized what an idyllic setting this was. I couldn't, I wouldn't, toss a grenade into the middle of this lovely family on Christmas Eve. I needed to leave. I didn't belong here. I needed time to think.

"Andrew," I said plainly, "I need to go back to London. I know Ellie offered to give me a ride to the train station, but do you think I might be able to ride with you and Katharine instead? I need to leave right away."

"Are you sure you want to be leaving?"

"Yes. If you don't mind."

Andrew tilted his head and slowly began to wag a finger. "You know what it is? It's the eyes. That's what it is."

He looked at the photo of Sir James on the mantel and back at me.

"Aye, that's what it is. It's the eyes. Like a mountain stream in the highlands, that's what they are. You have the clearest blue eyes I've seen since Sir James, rest his soul."

I swallowed and looked away.

"Now, he was a man of honor, he was. Why, we wouldn't be having the Dickens performances if it weren't for Sir James and his generosity to the town and to the preservation of the theater. He was a man of great benevolence. I like to think he would have enjoyed our humble show this year."

With a nod, he turned to his wife, who had joined us in the middle of his speech. I didn't look directly at Katharine. I didn't know how much of Andrew's oration she was taking in, and I also didn't know how strong her powers of deduction were. She was the only person to whom I had shown the photo. And she was standing only a few feet from the mantel. It would be too easy for Katharine to connect the dots.

"Miranda is in need of a ride. To the train station. I offered our services, Katharine. Are you ready to be on our way?"

Katharine hesitated before asking in her firm, gentle voice, "Did you find what you were looking for when you came here, Miranda?"

I paused before answering carefully with one word. "Possibly."

Katharine stood with her hands folded in front of her elegant red evening gown, and I knew that she knew. I can't explain how I knew, but I did.

I ventured a glance in her direction. Katharine was looking at me with the sort of smile that is shared between two women when one is holding the other woman's secret as carefully as a bird's egg that has fallen from its nest. It was easy to believe she wouldn't drop the precious bundle. At least not here. Not on Christmas Eve.

Chapter Twelve

Ellie strode across the drawing room toward us with my coat over her arm. Pink sparkles danced in her wake.

"I'm so sorry, Miranda. I got sidetracked. We should be on our way, don't you think?"

Before I could answer, Andrew said, "We'll be cartin' her off, so you won't have to drive in the snow." He stepped closer to Ellie and gave her a good look up and down, as if he had just noticed her outfit.

Turning to Katharine, he said, "You may need to drive, my love."

"Why is that, Andrew?"

"I avoided overdoing it on the punch, and yet I do believe I'm beginning to see pink Ellie-funts."

His pun took only a moment to sink in. As soon as it did, a chorus of groans followed.

"I will remember that one, Andrew MacGregor." Ellie held out my coat.

Andrew intercepted and held the coat for me so I might slip my arms in more easily.

"Ian will be disappointed." Andrew's boldness took over. "He would've wanted to meet you, Miranda. And what a pity you won't be staying through Christmas."

"Miranda, you are welcome to stay here with us, if you like," Ellie said. "Our guest room is ready. As I said before, we would be honored to have you for as long as you like. Truly."

Before I could slide my other arm into the coat, Andrew lowered it nearly to the floor. I turned to see what had happened, and he said, "You won't be needing this in the guest room, now, will you?"

A string of objections rolled off my tongue. I had already paid for a hotel room in London and my suitcase was sitting in that room, unopened, with everything I needed for an overnight stay.

Ellie quickly made mincemeat of all my objections and indicated with her expression that the decision had been made. I had the feeling that if I made another peep, I would be viewed as an annoyance and the invitation would soon be regretted.

My adrenaline must have been running low by that point because I took the path of least resistance and decided I would stay the night. I could collect my thoughts in the solitude of a guest room or a hotel room. The guest room was closer.

"All right. I will stay, if you're sure it's okay." I was, in a way, asking the question of Katharine as much as I was asking it of Ellie. My glance went to Katharine first.

She closed her eyes only a moment and gave her head a slight nod. It seemed as if she was granting me approval.

Ellie was much more effusive. "Of course it's okay. The more the merrier! Katharine already knows this about me, but I don't know if you do, Andrew. When I was a university student, I had the romantic notion of spending a semester in Portugal. I was alone in Lisbon over the holidays, and it was the worst Christmas of my life. The thought of you going to London but not meeting up with family or friends once you get there, well, I'm not one to tell you what to do. I can only say that, when I spent a Christmas by myself, it was desperately depressing. So you see, I have my own reasons for wanting you to stay."

I knew this group of kind-hearted people would be stunned to know that most of my Christmases had been spent alone. Ellie's invitation was offered from her heart, and from a frightened yet awed corner of my heart, I accepted.

"Now that we have that settled, we'll be on our way, then." Andrew said. But he and Katharine chatted a few more minutes with Ellie about joining the Whitcombes for Christmas dinner after the morning church service. All the plans were set, and the two of them made their way to the front door, along with most of the other guests.

I followed, not sure what else to do. At the door, Katharine turned and gave me a look that I interpreted to be reassurance that I had made the right decision and everything was going to be okay. I raised my hand in a good-bye wave as she followed her kilted Christmas Present out into the drifts of snow.

"The guest room is upstairs, third door on the right." Ellie explained that she would gather a few overnight items for me and leave them on the bed. She also said she and Edward would be up for a while longer because she had a few more gifts to wrap.

"Christmas services are at ten thirty. Christmas dinner will be at two o'clock."

The awkwardness that should have been present when

trying to fit a stranger into a family's holiday schedule was absent around Ellie. That grace was due, I think, to her easy-going manner. She seemed content to let the rest of the night and the holiday roll along at its own pace.

"Is there anything I can do to help clean up?" I asked.

All but two of the guests had gone, and one of them was clearing the serving table and carrying the dishes into another room. The other guest was leaning against the mantel, deep in conversation with Edward, who looked respectfully concerned about what the older man was saying.

"Whatever would make you feel the most comfortable, Miranda. That's what you should do. And just for your reference, the kitchen can be reached through the hall and to the far right."

Ellie took my coat from me once again and flitted off. I stood in the almost empty drawing room and didn't know what to do. Edward was still occupied with the man wearing a tweed jacket and a red woolen vest underneath. I should have been ready to head to the isolation of the guest room but, in that moment, helping to clean up seemed the right thing to do.

The other woman, a white-haired worker bee, gave brusque directions to me, as if I were her servant girl. I didn't mind. She seemed to have a system going. She also seemed to be the sort who lived to serve and loved to be commended for her service.

I cleared all the plates that had been left in the drawing room on end tables, chair arms, and bookshelves. The bee woman had a tray ready for me to stack all the plates and carry them to the kitchen. I followed the directions Ellie had given, out into the large entry hall, then to the far right.

The kitchen was well lit and surprisingly modern compared to everything else I had seen of the house so far. A large center island was at the hub of the kitchen. The island and all the counters were black marble. Gleaming copper pots hung above the stove. A painted clay pot in the window held a long-stemmed orchid that exploded with three exotic purple blooms. Beside the tropical flower was a nativity scene carved in wood and painted in primary colors that had faded since the set's debut.

Stepping closer to the kitchen sink that was directly under the wide window, I examined the crèche. The irregularities of the pieces made it look handmade. The cast seemed to be all there: Mary and Joseph, the shepherds with their lambs, the wise men in turbans with a long-legged camel, an angel with outstretched wings, all of the walk-on characters of the nativity faced the star of the evening, Christ. The infant lay in a manger lined with straw and was attended by a kneeling blue Madonna and a yellow-robed Joseph, who leaned on a staff.

I made the decision then that I would go to the church service in the morning with Edward, Ellie, and their children. I had never been to a Christmas church service. My gift to my mother had been setting foot inside a theater once again. My gift to Aunt Doralee would be to set foot inside a church.

At that moment, I knew I had made enough decisions and taken in enough information for one day. One very long day. I needed to find the guest room and let sleep cover me with a blanket of time and space so all the spinning orbs in my personal cosmos could realign themselves. The world I now moved about in was not the same world I had known for the past twenty-nine years. I needed to find my center of gravity.

I tiptoed up the stairs that had bid me to climb them ever since I entered the house. After eight stairs there was a landing with a padded window seat and a large lead-paned window that looked out on an expansive garden. I paused and watched the storm illuminated by the dim light coming from the windows on the lower floor. The garden was quickly being covered with snow.

Having spent most of my life on the West Coast, I knew little about snow. I did know that sometimes it comes to the earth as gently as a dove, leaving a feather-like covering of white on homes, trees, and country fence posts. Other times, snow comes blasting into a quiet village on vicious gales of wind and heaving sheets of ice at everything in its path. Such was the snowstorm—no, such was the tempest—that I watched that Christmas Eve.

Yet I was safe, tucked away in a spacious guest room in a home built by Edward Whitcombe's great-great-grandfather. A man who, quite possibly, could be my great-great-grandfather, as well.

Chapter Thirteen

The sort of crying I gave in to that night in the guest room was important crying. I wept as a woman in mourning. I mourned the absence of a father in my childhood. I mourned the loss of my mother at the onset of my teen years. I mourned the loss of Doralee at the launch of my young-adult years.

And I cried for myself. For the fragments of my life that might have been about to line up.

I cried into the plump pillows that lined the tall wooden headboard of the elevated guest bed. Like Shakespeare's Miranda, in the wake of the tempest, I watched and waited with a tenacity born of unfounded hope and idealized trust. The crisp white pillowcases caught all my tears and held them the way the sails of a ship gather wind.

My tears came without much sound. The few muffled sobs that leaked out went deep into the pillows and stayed there. Once the storm ceased, I knew that a season of my life had ended in that guest room. My breath returned to me in calm measures, and I began to think about what was to come. In that place of peace, I made a decision.

I would keep my possible connection to Sir James a secret. I would take the secret with me to the grave, as my mother had.

I also decided that as soon as I had a chance to see Katharine again and pull her aside, I would make her promise that she wouldn't reveal any of our shared speculations. She seemed the sort of woman who could keep a promise.

As I drifted into deep sleep, I thought about my reasoning for such a decision. My connection to this family wouldn't change anything. Whether or not Sir James was my father wouldn't change who I was or what I did or how I chose to live my life. The possibility—the evidence that seemed clear to me—was enough to satisfy me. What kind of disruption would my declaration make in this home where "grace" and "peace" were the sentries at the front door? I liked the thought of being noble. Keeping the speculations to myself seemed the most noble route I could take.

I awoke from a deep and dreamless sleep while it was still dark. The small clock beside the bed told me it was 7:09. Christmas morning.

To pad down the hallway to the bathroom, I needed to pull on my travel-rumpled gray pants, white T-shirt, and V-neck sweater. Inching the door open as quietly as possible, I tiptoed across the runner on the wood floor of the long hallway. Every third or fourth step the floor creaked, making it impossible to cover the distance without creating a dreadful amount of noise.

Attempting to run the water quietly, I washed my face, holding the cool cloth over my tear-swollen eyes. With a squirt of toothpaste on my finger, I gave my teeth a less-than-effective scrub. At least my hair was easy to catch up in a clip in the back. I didn't look my best, but I felt okay. Ready to meet whatever was ahead. My center of gravity was returning and that center was me, just as it had been out of necessity for the past decade and a half.

I was a few feet past the bathroom door when one of the bedroom doors along the hallway opened. Five-year-old Julia appeared wearing a pink nightgown and fuzzy, duck-shaped slippers. She looked out at me expectantly.

Her expression turned to a frown. "You're not Father Christmas."

"No," I whispered, with a finger to my lips, "I'm not Father Christmas."

"Who are you?" She didn't lower her voice on my cue.

"My name is Miranda. I'm . . ." I didn't know how to explain who I was. "I'm visiting your mother and father."

"Why do you talk like that?"

I kept whispering, hoping she would take the hint to keep her voice low as well. "I don't live here in England. I'm from America."

"Are you a film star?" She looked hopeful.

I shook my head.

"One time when I was little we had a film star who came to our house, and he stayed in that room." She pointed to the guest room where I had just come from. "He came to our house the day my grandfather went to heaven."

She looked at me more closely. With a tilt of her head she asked, "Did you know my grandfather?"

A knife went through my heart. "No," I barely whispered. "I didn't know your grandfather."

I bit the inside of my lip and then added before the tears could come, "I wish I could have met him."

She yawned a kitten-sized yawn.

Redirecting all my emotions, I said, "You should probably go back to bed. At least for a little bit."

"But I want to go downstairs to see if Father Christmas has come with the presents." Her dark eyes twinkled. "Will you go downstairs with me?"

My experience with appropriate protocol when visiting a family on Christmas Day was nil. The only point of reference I had was American movies in which eager children in pajamas bounded down the stairs at dawn and found a massive collection of wrapped gifts under the Christmas tree.

My childhood memories included gifts wrapped in playbills and scrawny trees decorated with silver tinsel. On Christmas morning, my mother and I didn't scramble to open our few gifts. Our tradition was to stay in bed and share a box of Whitman's Sampler chocolates for breakfast. Then we opened our presents.

My mother always clapped as I opened my gifts, which were usually items such as new socks that hadn't come from the thrift store like the rest of my clothes. Every year, I wrapped up the little bottles of hotel lotions and shampoos, and she never failed to act surprised and pleased. She would open the tops of the bottles and breathe in the scent as if I had given her a bottle of perfume direct from Paris. The rest of the day we watched holiday movies, and sometimes my mother took a nap.

"Will you come with me? Please?" Sleepy-eyed Julia tugged on my sleeve and looked adorable in her yellow ducky slippers.

I glanced up and down the hall and fell into a role I didn't know I could play. "All right. I'll go with you, but we must be very, very quiet. We don't want to disturb Father Christmas if he's still downstairs."

"Do you think he's still here?" Julia's eyes widened the way I'm sure my eyes must have widened whenever my mother verbally turned an unseen combination lock and opened to me a parallel world of make-believe.

"I don't know. We can go see. Your feet must make only the softest of tiptoeing sounds as we go down the stairs. Are you ready?"

Julia nodded and slipped her small hand into mine.

With tiny steps, we made our way down the hallway to the stairs. Nimble Julia made an "oh no" face at me when our weight on the second stair produced a loud creak.

From behind one of the other bedroom doors at the end of the long hallway I heard sounds as if someone else in the house was stirring. I hoped what I was doing with Julia was okay. I didn't know if I might be spoiling some family tradition with our descent to the lower level of the quiet house.

We made it to the landing where the stairs took a turn before continuing with the final eight steps that led into the grand entryway. I was prepared to start the next flight of steps when Julia stopped and let go of my hand.

She let out a little gasp and flew to the window seat. Outside, in the pale rose shade of the rising dawn, the world appeared as soft and airy as a pure white dove. The blush from the winter sun enlivened the snowy horizon with a glistening glow of otherworldly first light. One glance was not enough to take it all in.

I stood beside mesmerized Julia, and together we watched

the day come forth on white-feathered wings. With a touch of splendor, the undressed trees seemed transformed into regal maids-in-waiting, shimmering with icicle-shaped diamonds dripping from their elegant ears and slender arms.

"Is that snow?" Julia asked, whispering for the first time.

"Yes, that's snow. It's beautiful, isn't it?" I whispered back.

Julia nodded, her gaze still fixed on the unparalleled show outside the large window, where the day before a sleeping garden had stretched out brown and unnoticed.

I sat beside her on the padded window seat. With complete trust, she curled up in my lap, leaning her head against the soft inner curve of my shoulder.

Never before did I remember feeling as if another human was so completely at ease, sinking into me for companionship and comfort. I used to snuggle this way with my mother any chance I had. She didn't seem to tire of the positions I chose or the times when I needed the security of her touch. It hadn't occurred to me that I might one day provide that same source of tenderness for a young life.

Then it came to me that Julia was more than just any little girl. If Sir James was my father and Edward was my half brother, then Julia was my niece.

Drawing a breath for courage, I faced the fact that if I walked away from an exploration of my possible heritage, I would lose more than the sure knowledge of who my father was. I would lose the only half brother I would ever have, along with his Sugarplum Fairy wife. I would lose a twelve-year-old nephew I hadn't met yet. And I would lose my only niece, the adorable embodiment of sweetness, who was now cuddled up in my arms and whose soft brown hair smelled like warm maple syrup.

The price of my decisive nobility was going to be much higher than I had first estimated.

Chapter Fourteen

Father Christmas and gifts under the tree forgotten, little Julia stayed close to me in the window seat. Together we watched two red and brown birds flit from the icy branches of an apple tree and land in the fresh snow. The early birds hopped across the clean white carpet, leaving their tiny footprints to mark their trail to the snow-covered bird feeder. With a flutter of their wings, the two birds pecked and flicked through the snow before reaching their chilly breakfast.

I stroked Julia's silky hair and hummed the only Christmas carol I could remember at the moment—"Silent Night."

Julia leaned into me and released a contented sigh.

All was calm. All was bright.

The gift to me in that timeless moment on the bench seat was a gift of understanding. I experienced in a small way the bliss my mother must have felt when she held me in her arms. I was her baby doll. To her credit, she did the very best she could at loving me despite her disjointed life.

The years of blame I had assigned to my mother for choosing to live within the fairy-tale castle of her own mind all seemed to evaporate when I felt the unlabored breathing of small, trusting Julia. How could a woman not choose to gather up a tiny version of herself and valiantly protect, nurture, and delight in such a marvel?

By my best estimations, my mother was eighteen when I was born. Maybe nineteen. If she had relatives she could have sent me to, she never hinted at it. If she considered handing me over to an adoption agency, it was only a private contemplation.

Her decision had been to keep the two of us together, and now I understood why. This. This closeness. This chance to share the moments of wonder together. My mother wanted me. That in itself was a precious gift.

That truth was the gift I received that Christmas morning. My mother wanted me. She wanted me close to her heart. And she always kept me there.

In that Christmas morning moment, with little Julia enclosed in my embrace, I looked out the frost-laced window and released Eve Carson, the actress, from all her failures toward me, her miniature self. I then thanked Eve Carson, the mother, for every right thing she did in proving how much she wanted me.

I wondered: If she had lived, and if I had asked, would she have told me who my father was? And if she did tell, would she have told me the truth? I knew I would have wanted the imaginary answers more than I would have wanted the unbendable truth. But still, I wondered. What would she have said if she knew I was here, in this home, with these people? What details of my existence would she at last reveal to me?

"What about Father Christmas?" Julia reached up and patted my face. "And the presents. We must go see the presents!"

I helped her off my lap, and we were about to tiptoe down

the remaining eight steps when I heard a door open in the hallway above us.

"We must hurry!" Julia whispered, circling back to the playful excitement of being on a secret mission. She padded down the stairs in her yellow slippers, reaching for my hand as she went.

I followed eagerly.

The grand entryway was even grander in the faint daylight. Soft rays of steady sunlight pierced through the colored glass in the two tall arched windows that rose like pillars on either side of the stairway. A bucket of morning glorious colors spilled over the wooden floor and caught a gathering of dust particles in the spotlight right in the middle of their waltz.

I stopped just a moment and held out my hand as if I could catch one of the lit-up dust particles the way I had long ago stopped to catch a raindrop in my palm on an Oregon afternoon. Julia tugged on my hand. "Come on!"

Scrambling, I followed her into the drawing room. All evidence of the party from the night before had been cleared away. In the corner, the full green Christmas tree was lit up with twinkling lights. Under the tree was a mound of fabulously wrapped gifts. Ellie had accomplished her late-night goal with panache.

"Oooh." Julia's eager expression was worthy of a picture. I wished I had a camera just then to capture the magic in her eyes. She hung back, looking without touching. Maybe she knew the family traditions. I guessed she knew she must wait for the others. Or maybe all she wanted was to have a peek at this feast for the eyes. Everything about the room was enchanting in the thin morning light. The dark wood of the fireplace along with the deep cocoa brown leather of the chairs set the tone of sophistication, but all the added touches gave the room its regal feel.

I joined Julia in taking in the elegance of this room that was dressed up for Christmas morning. In addition to Ellie's pink touches throughout the greenery swags and the strings of gold beads that hung from the chandeliers, I noticed other details that had been hidden last night when the room was brimming with guests. My eyes went to the hand-painted blue Delft tiles that lined the inside of the fireplace and to the large floor rug with the small red birds woven into it. An engaging pattern of waving green and gold vines was laced throughout the thick curtains that hung from the ceiling to the floor alongside the front window. The drapes were drawn back with golden cords, making a soft frame for the pristine view of the snow-blanketed world outside the window. All the room needed was a fire in the hearth to warm things up, and it would be as perfect a setting for a Christmas card as ever there could be.

A thought both tender and sad settled on me. This time it wasn't a thought about my mother or my father or my past. The thought was of my future. One day I wanted to be married. I wanted to have a daughter. I wanted her to know who her father was and to have a precious, close relationship with him. I wished that if I did have a daughter someday, I could bring her to this home, this room, on Christmas morning. I wanted her to have all this wonder.

The tender sadness covering my wish was that I didn't belong here. Not really. This wasn't my place or my world to dream about.

And yet I was here. Against all the odds, I was here. On Christmas Day. With family, really, even though they didn't know that. In my heart I knew this place, these people, were my people. And I didn't know who to thank for that. How had I ended up here?

The coincidences were too many. If there truly was a heavenly Father over us all, as Doralee had proclaimed until the end, then he had chosen to play the part of Father Christmas for me and had given me this gift of knowing, of being reasonably certain of who my father was.

Standing alongside Julia, hand in hand in this room of gifts, warmth, and light, it seemed almost possible to believe in God the way a child believes in Father Christmas.

Thinking of the line that Andrew delivered in the performance—"Come in, come in, and know me better, friend"—I saw myself as the trembling Scrooge, standing on the doorstep of Christmas Present. All this bounty was being opened to me, and yet I couldn't come in. Not all the way. I couldn't enter. It wasn't mine to receive.

Julia looked up at me with a different sort of "ooh!" expression. This one was along the lines of "Uh-oh, I forgot something!"

"Our stockings," she said. "I didn't look for my stocking."

My eyes went to the fireplace. No stockings hung there. They were the only key Christmas item missing from this cozy setup.

"You're right. There are no stockings hanging by the fire. Maybe Santa Claus—I mean, Father Christmas—forgot to bring them this year."

"You silly! Father Christmas doesn't hang our stockings by the fire. He hangs them on our bedposts."

"Oh. Well, then let's sneak upstairs and see if Father Christmas remembered to hang a stocking from your bedpost."

"No. I was the one who put the stocking there." Julia gave me a don't-you-know-anything look. "Father Christmas comes and puts the sweets in my stocking. I hope I get a Lion Bar this year. They're my favorite. Do you like Lion Bars?"

"I don't know. I don't think I've ever had a Lion Bar."

I could tell by her amazed expression she thought I had come from Jupiter because Jupiter had to be the only place in the universe that didn't have Lion Bars.

"If Father Christmas didn't put a Lion Bar in your stocking and if he put two in mine, I'll give you one of mine," Julia said.

Stroking her soft cheek I whispered, "Thank you."

Together we retraced our trail upstairs with more noise than we had managed on our way down. Julia raced to her room. I followed, still not sure if I was aiding and abetting a wild little tradition-breaker running free in the Whitcombe household.

When Julia pushed open her bedroom door, she gave a happy squeal, and I knew that Father Christmas had plumped up her stocking. I also heard another bedroom door open farther down the hall.

Assuming either her brother or her parents were up and about, I slipped back into my guest room and closed the door. I didn't want to be in the way.

To my surprise, Father Christmas had visited my room while I was downstairs with Julia. On one of my bedposts hung a long red sock. My name had been written with curling letters on a piece of white fabric, which was attached to the top of the stocking.

I sat on the end of the bed and examined the stocking. I had never had a Christmas stocking before. The gesture of sweet hospitality was almost too much to swallow. In the toe of the stocking was a mandarin orange that made a nice bulge and added a fresh, sweet scent to the room as I emptied all the goodies onto the top of the down comforter.

Along with the orange, my treats included a purple pen attached to a notepad, six pieces of candy (four hard pieces and two chewy), the highly praised Lion Bar (a chocolate candy bar), and a small bag of cashews.

Snuggling back under the covers, I started with the chocolate bar, remembering all the times my mother and I had dined on chocolates for our Christmas morning breakfast. The Lion Bar had a strip of caramel inside. My mother would have liked that. One bite, and I knew why it was Julia's favorite.

I moved on to the cashews and the two chewy pieces of candy. The orange I saved for last. I sucked each wedge slowly, savoring the fresh taste in my mouth. Glancing up, I caught my reflection in the large mirror above the dresser across the room. Positioning the orange slice just right, I spread my lips and flashed a wide, orange-toothed smile at my reflection.

The image made me laugh. I kept smiling and realized it had been a long, long time since I had laughed. A happy thought settled on me. Could it be that after all these years of winter in my life, it was finally, at long last, Christmas?

I dared to believe it could be so.

Chapter Fifteen

Remaining under the cozy down comforter, I smiled to myself, thinking of being here on Christmas morning and not alone in a London hotel room. Father Christmas had brought me something else for Christmas—being here, in this place, with these people. And I felt blissfully young.

Decisions regarding some strategic conversations would have to take place eventually. But for now I could linger, open my gifts of Christmas morning ever so slowly, and relish the lavishness of it all.

That's what I told myself as I lounged in the puffy comfort of the guest bed, gazing outside at the sunlight on the new-fallen snow.

A soft tapping came on the bedroom door. It was more like a patting than a tapping. I guessed it was Julia and called out, "Come in!"

Instead of Julia, Ellie's curious face appeared when the door opened. "So you are awake. Good morning and happy Christmas!"

"Happy Christmas to you, too."

"Julia said you showed her the snow and the presents under the tree."

"I hope that was okay." I sat up in bed.

"Yes, yes, of course it's okay. I told you to feel at home, and that's exactly what we want you to do." Ellie's hair had returned to its natural brunette shade, sans sparkles of any kind. She was wearing a plush white robe and fluffy slippers on her bare feet. The ensemble was quite a departure from the Sugarplum outfit of the evening before.

"I've come to see if you would like to join us downstairs around the tree."

I hesitated, still not sure how it could be okay for me to crash another one of their parties. "I think I'll stay here," I said. "But I would like to go to church with you later."

"Lovely!" Ellie surveyed the combat zone on my bed where all the food items had been annihilated quickly.

"Thanks for the stocking," I said, feeling shy. "I loved it, as you can see."

She smiled. "I'm sure Father Christmas would be pleased to know how much you enjoyed the gifts he left for you. Now, would you like a cup of tea, or perhaps some hot chocolate? I always make hot chocolate for the children before they open their gifts."

I smiled and nodded. "I can come down to the kitchen and get it."

"No, no, no! You stay right where you are. I'll bring it to you."

Ellie backed up and closed the door behind her before I could protest. I was still having a hard time believing her generosity. What woman with a husband and two children wouldn't consider a stray houseguest to be a burden on Christmas Day? Especially a houseguest who was a stranger?

Ellie returned with a red Christmas mug on a tray and served it to me while I was still in bed. Along with the cocoa she had brought a small croissant, a slice of well-toasted wheat bread, and a little dish of orange marmalade. I felt foolish, like a child being showered with kindness on a day she had faked an illness to play hooky from school.

"Come downstairs whenever you wish."

"Thank you."

With a flutter of her hand Ellie closed the door, but the end of her long robe got caught. Giggling, she opened the door, pulled up her robe and, with a swish, closed the door again. She may have washed away all the sparkles in her morning shower, but from where I sat, she still appeared to be a Sugarplum Fairy.

I leisurely finished my breakfast in bed and then slid back under the inviting comforter for a little doze. I was beginning to see how my mother could so easily fall into nap mode on Christmas after our breakfast of chocolates. So much chocolate at one time may release lovely endorphins, but that much sugar on an empty stomach could cause a lull, and that's exactly what it did to me.

The sleep I swam into was soothing. I dreamed of Ellie and Edward wanting me, inviting me to dine with them. The table was heavy with all sorts of wonderful things to eat. The laughter echoed off the walls, and Julia came over and climbed into my lap.

I woke and stretched. I had slept for probably only ten or fifteen minutes, but the nap had rejuvenated me. I reached into my shoulder bag beside the bed and pulled out the blue velvet pouch with the golden tassels. The photo was still there. I stared at it and knew I hadn't imagined any of this. It was the same photo as the one sitting on the mantel downstairs.

My birth certificate had been locked up long ago in a home safe in the closet of my San Francisco apartment. The folded-up playbill lay in the velvet pouch. I had a look at it and ran my eyes over words I had read many times.

"Lake Shore Community Theater Presents Shakespeare's *THE TEMPEST*."

My mother's name was listed beside the role of Miranda. It would have been so helpful, so obvious, if the name "James Whitcombe" appeared next to one of the other characters' names. It would have all been there in black and white, and I could explain how my mother had fallen for one of the other actors, who happened to be James Whitcombe, and nine months later I had made my grand entrance onto the stage of life.

But like every other detail of my mother's life, this one wasn't that easy or that obvious.

I studied the playbill one more time. At the bottom of the paper, in small print, I read the words, "With a special thank you for the support given by the Society of Grey Hall Community Theatre."

Sitting up more fully, I read the fine print again. The Society of Grey Hall Community Theatre was the name on the plaque in front of Grey Hall where the performance had been held last night. I hadn't made the connection then.

In front of me was another small clue. Had James Whitcombe been involved in the Society of Grey Hall Community Theatre? Andrew said Sir James had contributed much to this community with his status and dedication to the theater. Had his involvement led him to the US and to this small-time community theater performance of *The Tempest*?

How was the Lake Shore Community Theater connected to the Grey Hall Community Theatre? Lake Shore group was in Michigan. I was born in Michigan and somehow ended up on the West Coast soon after. Did my mother have family in Michigan, or was she simply passing through when she joined the theater group?

It seemed that with each clue I uncovered, I picked up another string of questions. Many of those questions would never, could never, be answered. Other answers seemed to be so close, so nearly within my reach.

Tucking the photo and the playbill back into the blue velvet bag and setting it on the nightstand, I decided to venture downstairs and find a way to begin my very necessary conversation with Edward and Ellie. The evidence was mounting. I needed to say something.

I found the Whitcombe family poetically gathered around the tree. A fire blazed in the hearth. From where I stood, all the gifts appeared to have been opened. Julia was busy brushing the long hair of a new doll, and Mark, who looked tall for a twelve-year-old, stood beside his father, who was trying to fit together a control box of some sort.

"They don't exactly make this easy, do they?" Edward asked.

Ellie leaned closer. "Do you need the instructions?"

"I can get them, Father. Are they in the box?" Mark looked up and noticed my slow entrance. "Hallo. Are you Miranda?"

"Mark, mind your manners," his father said. "You should walk up to our guest, offer your hand, and introduce yourself."

Bounding past the patches of cast-aside gift wrap, Mark followed his father's instructions and came skidding up to me with a free-spirited expression that I was sure he inherited from his mother. "I am ever so pleased to make your acquaintance, madam. I am Master Mark Robert Whitcombe."

"Mark, don't be pert," Edward said.

"I'm not Pert. I'm Mark."

He received a stern look from across the room.

"Yes, Father."

"It's nice to meet you, Mark." I shook his outstretched hand. "My name is Miranda."

"My sister said you're from America, but you're not a film star."

"She's right. I am an American, but I'm not a movie star."

"Are you an actor, then?"

"No, I'm not an actor."

"Do you know any actors?"

"Yes, I have met a few."

"Really? Any ones that I would know?"

"No, none you would know."

"Mark, I have this put together now. Will you come have a look?"

Like a gazelle, the lanky twelve-year-old bounded across the room and eagerly took the controls from his father. Mark pressed a button, and out from under the camouflage of gift wrap a remote-controlled truck rumbled across the floor, heading directly for the wall. Mark used his whole body as well as his thumbs to urge the rolling vehicle to make a turn toward the center of the room.

"Well done, Mark," Ellie said.

"This is brilliant!" Mark directed the truck around a leather chair as the revved-up vehicle made a louder humming sound.

"Make it go up the wall, Markie." Julia was on her feet, watching the new toy do its stuff for the small audience.

"It doesn't go up walls. Just on floors. Don't get too close, Ju-Ju. Step back."

Ellie motioned for me to come closer to where they gathered around the tree. "If you dare," she said with a smile.

I slid onto the end of the sofa and took in the full view of the tree. Julia came over and sat beside me, showing me her new dolly and chattering about all the doll's special features, including its pony. She hopped off the couch, went for the unwrapped pony under the tree, and showed me how the doll could fit on the pony. Then Julia galloped around the room with her new toy.

Ellie shuffled the wrapping paper into a mound. Edward looked over at me and said, "Did you sleep well, Miranda?"

"Yes, very well, thank you."

"Glad to hear it. I understand you'll be joining us for church this morning."

"Yes. I hope what I'm wearing is okay for church. My luggage is still in London."

"What you're wearing will be fine," Ellie said. "You might need a warmer coat. I have several you're welcome to choose from to borrow."

"Thanks. I do need a warmer coat."

Edward seemed to be studying me. "If you don't mind, may I ask you a personal question, Miranda?"

"Certainly."

"How is it that you came to visit Carlton Heath? Our little town isn't exactly one of the usual tourist sites."

My heart beat faster. This was the opening I needed. I just hadn't prepared what to say. "I, um, I came here because—"

"Didn't Katharine say you were going to meet someone?" Ellie inserted. "Or did she say you were trying to find someone?"

"Yes," I said plainly. "I was trying to find someone."

"And how did that turn out?" Ellie asked.

This was it. This was the moment to tell Ellie and Edward who I was and why I was here. I drew in a deep breath and sat up straight.

Chapter Sixteen

Before a full sentence could tumble off my lips, everyone turned to the front window, where the driveway was visible. Up to the front of the house came a large farm horse wreathed in a harness of loud jingle bells and saddled with a big red sack of wrapped gifts. Holding the reins was a merry rounded fellow with a long, flowing snowy white beard and a long robe.

"Father Christmas!" Julia shouted, leaving her doll and pony and rushing to the front window. "It's Father Christmas!"

Mark stopped pushing the buttons on the remote control and hurried to the window. Edward and Ellie exchanged surprised glances. I stood for a better view, and for the blink of a moment, I almost believed.

"Father Christmas! Father Christmas!" Julia beat her flat palm against the front window.

"Come on, Ju-Ju." Mark was already sprinting toward the door.

Ellie and Edward followed, and I was right behind. We stepped into the crisp air. Pillowed snowdrifts lined the rounded drive. As Father Christmas strode toward the children, he hitched up his robe to reveal argyle socks that I knew had to belong to Andrew.

"Happy Christmas, one and all!" Father Christmas's booming voice caused a layer of peaceful snow to quiver off a nearby tree branch and sift its way to the ground.

Bright-eyed and full of glee, Julia gave a little hop that landed her in the snow in her yellow ducky slippers. "Hallo, Father Christmas! It's me, Julia!"

Father Christmas came close and cupped her chin in his gloved hand. "And so it is!"

"We already got our presents," she proclaimed. "We've opened them. I already ate the Lion Bar. They're my favorite. Did you come back because you have more presents for us?"

"Indeed I do."

If Mark recognized Andrew, he was to be commended for keeping a straight face and playing along for the sake of his sister. However, it seemed that Mark may have been convinced that the larger-than-life man who stood before him *was* Father Christmas.

"I understand you have been a most helpful chap this year," Andrew said, doing a fair job of masking his Scottish accent.

Mark nodded.

"That's very good. Very good indeed. I happen to have a special gift here for a young man such as yourself. Young Mark, this present is for you." He reached into the red sack tied to the saddle of the old horse and handed Mark a long box that was wrapped in gold foil and tied with a big red bow.

"And for you, young Julia . . ." He hesitated, and she shivered with excitement, giving two little hops. "Ah, yes, here it is. A gift for a special young lady who has also been a good helper to her mother this year."

"Thank you, Father Christmas!" Julia took from him a box also wrapped in gold with a red ribbon.

"I have another gift here for the master of the house and his lovely wife."

"That's my mum and dad! Mummy, you get a present, too!"

The smiles on Edward and Ellie's faces as they received the gold box were more than pleasant expressions. Both of them seemed touched by what Andrew was doing for their children. The couple slipped their arms around each other, and Ellie rested her head on Edward's shoulder.

I wondered if, by this grand performance, Andrew was picking up the Father Christmas gap that had been left when Sir James passed away. Whatever the reason, Andrew's magical appearance was a gift to all of them.

"I have one more present here. Let me see. Who is this for? Oh, yes. Miranda." His rolling brogue peeked through when he said my name. I think that one slip unveiled to Mark the identity of Father Christmas, if he hadn't figured it out before. Mark was a good big brother, though, and kept the discovery to himself.

Andrew, or rather, Father Christmas, handed me a small gold box with a red ribbon. I thanked him politely and played along by adding a bit of a curtsey. Julia followed my cue and gave a curtsey as well, jiggling with joy.

"Happy Christmas to you, one and all!"

"Happy Christmas to you, Father Christmas!" Julia could barely contain herself as Andrew mounted the stout horse and urged it to trot away.

"Thank you, Father Christmas!" Mark called out as the

endearing man and his horse etched a trail in the snow down the long driveway. "Come back next year!"

"And bring me a pony!" Julia called out.

Edward and Ellie laughed.

"May I open my present now?" Julia wiggled like a jitterbug. "Please, Mummy?"

"Of course, but wouldn't you like to go inside first?"

"Yes, my feet are cold!"

We all agreed, stomped our feet, and returned to the comfy drawing room by the fire where we sat with our gifts on our laps.

Julia and Mark didn't need to be invited twice to open their gifts. Julia unwrapped a little girl's tea set and gave a squeal of delight. She immediately went to work, placing the cups and saucers on one of the end tables.

Mark pulled from his opened box a bow-and-arrow set, complete with a quiver and its long strap to position over his shoulder. His excitement was uncontainable.

Ellie and Edward exchanged glances that said, "We're going to have a talk with Andrew about this later."

"May I try it out now?" Mark asked. The strap was in place, the three arrows were in the quiver, and his feet were heading out of the room.

"Go in front of the house," Ellie said, "so we can watch you."

"And aim away from the house," Edward added.

Mark gave his parents a gleeful smirk over his shoulder, as if they should know he was mature enough to aim the arrows in the right direction without their having to tell him.

"What did Father Christmas bring you?" Julia moved toward

me, eyeing the only unopened gift left in the room. Ellie had opened the box of candy that had been given to her and Edward.

"I don't know." I shook the small box next to my ear. "I can't imagine what it could be. Can you guess?"

"I think it's a turtle," Julia said.

I smiled at her whimsical answer. "It might be. Would you help me open it?"

I handed the gift over to our expert, and she put her five-year-old fingers to fast work, peeling back the gift wrap.

"It's not a turtle." She looked up, a little disappointed. "It's only a teapot with a ribbon."

Julia dangled the dainty Christmas tree ornament in front of me.

"Lovely," Ellie said. "And fragile, isn't it, Julia? We must be careful not to drop fragile ornaments."

"I love it." I received the gift as Julia carefully placed it in my open hands. It was the first Christmas ornament I had ever been given. I found the kindness shown to me by Ellie and now by Katharine to be far beyond my ability to understand. Were all British people this trusting and generous to strangers? Or had Katharine and Ellie sensed the same inexplicable connection to me that I felt to them?

"I know where you can keep the teapot safe," Julia said.

"Where is that?"

"You could put it in your stocking. Your Christmas stocking."

"That's a good idea, Julia. I'll do that."

"If you like, I could put it in your stocking for you. That way it won't get broken, will it, Mummy?"

"That's right, darling. A stocking is a good place for a delicate ornament."

I handed over the little teapot to Julia for safekeeping. She scampered off, and Edward went over to the front window, nodding at Mark, who was ready to take aim at a tree with his bow and arrow. Ellie tidied up the room, chattering about the explosion of gift wrap being messier than in years past.

I realized this would be a good time for me to speak up. A much better time than earlier, when the children were in the room. What I had to say was for Edward and Ellie to hear.

"Keep your elbow up, Mark," Edward called out through the front window, pointing to his elbow. In a lower voice he added, "Andrew is going to have a piece of my mind before this week is out."

"He was being kind to the children. So kind. And Mark is twelve, you know."

"Of course I know he's twelve. And he's holding a better stance than I thought he would. Has he done archery before?"

"Last summer. At the Culliford's lawn party. Do you remember how young Anna challenged Mark and the other boys to an archery contest and then bested them all?"

"Oh, yes, that's right. I had forgotten about that." Edward waved and nodded at his son, as Mark made an improved shot that glanced off the side of the tree trunk. "It might be all right after all. He does have the posture, doesn't he?"

"He's your son." Ellie sent a soft smile across the room to her husband's back.

A brief pause hovered over us, and I opened my lips to speak. Nothing came out. I began to tremble. Swallowing and stepping over to the fireplace, I reached up for the framed picture. Gathering all my courage, I tried to speak again, this time with a visual aid.

"Edward, Ellie, I wanted to say something to you both, and now seems like a good time."

They turned to face me.

I smiled.

Go ahead. Tell them.

As my lips parted, Julia skipped into the room. "Miranda, is this yours? This little blue pillow?"

Chapter Seventeen

"Julia, no!" I nearly dropped the framed photograph in my hand as I rushed to snatch the blue velvet purse away from startled Julia. Her lower lip quivered.

"It's all right," I said quickly. It didn't appear that she had opened the purse. "I was surprised to see you with this, that's all. I didn't mean to frighten you."

"Julia, it's not polite to touch other people's belongings," Edward said with a fatherly firmness.

Realizing I was still holding the frame, I took the admonition along with Julia and returned the photo to its rightful place on the mantel.

"Sorry, Miranda," Julia said in a small voice.

"It's okay, sweetie." My voice came out light and softer. I smiled in her direction, and she seemed to perk up. "Really, honey, don't feel bad."

"Julia loves to help out, don't you, darling?" Ellie went to her daughter and gave her some reassuring pats. Looking at me Ellie added, "She's forever fetching items for me. Coats and purses. Is everything all right, then?"

"Yes, fine. Sorry I jumped the way I did."

"Don't worry. It's all right. Julia, why don't you set up a tea party for us? Would you like that?"

Julia gave a timid nod and went to the end table where her tiny tea set was waiting.

"Shall I pour, or will you?" Ellie asked.

"I'll pour, silly Mummy. It's my party." Julia cast a shy glance at me.

I smiled, hoping my outburst hadn't ruined the closeness I had felt with Julia earlier.

She looked at her tea set and then back at me. "Would you like to come to my tea party, too?"

"Yes, I would like to come very much."

"Then you can sit right there." She went to work pouring invisible tea into one of the four cups.

The three of us "ladies," as Julia now called us, sipped our invisible tea while Edward remained at the window, watching his pajama-wearing son shoot another arrow into the air.

"It's a wonder he isn't frozen solid yet." Ellie glanced over her shoulder at Mark. "We should call him inside, though. We do need to get ready for the Christmas service."

Edward left the room, and Ellie excused herself from the tea party, thanking her hostess before turning back into the mother and sending Julia upstairs to dress for church. I offered to help in any way I could. Ellie assured me there was nothing more to do.

"The turkey is already in the oven," she said. "I've managed to organize everything this year, so I think there's only one thing for you to do, and this is only if you would like, because I can certainly do it later. But the cutlery needs to be laid out on the dining table."

I assumed she meant I could set the table with the silverware, but I didn't see a dining-room table in the drawing room.

"It's all on the sideboard in the dining room, which is the room directly across from the study. I can show you now, if you'd like."

Clutching the blue purse, I followed Ellie into the dining room where she showed me how she wanted the table to be set. The china plates were a cheerful seasonal pattern with sprigs of holly and bright red berries circling the edges. Each of the twelve places had a dinner plate and a bread plate. Silverware of all shapes and sizes accompanied the various plates and needed to be positioned on the table just so.

Down the center of the ivory tablecloth ran a winding swath of fresh evergreen boughs. The fragrance enlivened the rather small formal dining room. Tea candles were tucked here and there, ready to give a soft glow when the time came for the Christmas feast. Over the table hung a simple chandelier with red and green ribbons entwined around the dangling crystals.

Edward appeared in the doorway. "Ellie, did you have a chance to give one last look to the papers on the desk?"

"No, I didn't. Do you need to make the decision today, or can you wait?"

"I can wait, of course, but I will be seeing Robert at the service this morning. He is eager for an answer, you know. After the party last night, he and I put our best efforts into the discussion, but I'm afraid we have failed to come to an agreement."

"Right." Ellie handed me the forks. "The papers are still on the desk?"

"Yes."

"I'll come have a look. Then we really must dress for church."

Ellie and her husband stepped into the study across the hall.

I could hear their voices but didn't think they realized how clearly their words carried from room to room.

"It does seem, Edward, that finding this paper in your father's wallet should be reason enough to include it in the collection."

"Robert would agree with you, of course. I was only hoping for some possible clarification."

"What we really need is a fresh pair of eyes on this," Ellie said.

I heard Edward's brisk footsteps returning to the dining room. He stuck out his jaw and looked at me through the lower portion of his glasses. His stance reminded me of a scientist examining a rare bug. "Are you by any chance good at word games, Miranda?"

"Not especially."

"Pity." He sighed. "Would you mind coming and having a look anyway? We have a small problem with a short poem."

Mystified, I followed him across the hall into the study. In front of us was the fabulous, wide desk. The top of the desk was covered with papers that seemed to have been placed in a specific order. The handwriting on all the pages matched. Some of the pages were filled with words and spaced like a handwritten letter. Other pages had only a few words. Even though the pages were upside down from where I stood, I could see the consistent slant of the author's penmanship.

"It's this one." Ellie pointed to a piece of paper in the far corner. The page at one time had been folded into a small rectangle and was now yellowed along the many creases.

"We're trying to make a final decision on several pieces of my father's works, which are under consideration by the British Theatrical Preservation League for a historical collection. We're certain the piece in question is in his handwriting. It matches all the other pieces. However, this poem simply doesn't follow the pattern or logic of his other works."

"In other words, none of us understands what the poem means," Ellie said.

"We believe it was an original piece and not copied from a quote. The challenge is that we're being asked to provide some reference data and, quite frankly, we're puzzled. If there is a meaning to the piece, it certainly has escaped us."

By that point in the conversation, my heart was pounding. These were my father's papers. I was looking at his letters, in his handwriting.

Stepping to the other side of the desk, I held my racing pulse in check as I read the five lines that solidified my birthright.

by lake shore in moon glow
first time only time
as it was at the beginning of time
beguiling eve once
now ever in this failed heart

I knew what the poem meant.

I knew all about the moonlit night beside a lake on a feathery bed of moss. James Whitcombe slept there with beguiling Eve Carson, the actress, and the memory of her had never left him. It was the first time, the only time, he was unfaithful to his wife. My mother had taken the photo from his wallet, and in its place he had inserted this small clue. A poem. An ode to beguiling Eve, and perhaps a temperate reminder to his failed vow of faithfulness.

"It's a mystery." Ellie shook her head. "I'm not sure anyone can explain the meaning. Apparently, it was special to him. That is the part we can choose to honor."

I clenched my jaw, hoping my expression wouldn't give away any of the emotions that came rushing forth. Long ago I had chosen to believe in my father. After seeing the photo, seeing the name of his community theater on the playbill, and hearing this poem, I knew my father was real. His name was Sir James Whitcombe. The sweetest part about these words, written in my father's hand, was that my mother had meant something to him. He had carried a memory of her in his wallet.

"Any thoughts, Miranda?" Edward turned to me with his bug-examining expression.

I hesitated far too long. Edward and Ellie stared at me until I finally spoke, my voice cracking as I said, "I think the poet was writing about a woman. The woman was named Eve. He wanted to remember her."

By the stunned expressions on their faces, I knew they never had considered the possibility that the "eve" in the poem might be a person and not a reference to the time of day.

Ellie read the words again and shook her head. "That couldn't be right. If it's a love poem, the name would be Margaret. Not Eve. He and Margaret were married for fifty-eight years. He wrote a number of poems to her."

Obviously, James had experienced a season, or perhaps only a moment, with Eve. I was the living proof of that.

"Maybe," I said gingerly, "your father had a moment, so to speak, with another woman, and—"

Before I could finish, Edward brusquely squared his shoulders. "That's not possible."

"It's certainly not probable." Ellie gave me a sympathetic expression the way one would look at an outsider who didn't know anything. "We do appreciate your willingness to offer an opinion. That is why we asked you. But, you see, that possibility is not probable."

"Not at all probable," Edward stated firmly. "Not probable and certainly not possible."

"But she wouldn't know that, Edward, because, after all . . ." Turning to me, Ellie said kindly, "You didn't know Edward's father."

Clenching my jaw and looking away I said, "You're right. I didn't know him."

"We'd best be getting ready for church, Edward."

The two of them turned to leave the study, but I longed to stay where I was, right there, in the midst of my father's letters.

Edward stopped at the doorway and cleared his throat.

I looked up and with my bravest smile said, "Would it be all right if I stayed in here?"

"Certainly," Ellie answered. "It's a wonderful room, isn't it?"

"Would it also be all right if I had a look at the rest of these papers?" I knew my request was bold, but I longed to touch something my father had touched. I knew these papers might be the only chance I would have to glimpse his heart.

Ellie looked to Edward for his answer to my strange question.

"You're not a reporter or anything, are you?"

"No, I'm not a reporter."

I'm not a lot of things. But I am the daughter of Sir James Whitcombe, whether you think such a thing is possible or probable or not.

I waited a moment. Did I only think that, or did I say it aloud? Edward and Ellie didn't look shocked. I must have only thought it. How disastrous if that declaration had slipped out.

Edward looked at Ellie's kind eyes and then back at me. "I don't mind your having a look as long as everything remains as it is." As an afterthought he added, "We've nothing to hide."

Chapter Eighteen

We left in a flurry for the Christmas morning service. Julia sat beside me in the car's backseat. Holding my hand, she chattered like a little bird. I was glad for her prattle because it meant Edward and Ellie weren't compelled to converse with me about what else I might have seen in the letters in the study.

Most of the papers were cordial correspondence, thanking a colleague for a dinner invitation or a theater critic for a good review. One of the letters was a note to his brother Robert, expressing appreciation for a pocketknife Robert had bought James on a trip to Switzerland in 1975.

One other poem in the collection, the one that referred to "Margaret of the Midnight Sun," preoccupied my thoughts as we drove to church.

you touch
with light
the arctic hollow of my
pilgrim soul
margaret of the midnight sun
with you

i journey through always summer
and never night

The poem opened my mind to the depth of Sir James's love for his wife Margaret. It made me dwell on the thought that he had no business sleeping with my mother.

He had a wife. He loved her. What was he doing allowing himself to be "beguiled" by Eve?

I was aware of a sense of guilt simply for being born. I felt bad about being the result of my mother's "moment" with a married man. I never had felt remorse because I hadn't known any details surrounding my existence. My mother's choice not to tell me about my father had kept me from lingering over such possible revelations. Her silence had kept me buoyant on a sea of secrecy.

I looked down at Julia's little hand in mine and knew that no child should ever be handed the self-destructive seed of feeling guilty for being born. None of us gets to select our parents. How can any of us feel responsible for coming into this world? It wasn't my idea to be born.

I remembered a conversation I'd had with Doralee when she was trying to find my father the second time. I told her my life must have been an accident. My guess, I said, was that my mom must have done something that "put her on God's bad side," and that's why she didn't want me or anyone to know who my father was. We were cursed.

Doralee got pretty revved up and said my life was *not* an accident. She said all of us start life "on God's bad side," under a curse. She said we all need someone who will make things right for us with God.

That's how she explained Jesus to me. He was the only one since Adam and Eve who wasn't locked into the curse when he was born.

"God is supreme," she told me. "Your life was no mistake, Miranda. God can do whatever he wants. Isn't it obvious he wants you?"

At the time I said I much preferred the premise that I was an accident of nature and in control of my own destiny. At least my destiny in this life. After that, I wasn't sure what happened.

Julia gave my hand a gentle squeeze, checking to make sure I was still listening to her chatter. I gave her little hand a squeeze back and decided that going to church on Christmas morning felt right, as if a part of me was saying to God, "All right, I'm here. Go ahead. Show me what you've got. This is your chance. Prove to me that I'm not a fluke of evolution."

I didn't mean those words in a disrespectful way. I was looking for affirmation. Much like Julia squeezing my hand, I wanted to know if God was paying attention and if he would squeeze back.

As I became more curious about what awaited me at the church service, we arrived at the same charming village chapel I had walked past the night before. Sunlight spilled over the top of the spire and warmed the quilted earth that trailed from the rose bed and covered the quarried gravestones. The image was glorious. If ever I felt in the mood to set foot inside a church, this was the morning.

We arrived early because Mark and Julia had parts in the Christmas service. Julia was jumping up and down on one foot by the time we filed through the arched entrance. The inside of the stone church felt as chilly as the outside. Small electrical heaters were plugged into a long orange extension cord. The metal grates were glowing red, huffing and puffing out their heat in an effort to warm the cavernous space.

Ellie took the children to where they were to report for their part in the service. Edward and I filed into a wooden pew four rows from the church's front. I kept my coat on after I sat down. Actually, the coat was Ellie's and much warmer than mine. It came past my knees, and the collar was made from white rabbit fur, warming my neck and shoulders luxuriously. I was grateful that none of the well-dressed worshippers could see my casual apparel under the coat. On the outside, thanks to Ellie, I fit in.

As others from the village entered the church and took their seats, I looked around the sanctuary. The church was designed with the same feel of ornate Victorian splendor as the theater the night before. A variety of textures dominated the floor, ceiling, and walls. The stained-glass windows along the sides of the chapel seemed to come alive in the morning light, showing off the tranquil expressions of the subjects.

I gazed at all four of the tall windows that balanced each other on the sides of the chapel. I didn't know who any of the people were supposed to be. Doralee would have known. Aside from Mary and Joseph, the only biblical character I was familiar with was Christ.

His image was the central figure in a stained-glass window at the front of the chapel, behind the altar. The representation was Anglo-Saxon looking, which I found amusing. The artist who designed the stained-glass window had given the Christ figure long, flowing blond hair. That seemed odd to me since I knew Jesus lived in the Middle East and therefore would have had dark features.

I liked everything else about the window. Christ was portrayed as a ruling king seated on a throne. Instead of appearing aloof in his majesty, this Jesus had a compelling expression. His arms were extended out in a gesture of invitation. Clearly visible were red pieces of stained glass strategically placed where the nails had been driven through his wrists.

With the sunshine so perfectly centered behind the front of the church, the emblazoned image of Christ shone with a golden intensity. I didn't have the impression that he might lunge across the open expanse and devour me, like a one-eyed dragon might. Instead, his open arms reminded me of how welcoming Andrew was when he greeted me at the Tea Cosy with, "Come in, come in, and know me better, friend."

Ellie slid into the pew next to me and gave my arm a pat. I smiled at her, but all I wanted to do was shrink down into the warm coat. I felt the fur come up to my ears. As warm as the coat made me feel, I couldn't suppress a rising sense of discomfort that started in my stomach and worked its way to the top of my head. I knew this discomfort. I had felt it the day I had decided to believe in my father. That day all the old myths were abolished. The new belief took over. And that belief in my father had been true.

Adjusting my posture, I reminded myself that if—and only *if*—I was going to believe in God, I would have to let go of some strongly held presuppositions to make way for the supernatural. Then I remembered all the coincidences since I had arrived in England and how they begged for an explanation. Along with these coincidences was all the kindness I was being shown for no earthly reason. Could any of this have to do with God?

An even more unsettling thought came over me, intensifying my discomfort. Could it be that God was the one who had offered the first squeeze of my hand, so to speak, and now it was my turn to squeeze back?

A woman wearing a red floral shawl over a simple black dress stepped up to the front of the church with a violin and bow in her hand. The congregation hushed as she tucked the polished instrument under her chin and played. Her passion for her music was evident. This was not a production. She felt what she was playing, and it flowed from her fingertips. The beauty of her expression was something I hadn't expected to see or experience in a church.

At the end of her piece, a man who had been standing to the side took the last note she played and began to sing a capella. The words that rolled from his deep chest were of the omnipotent God and included the words, "Wonderful," "Counselor," "Everlasting Father," and "Prince of Peace."

He concluded with a long note that resonated with such depth that it seemed to warm the pews. Stepping to the side, he made way for four children, including Mark and Julia, to tromp down the center aisle. The children took their places. Julia looked adorable in her red and white Christmas dress and red rubber rain boots. She held her hands behind her back and grinned widely at her mom. Mark stood tall and unsmiling, looking straight ahead. He was wearing a robe over his clothes and a fancy silk turban on his head.

The first boy in the lineup was dressed as a beggar with

appropriate soot smudges on his face. He took a step forward and in a blaring voice shouted, "'My Gift' by Christina Rossetti. 'What can I give Him, poor as I am?'" He stepped back in place.

The next boy stepped forward holding a shepherd's staff. He also was wearing a robe. "'If I were a shepherd I would bring a lamb.'" He held up a stuffed lamb the size of a football.

Mark stepped forward with all the dash and drama that must run in his veins and said with perfect inflection, "'If I were a wise man I would do my part.'"

He stepped back.

Julia was still looking around, hands behind her back, grinning at every parishioner she recognized.

Whispering from the side of his mouth, Mark urged his sister forward.

She took a big step in her oversized boots. Swallowing and extending her round little chin, she said her line with sweetness. "'Yet, what can I give Him? Give my heart.'" From behind her back, she pulled out a big red Valentine-shaped heart and held it for all to see.

The congregation's approval was instant, though formal. If it's possible to "feel" a room of people smiling, that's what I felt.

Mark and Julia wedged into the pew with us. Mark sat next to his father, and Julia squeezed in between Ellie and me. She held the red heart in her lap with great care and swung her crossed ankles demurely. It was evident that the little star was quite pleased.

A minister took his position behind the carved wooden pulpit and read from an enormous book. I soon guessed it to be the

Bible because the passage was about shepherds abiding in the fields at night to keep watch over the sheep. I recognized the story from watching a rerun of the old *A Charlie Brown Christmas* a few years ago on TV. One of the cartoon characters, I think it was Linus, recited the same lines about how an angel appeared and told the shepherds not to be afraid. Unto them was born that day a child. The angels sang. The shepherds hurried to Bethlehem where they found Mary and Joseph and the baby, who was lying in a manger.

My gaze rose to the stained-glass image of Christ, who was seated as a ruler. The Prince of Peace, with his arms extended in an invitation. Accessible. Willing to make things right with me before omnipotent God.

Access to a father. My father. That was all I ever longed for.

My eyes teared up.

The minister concluded the reading, and the congregation stood. I stood with them. The minister recited a prayer. "Our Father, who art in heaven, hallowed be thy name."

Everyone around me joined in and recited the lyrical prayer, but I didn't. I didn't know the words. That's because he was their Father, not mine. They could climb up on his strong shoulders and make daring leaps into the mysterious depths without fear. They had the relationship. I did not. And yet, I was invited to come.

Blinking away my tears, I stared across the watery distance. There, at the deep end of the church, the golden Savior seemed to be staring back at me.

I didn't move. Neither did he.

Chapter Nineteen

On the drive back to the house after the Christmas service, I kept blinking. I'd gone too deep at church. Too deep into the mystery of all that couldn't be explained. It felt as if we were driving away from a singular presence and I was dripping with whatever the spiritual equivalent might be of pool chlorine. It would be too easy for him to follow my trail. I wanted Edward to drive faster before the golden-eyed Savior came after me.

Closing and bolting the door of my heart, I didn't peek out to see if he was still there. Instead, I pressed all my thoughts to picturing how I would finish this day. A sketchy plan formulated. First, I would draw Edward aside before Christmas dinner was served. I would lay out the facts for him, even though he wouldn't want to hear what I had to say. I would show him the poem, the photo, and the playbill and tell him the name that appeared on my birth certificate. I would put the information out there. That was fair.

Then I would leave. I would return to the London hotel. If Edward wanted to tell his wife or anyone else, it would be his choice. If he wanted to contact me before I left London, I would leave the name of the hotel with him.

That way I wouldn't intrude any longer on this family. If Edward chose not to believe me or take into account the evidence, it didn't matter. I knew. I had received what I came all this way to find.

We arrived back at the house, and the children moaned that the snow was melting. Edward said he would take them into the back garden to build a snowman and sent them upstairs to change into what he called their "woolies."

I knew that would give me the ten minutes I needed alone with Edward before slipping out of the house and returning to London. Ellie would understand. I knew she would.

In an effort to put all the mannerly pieces in their proper places, as we climbed out of the car, I said to Ellie, "Thank you so much for your hospitality. I especially appreciate the handkerchief you gave me. Are you sure it's okay if I keep it?"

She waved her hand. "Oh yes. Definitely. I have quite a few. My mother-in-law has been embroidering them for years."

"Margaret?" I asked. "Your mother-in-law, Margaret, embroidered the handkerchief?"

"Yes. It's a bit of a hobby for her, really. She paints as well. You'll meet her this afternoon when she arrives. You'll love her. She's a beautiful person."

I stopped in my slushy tracks. "Margaret is coming here? This afternoon?"

"Yes, of course. She lives here with us, you know. She went to Bedford for a few days to be with Edward's sister, Marion, for Christmas Eve. They usually come here, Marion and Gordon and their brood, but this year they decided to huddle close to the home fires. Margaret is an absolute sweetheart. You'll see."

"I didn't know she was still alive."

"Oh yes, very much alive."

My plan to disclose my secret and then flee now seemed like a bad idea. It was one thing to tell a grown man his father had been unfaithful. That was stunning enough. To reveal to an elderly widow that I was the result of her husband's indiscretion thirty years earlier . . . it felt cruel.

Ellie stepped into the house and looked at me over her shoulder. "Are you coming in? I'm going to get straight to work in the kitchen, and I will tell you now, I absolutely don't allow anyone in there when I'm creating. I'm rather selfish that way. I hope you understand. I will accept assistance on the cleanup, though."

She grinned and set off for the kitchen.

I stepped in under the "Grace and Peace Reside Here" motto and closed the front door. Alone in the entryway, I thought that leaving right then sounded like a good choice. The best choice. No one in Carlton Heath needed to know. Ever.

However, Katharine knew. I knew she knew. If Edward, Ellie, or Margaret ever heard of this missing piece of Sir James's life, it shouldn't come to them because Katharine felt compelled to speak up after I had gone. That wouldn't be fair to the Whitcombes or Katharine, either.

I also knew that Katharine and Andrew were still planning to come to Christmas dinner because they had discussed what they were bringing when we chatted in the church after the service. I was feeling hemmed in.

Climbing the stairs to the privacy of the guestroom, I entered and closed the door. My exhaustion was real as I stretched out on the bed. I had been in England for only twenty-four hours, yet everything in my heart and life had spun off into another galaxy.

"What should I do?" I whispered. "What should I do?"

I rolled over on the bed, and a beam of winter sunlight slipped through the thickpaned window and touched the side of my face.

I bolted upright and looked around.

He was here. He had followed me into this room, through the closed door. Not literally followed me, of course, but I knew he was there all the same. He hadn't stayed on his stained-glass throne. He had come to me and was with me now. I couldn't shake him.

"What do you want?" I whispered in a trembling voice.

All was silent. Peacefully silent except for the pounding of my heart. And in my heart I knew why he was there. I knew what he wanted. Wasn't it obvious, as Doralee had said? He wanted me.

Inside the silence, surrounded by the mystery, I spoke the single word that had been lying in wait all these years. "Father."

His name tasted like golden syrup on the tip of my tongue.

I remained still. Very still.

The only sound I heard was Mark and Julia shouting and squealing as they played in the snow in the back garden. A moment later I heard another sound. Loud, cheerful voices echoed in the entryway. Doors opened and closed. I heard Ellie's laughter. Margaret had arrived.

I didn't want to go downstairs. I didn't want to meet Margaret. I didn't want the woman who had shared her life with

Sir James Whitcombe for fifty-eight years to look into my eyes and note that they were clear and blue like her husband's.

I wanted to evaporate. To turn into a snowflake, fly out the bedroom window, and melt in the arms of some inconspicuous shrub.

But an unfamiliar sense of hope covered me and coaxed me out of my fear. He was still here. He hadn't left me alone. Even though I had spoken no specific words nor understood entirely what had transpired, relinquishing my heart to him had been distinct and fixed forever. He had come to me, and I had folded myself into his greatness. I believed.

A light tapping on the guest-room door kicked my heartbeat up a notch or two. I didn't respond. The knock repeated.

"Miranda?" It was Andrew's voice, his Scottish brogue rolling the "r."

"Yes?"

"Ah! Miranda, I've been sent to invite you to come downstairs and join the festivities."

Without moving from the bed, I timidly called out, "Andrew?"

"Still here," he replied from behind the closed door.

"Who else is here?"

"Katharine is downstairs, if that's what you're asking."

"Anyone else?"

"Ah! You're wondering if my son has arrived yet. You can put yourself at ease. For the time being, the only MacGregors downstairs would be Katharine and myself. Now, shall I tell Ellie you'll be joining us, or are you looking for a little peace and quiet?"

"I'll . . . I'll be down in a few minutes."

I looked up just in time to see an arrow hit the window and drop to the ground. Sliding off the bed I hurried across the room, expecting to see Mark with a grimace on his face.

Instead, I looked down on Edward, who stood with the bow still in his hand. His surprise was evident. Mark appeared equally stunned. By the way the two of them were positioned, they seemed to have aimed for the apple tree in the opposite direction of the house. How did the arrow manage to flip back and hit the window?

I waved and offered a smile, trying to let them know that all was well. Except for a tiny crack that appeared in the beveled glass, the window was still intact.

Julia, who had been standing to the side with her mittened hands over her mouth, waved at me, calling out something I couldn't hear.

Edward put down the bow and offered a sheepish shrug. The children then laughed along with their father, and I felt overcome with a bittersweetness. This family was a cohesive unit. Each had his or her place. My intrusion worked as long as I was the foreign stranger whom they had taken pity on and invited in for the holidays.

That's what I wanted to remain to them. A stranger. Not the illegitimate daughter of Sir James, their beloved patriarch.

Slipping the teapot ornament out of the Christmas stocking, I tucked it into my shoulder bag and prepared to make a beeline for the front door. Grace and peace did reside here. I refused to be the one to disrupt that blessing.

Chapter Twenty

I made it as far as the bottom of the stairs. Katharine met me there, saw my shoulder bag, and quietly began her "che-che-che" sounds, as if I were a frightened bird and she could calm me.

"I need to go," I told her in a low voice, trying to sound as firm as I could.

She didn't move.

"It's not fair to them, Katharine. I found what I came for, and that's enough. They don't need to know."

Her expression was compassionate yet reluctant to agree with me.

"Katharine, I know that you know. I saw it in your eyes last night. I'm begging you, please, please, don't say anything to anyone, ever. I want to leave this place and this family just as they are. Will you promise me, Katharine? Promise me you will never say anything?"

"I cannot promise you that, Miranda. I'm sorry."

"Why?" I felt panic rising in me. Katharine was the only obstacle in my path. Why couldn't she see the urgency of and the clear reasoning for keeping my secret? "Have you already told someone? Did you tell Andrew?"

"No, I haven't said anything. I believe it's your place to open this gift."

"But it's not a gift, Katharine. It's a bomb. It's a tangled mess. It's—"

"It's the truth, Miranda. That's all it is. The truth."

"Okay, it's the truth. Don't we all know that the truth can hurt others too much sometimes?"

She dipped her chin in acknowledgement of my statement, but she wouldn't leave it there. "And sometimes after the hurt, the truth heals."

I knew the longer I stood there, the less likely I could slip out of the house unnoticed. Pressing in closer to Katharine I begged her, "Do not tell. Please. This isn't your secret to share with anyone. This is my life. Please. Keep this secret for me. They don't need to know, Katharine."

Her lips remained pursed, but her eyes welled with tears. "I can't promise you that."

Anger flamed up inside me, turning my face red as I pushed past her and strode toward the front door. Her unreasonableness was forcing my hand. Fine. I would tell Edward. But not face to face. He would have the truth in writing. The letter would arrive after Christmas. After I had flown back to San Francisco. That would only be fair to him.

Too flustered to even say good-bye to Katharine, I reached for the handle and flung open the door. Then I realized I wasn't sure how to get to the train station. If I could reach the church we went to this morning, I could probably get there. But even if I remembered the way to the church, I couldn't walk that far in the slushy snow.

To add to my humiliation, I wasn't sure how to place a call on a British phone to arrange cab service. Did "411" work on the other side of the pond?

I needed help.

Closing the heavy front door with a thud, I slowly turned around, knowing that Katharine would still be there.

I spoke firmly without looking at her. "Would you please tell me how to call for a taxi?"

Ellie popped into the entry hall, wiping her hands on an apron that covered the front of her outfit. "I thought I heard the door. Has someone else arrived?"

"No," Katharine said.

"If the children come in through the front, would you two make sure they leave their wet things by the radiator?"

Before bopping back into the kitchen, Ellie looked at the two of us standing in our tense positions and cautiously asked, "Is everything all right?"

"I need to use your phone, if you don't mind."

"Not at all. Would you like to use the one in the study?"

"Yes, thank you."

I was about to slide past Katharine when she said, "It would be better if you stayed, Miranda. It really would."

Before I could respond, the latch jiggled on the front door. Two people entered. First came a round, rosy woman with fair skin, white hair, and wire-rimmed glasses. She was dressed in a long coat with a matching fur-lined hat, and she carried a Harrods shopping bag in her leather-gloved hand.

The other person was a uniformed chauffeur who was carrying two small pieces of luggage.

"Hello, hello!" the cheery woman greeted us. She motioned for the driver to put the luggage in the corner and then pulled her gloves off finger by finger.

Katharine and Ellie went to the woman and greeted her warmly. I hung back, stunned.

Could this be Margaret?

I had expected the wife of Sir James to be tall and elegant and to fill the room with the fragrance of Chanel perfume upon her entrance. This woman who chuckled merrily and exuded the essence of cinnamon rolls didn't seem like the wife of a famous actor. If this was Margaret, then she had turned out to be everything my mother was not.

"You must meet Miranda." Ellie stepped back so the woman could have a look at me. "She's our special guest all the way from America. Miranda, this is Margaret, my mother-in-law. Margaret Whitcombe."

Propelled by the few manners I had left in me, I stepped toward her, keeping my gaze diverted. I didn't want Margaret to look into my eyes.

"Lovely to meet you," she said. "Welcome and happy Christmas."

"Thank you. Merry Christmas to you, too. You have a beautiful home."

"That's kind of you to say."

I could feel Katharine's gaze on me, but I couldn't say anything else. I didn't know what to say. I was thinking about the driver, who was standing only a few feet away. He had a car waiting out front. More than likely he would be willing to drive me wherever I wanted to go for the right price. All I had to do was open my mouth and say something.

Yet I remained silent, caught off guard in the unexpectedness of the moment.

As soon as Margaret had removed her coat and hat, she settled her account with the driver. I knew this was my chance to arrange a ride, but as I looked at him, nothing came out of my mouth. The driver left, and I stood there as a victim of my own sabotage. Either that or I was being compelled by something larger than myself.

I somehow found it easy to believe it was the latter.

"Your timing is perfect," Ellie said to her mother-in-law, taking her coat from her. "We're just about ready to eat. The children are in the back with Edward and Andrew. You won't believe this, but Andrew arrived at the house this morning dressed as Father Christmas. He had the Bromleys' old horse decked out in bells. The children were enchanted."

"It must have been lovely," Margaret said. "Did the children recognize Andrew?"

"Julia believed Andrew was the real Father Christmas. I'm not sure about Mark. The whole thing was quite touching for Edward. He told me he remembered all the years his father had played that role and how grand it was of Andrew to pick up the tradition now with our children. Really, Katharine, it was exceptionally good of Andrew to surprise us all that way."

"You must know," Katharine added, "that Andrew was much more excited about it than the children or even Edward could have been."

"I'm sorry now that I missed all the happenings around here," Margaret said. "It sounds as if you had a lovely Christmas morning."

"The best," Ellie said. "And what about you? How is everything with Marion and Gordon and the rest of them? Are you tired from the drive?"

"I'm not at all weary, thank you. Is there anything I can do to help with the dinner?"

"No, not a thing for you to do. The turkey is nearly ready, but you know how particular I am about presentation. We should be able to sit down in about twenty minutes. Will that work for you?"

"Yes, of course. Do keep in mind that I am available for assistance if you need me. I'll take my luggage to my room. Marion and the others all send their love, by the way."

"Oh Miranda, would you mind helping her lift those?" Ellie asked.

"They aren't heavy," Margaret protested.

"Nevertheless, you shouldn't be lifting them," Ellie said. "And Katharine, I wonder if you might be willing to go to the dining room for me, light all the candles, and then help arrange the nibbles before the children come dashing inside."

Katharine sent a final comforting glance my direction before going to fulfill her duty in the dining room. I returned an appreciative expression. *Grace and peace,* I kept saying to myself. *Grace and peace.*

My shoulder bag was still over my arm, positioned and ready for my exit. Instead of heading for the door, I reached for Margaret's small suitcases and found them light and easy to carry.

"How awfully kind of you." Margaret headed to the left, toward the study. "My room is just this way. It's not far."

I followed close behind, knowing only one thing for certain. Ever since I had arrived in Carlton Heath, nothing had gone the way I had expected—not that I had any ideas about what should happen. But it seemed that every time I made a small effort to move forward, the next step would come rushing to meet me. So at this point, I figured I should keep making my small efforts and see what happened next.

A distinct impression continued to rest on me: I was not alone.

Chapter Twenty-One

Margaret led me down the hall past the study on the left and the dining room on the right. We walked by what appeared to be another bedroom on the left. To the right was a series of small rectangular windows positioned at eye level. A small pink rosebud was painted in the center of each window. I could guess who the artist was.

Pausing, Margaret looked out one of the windows. The view opened to the garden where the children were throwing snowballs at each other with the remnants of the quickly melting snow. I noticed that Andrew was now the one with the bow and arrow. He was wearing slacks and a thick sweater instead of his kilt. Edward stood close, appearing to be intently giving instructions to Andrew, who looked quite confident without Edward's assistance.

"Someone received a new toy," Margaret said with a grin.

"The bow and arrow were Mark's gift from Father Christmas," I said.

"Oh, I'm sure they were." I noted a twinkle in Margaret's eye. She caught my eye for a moment. I looked away.

We continued down the long hall, heading for the room at the far end. Next to the room was a door that opened to the back garden. As we passed that door, it swung open and in came Julia, squealing.

A poorly aimed snowball followed Julia through the door and hit the wrong target.

"Grandmother!" Julia cried. "Mark, you hit Grandmother!"

I dropped the suitcases and rushed to Margaret's side. The airy snowball already had begun to melt off her surprised face. She straightened her glasses and brushed off her cheek.

Julia stood in front of her grandmother, both hands over her mouth, her eyes wide. "Sorry, Grandmother! Sorry!"

"It's all right, Julia dear. Quite all right. Nothing broken. That in itself is a small accomplishment at my age."

I noticed then that Margaret was bleeding from the side of her mouth. Julia noticed as well.

"Blood! Markie, you made Grandmother bleed!"

"You must have bitten your lip." I reached into my shoulder bag and found the travel packet of tissues I had fumbled around for last night at the theater. Pulling out a tissue, I handed it to Margaret.

She looked at me as she dabbed the corner of her mouth. I should have looked away. I planned all along to look away, as I had done earlier with her. But when Margaret's eyes met mine, I returned the gaze.

"Mark, come here and apologize to your grandmother at once," Edward's stern voice called as he joined us by the open door. A chilly December breeze raced past us and went frolicking down the hallway.

Mark came forward and politely said, "I'm awfully sorry, Grandmother."

"Nothing to worry about. It was an accident, Mark. Now, do take off your boots before coming inside."

Mark did as she asked and padded down the hallway in his wet wool socks, leaving footprints as he went.

"Welcome home, Mother." Edward stepped up and gave her a kiss on the cheek. "Nothing like making an event of your homecoming, wouldn't you say?"

"Yes indeed."

"I can take it from here," Edward said to me as he picked up his mother's suitcases and escorted the luggage and Margaret to the room at the end of the hall.

Julia slipped her cold, mittened hand in mine. "Do you want to come outside and help me make a snowman?"

"I can help you for a few minutes, but your mother said it's almost time to eat."

"Are the nibbles ready?"

"I think so."

"Then I'm coming in now!" She kicked off her boots, pulled off her mittens, and wiggle-walked out of her coat.

I closed the side door to the garden, hung up Julia's coat on the hallway peg, and followed her to the dining room. Everything was ready for a grand celebration in the candlelit room. Anticipation glowed in the candles' reflection on the stemware and the shiny china plates.

"Mummy said I could sit by you so I can help you with your cracker."

I smiled my appreciation at Julia even though I wasn't sure why I would need help to eat a cracker. Sliding my shoulder bag inconspicuously under the chair she assigned to me, I drew in the scent of the bayberry candles and thought about what might happen next. I wasn't sure what I was going to do, but I knew I couldn't bolt just yet.

The rest of the clan found its way into the dining room, and everyone stood around sampling the appetizers and making small talk. I stood to the side and listened. The mix of all the voices with their British accents bouncing off the low ceiling felt different from the party the night before. Here the stories being told were softly personal and laced with a lightheartedness borne of familiarity. I began to grasp that moments such as these carried the same meaning for families like the Whitcombes that morning waffle breakfasts had carried for me and my mother.

Katharine sidled up to me and in a low voice said, "You're doing a good job."

"A good job of what?"

"You're doing a good job of letting the moment come to you. Stay steady. It will come."

I wasn't sure what she meant, but I could guess. One of my co-workers at the accounting firm would call it "going with the flow."

I decided to go with the flow and say something to Katharine that would release what felt like a weight tied around my leg. "Katharine, I want to apologize for the way I reacted to you earlier."

She looked confused.

"In the entryway, when I was trying to leave."

"Che-che-che." With that and a slow blink of her eyes, all was pardoned.

Just then, Ellie swept into the room holding an oval platter with a perfectly browned turkey, complete with two white chef's hats covering the ends of the drumsticks. Circling the turkey was a wreath of fresh parsley, and spilling from its steaming cavern was dressing that bubbled with bumpy bits of apples, cashews, and raisins.

"Well done!" Andrew spouted, clapping his hands.

"I hope it's not too well done," Ellie giggled. "Everyone, take your place, please."

Julia climbed into her chair beside me. "Mummy, may we do our crackers now?"

I looked around the table but didn't notice any crackers. There hadn't been any with the appetizers, either.

Ellie placed the turkey platter in front of Edward's seat at the head of the table and gave him a nod.

All of this fascinated me. I found these family traditions more lovely and calming than I would have expected. There was a system. A set of unspoken rules. Everyone knew his or her role. This home was a place of order and steady rhythm. Never again would I lambaste traditionalists and their conservative ways. Done right, convention and form were irresistibly comforting.

Margaret sat at the head of the table on the other end. Ellie sat in the middle, across from me and closest to the door. The children, Andrew, Katharine, and I filled in the remaining seats. The circle felt complete.

"All right. Shall we say grace then?" Edward asked.

I watched the others fold their hands and bow their heads. Even Julia knew what to do. I was the last to lower my head but did so willingly. Edward's respectful and warmly spoken prayer captivated me. He had no difficulty addressing God with a reverent familiarity. He spoke his prayer of thanks much like a grateful son would speak to his father.

In this room, around this table, with these people, I found it easy to believe that God was listening to Edward's prayer. I also believed that some sort of significant first step had taken place between God the Father and me. I was accepted. I had been invited to come in. And I had entered under an eternal banner of grace and peace.

What remained to be seen was how the Whitcombes would respond once they knew who I was.

Chapter Twenty-Two

May we do our crackers now? Julia asked as soon as her father finished the prayer.

"Yes. You first, Julia."

She reached for a paper party favor like the one each of us had by our china plates. The "cracker" was twisted at both ends, making it look like a large piece of wrapped candy. Julie held out one end to me. I never had seen a Christmas cracker before and had no idea what to do with it.

"You hold onto that end, silly," Julia said. "Then I pull like this."

With a loud snap and the scent of a snuffed match, the contents of Julia's cracker spilled onto the table. She picked up a folded piece of bright green paper, opened it, and placed the jagged paper crown on her head.

"Do you want me to read your riddle for you, Ju-Ju?" Mark leaned across the table eagerly.

"I can read it," she said.

"No you can't."

"Mark," his father said firmly.

We waited as Julia picked up a little piece of paper that had popped out of the cracker. It looked like a slip of paper from a fortune cookie, only wider.

She studied the message with great concentration. From where I sat, I could tell she had the paper upside down.

Jutting out her chin, she announced, "It's not very funny."

Everyone laughed.

Julia picked up the final prize from her snapping party favor. It was a small compass about the size of a thumbnail. She turned it this way and that and looked bewildered as to what it was or what she should do with it. Not willing to admit her befuddlement, she said brightly, "I was hoping it would be a tiny pony."

Everyone chuckled.

"Maybe I'll trade you." Mark took both ends of his cracker and gave it a good tug. Out of his cracker sprang a tiny top that landed on its point in the curve of his spoon and gave a "ta-da" spin before toppling over.

"Did you see that?"

"I'll trade, Mark." Julia quickly held out her compass. "But you should know I think this clock is broken because it keeps going wibbly-wobbly."

Mark placed his paper crown on his head and diplomatically said, "Let's see what everyone else gets first, Ju-Ju. Do you want me to read your riddle now?"

She handed it over, and Mark read to us. "What's black and white and read all over?"

"A newspaper." I hadn't heard that one for years.

"How did you know that?" Mark asked.

"I guess we have the same jokes in the US that you have here."

"Do your cracker now," Julia urged.

All the adults joined in, and a fabulous chorus of snaps around the table was followed by the rising scent of a snuffed match. To my surprise, everyone, including Margaret, placed the paper crowns on their heads. I played along and laughed as Andrew tried to read the small letters of his riddle without his reading glasses. He finally took Julia's route and announced, "It wasn't very funny."

We all compared our plastic toys. Mine was a ring that had a large pink "diamond." Julia was thrilled when I asked if I could trade her for her "watch." I told her I wanted a new watch for Christmas anyhow.

Our merry group was looking as silly as we could in our paper crowns when Ellie reminded Edward that the turkey was "going cold." He stood and began the grand carving of the Christmas turkey.

I looked down the table at Margaret. She appeared to be pleased with her son and his family. Everything felt idyllic. All that was missing was our own Tiny Tim and a rousing "God bless us, everyone!"

Katharine caught my eye and gave me one of her tranquil smiles. I held onto her calming expression all during the cozy meal.

We dined on turkey with dressing (or stuffing as the others called it), peas, and another surprising group favorite—steamed brussels sprouts. I found them to be as unexciting as the last time I had eaten them. But everyone else seemed to like them, including Julia.

The rest of the meal was delicious and the company delightful. I didn't join the cheerful conversation. It was so magnificent that I just wanted to sit back and be an observer. Aside from tiptoeing down the stairs with Julia just that morning, I had not fully entered into a moment of make-believe in years. Here, at this table, on this day, with these people, I found it easy to let myself slip into believing this was where I belonged.

I was buttering my last bite of dinner roll when Ellie said, "I hope you can forgive our company manners. We've been so chatty that we've barely included you in the conversation, Miranda. I do apologize. Please tell us about yourself. What part of the States are you from?"

"I live in San Francisco."

"My grandmother has been to San Francisco, haven't you, Grandmother?" Mark said.

"Regrettably, Mark, I have not been to San Francisco. I have been to California, but I visited Los Angeles, not San Francisco."

"Have you always lived in California?" Ellie asked.

"Most of my life."

"You weren't born in California, then?"

"No."

"Where were you born?" Mark seemed to like picking up his mother's lead and taking an adult part in the conversation.

"I was born in Michigan. But I wasn't there very long before we went to California." It felt odd inching into the topic of who I was and where I came from. Part of me wanted to blurt out the facts and be done with it. But this was the gentle route, Katharine's theory of "letting the moment come" to me. If this was going to be the truth-revealing conversation, then Margaret and her family deserved the gentle route.

Mark gave his plastic top a twirl again on his spoon. "Why did you go to California?"

"My mother had a job there."

"What did your mother do?"

"She was . . . she was an actress."

"My grandfather was an actress," Julia said.

"*Actor*," Mark corrected her.

"*Actor*," Julia repeated.

"What about your father?" Mark asked.

I swallowed, not expecting the question to come so blatantly. But then Mark expanded his question, explaining the reason for his curiosity. "Was your father an actor, as well?"

The answer, of course, was "yes," but I looked down at my hands and said, "I only lived with my mother."

"Why?" Julia asked.

I turned to Katharine, desperate to read in her expression that this was it. That the moment had come to me.

Without pause Katharine said, "Children, would you like to be excused from the table now? I would very much like to see what Father Christmas brought for you."

"Yes." Andrew rubbed his hands together.

"Andrew, I was asking the children if they would like to be excused."

"Right. I knew that. What do you say, Mark and Julia? Shall we go into the drawing room, and you can show us the presents Father Christmas brought you?"

"He brought me a tea set." Julia's eyes took on a sugarplum sparkle.

"How lovely." Katharine's expression made it clear that she was pleased with Julia's enthusiasm over the gift.

"Mummy," Mark said before pushing his chair back under the table, "what about the Christmas pudding?"

"I'll serve it in the drawing room a little later, all right, darling?"

Everything in me tightened as I anticipated the direction our conversation would go now that Katharine and Andrew were removing the small ears from the room. I felt uncomfortably hesitant to be the first to speak. It seemed there was no way to make this moment easy.

Margaret picked up the conversation thread. "My husband grew up without a father, as well. Professor Whitcombe was a casualty of World War I. My mother-in-law did an admirable job raising the two boys. But James often spoke of how difficult it was, not having a father around."

It touched me to know that my father had experienced his own measure of loss and heartache.

"I would imagine you experienced a few of the same challenges growing up without a father."

I nodded, trying hard to hold my thoughts and emotions in check. I didn't want to blow this. *If now is the time for me to say something, then please, God, let me say the right thing.*

"You said your mother was an actor." Edward leaned back and folded his hands.

"Actress," I corrected him, the way Mark had corrected Julia. I realized I had made the correction aloud instead of in my head, so I quickly explained, "She liked to be called an actress. Not an actor."

Edward appeared amused. "I now understand your comment at the party last evening when I told you my father was an actor. That line of work lends itself to a unique sort of position for the offspring, does it not?"

His sympathetic response to our shared life experience simultaneously consoled me and made the truth more difficult to speak. I hoped Edward would remember this brief moment of camaraderie once the facts were revealed.

"Did your mother perform on stage or in film?" Margaret asked.

"Stage."

I could feel my heart pounding.

"And is she still performing?"

"No, my mother passed away when I was eleven."

"Oh, Miranda, that's so sad. What a terrible shame." Ellie pressed her hand over her heart. "I'm sorry to hear that. Have you any brothers or sisters?"

I glanced at Edward and pressed my lips together.

"Oh, no siblings, either," Ellie concluded before I had a chance to speak. "That's really sad. How tragic to lose your mother when you're so young."

Edward leaned forward and asked a final question the way people do when they want to offer the freedom to speak honorably of the departed.

"What was your mother's name?"

This was it. I would not hop over the truth one more time.

I paused, drawing in a deep breath through my nostrils. The scent of bayberry from the candles made me nauseous. I knew that once I spoke her name, nothing in this room or in my life would be the same.

"My mother's name was Eve. Eve Carson, the actress."

The room went deathly still.

Chapter Twenty-Three

Margaret gripped the arms of her chair and stared at me without blinking. Her words came across the table like flat stones thrown into a still pond. Each word caused a ripple. Together they disrupted the entire ecosystem. "Eve Carson was your mother?"

I nodded, holding my trembling hands in my lap. I could hear Ellie exhaling the name "Eve," but I didn't dare look at her.

"Hold on there," Edward said, rising taller in his seat. "Are you trying to imply that your mother is the 'beguiling eve' in the poem?"

My throat tightened. I nodded. With dry lips I at last spoke the words. "I have reason to believe that Sir James Whitcombe was my father."

Edward pushed away from the table and stood up straight. Clasping his hands behind his back he said, "I am certain you are mistaken. And I must say this is not the sort of discussion I would have expected to take place in my home. Certainly not on Christmas and in the presence of my mother or my wife." Edward's scowl deepened. "I'm afraid I must ask you to leave, Miranda."

Stunned, I started to rise. My foot caught on my purse strap.

I remembered the picture and playbill and went for a last foray into the truth. "I'd really like to show you something before I go."

Edward clenched his jaw.

"Edward?" Ellie compassionately tilted her head.

Eye contact with his wife eased Edward's demeanor from blazing flames to slow-burning embers. Lowering into the chair he said, "What is it?"

I reached for the blue velvet pouch. Edward and Ellie seemed to recognize it as the purse that caused my panic when Julia brought it downstairs. Without an explanation, I handed the photograph to Edward.

The embers in his face were being fanned back into a flame. "Where did you get this?"

"From my mother's things."

He looked across the table at his mother and then back at me. "Why would your mother have this picture?"

"I think . . ." I glanced at Margaret and then down at the velvet pouch. This was so difficult. In a small voice I said, "I think perhaps my mother took the photo from your father. From his wallet. Many years ago. In Michigan."

"That proves nothing."

I slid the playbill across to him. "I was born nine months after this performance."

He glanced at the playbill and looked again at his mother. She stared across the table without blinking, her expression tightening into a pinch.

"Nothing here proves my father had any association with your mother. His name doesn't even appear on the playbill. You wouldn't have known about the 'eve' in the poem unless we had shown it to you—in confidence, I might add. I don't know what kind of a scam you're trying to pull on us, but I assure you, we will not fall for it. I believe you've had your opportunity to speak, and now I will once again ask you to leave."

Before I had a chance to point out the mention of the Society of Grey Hall Community Theatre on the playbill, Margaret let out a weighted sigh. Her lips moved as if she were talking in her sleep. "The play was *The Tempest.* Your mother performed the role of Miranda."

My heart did a flop. Margaret knew. She knew!

Edward checked the playbill and then stared at his mother. Ellie stared at me. Margaret wept silently. No one spoke.

I pushed back my chair and stood, ready to leave. Swallowing the tears that had puddled in my throat, I said, "Please understand. I did not come to England expecting anything like this to happen. My mother left only a few clues for me. The name of the studio on the back of the photo was what led me here. Yesterday, when I stumbled into the Tea Cosy . . . Well, it doesn't matter. All I want to say is I didn't plan any of this. You have all been very kind to me, and I want you to know that I never intended to hurt anyone. I'm sorry. I just . . . I just wanted to find my father."

That's when I broke down and cried.

"Miranda." Edward's voice carried the same gentle firmness that he used with his children. "Please sit down."

As I sat down, I tried to breathe, but all I could smell was the bayberry-scented candles.

"I can see how . . ." Edward took off his glasses and placed them beside his paper crown. The defeated prince sat with his hand covering his mouth, leaving his sentence unfinished.

Margaret produced a handkerchief from the cuff of her sleeve and used the rosebud end to blot her tear-moistened cheeks. With a wavering voice she said, "Miranda, it is clear—"

"Mother, if you don't mind, I would like to say something first." Edward cleared his throat. "I believe we can all appreciate your situation, Miranda. Losing your mother at an early age and not knowing the identity of your father are significant life obstacles. However, you must know that we are not novices when it comes to accusations and assumptions about my father. As he used to say, 'Such is the consequence of a touch of notoriety.' I may have reacted a bit too strongly in requesting that you leave. My apologies. We have all enjoyed your company. However, I must say I did not expect such an allegation to come from you."

"Edward."

"Just a moment, Mother. I have one more thing I would like to say."

He put on his glasses and looked more closely at me through the lower half. "The point is, you see, you have come to the wrong conclusion with, as you referred to them, the few clues your mother left you. I can guess at what you might have expected to gain from this, and yet I'm sure you can see how preposterous it is for you to expect any of us to—"

"No." I blinked away my unstoppable tears. "You don't understand. I don't expect anything from you. I don't even expect you to believe me."

"Then why have you brought all of this to the table?"

"I . . . I needed to find out the truth. And—"

"Well, the truth is that your mother may have had some slight association with my father and acquired the photo somehow. However, I'm afraid your search for your biological father cannot be resolved here."

"Edward," his mother said, her voice unnervingly calm, "I have something I must tell you."

I watched her words snuff out the fire from my half brother's face.

Margaret squared her shoulders and spoke in a resolute voice. "Edward, do you remember the summer you were twelve, when I took you and Marion to my parents' summer home?"

"Of course."

"That was the first time either of you had been with me to Sweden. Both of you kept asking when your father would arrive, and I told you he was working. What I didn't tell you, and never told either of you, was that your father and I were legally separated at the time. He had received an invitation from his colleague, Charles Roth—"

"Prospero," I said under my breath.

"Yes, Prospero." Margaret glanced at me and then returned her steady gaze to Edward. "Charles was cast for the role of Prospero. He had some sort of serious back injury a week or so before the play opened. That's when he phoned your father."

Edward looked down at the playbill. I knew he would see Charles Roth's name next to the role of Prospero.

"The playbills were already printed, you see, before your father decided to go to Michigan and take the part. All his life he spoke of that production as his favorite and his performance as his best ever. His only regret, he said, was that you children and I weren't there with him to see it."

Edward rubbed the back of his neck, slowly dissolving under his mother's confession.

"When your father returned to England that fall, we worked out our differences. Your father had been told that I was seeing someone while he was away. It was a lie. There was never anyone for me but James."

Margaret sighed and continued. "Many years later, perhaps you remember, your father had a bit of trouble with his heart."

"I remember," Ellie said softly.

"James believed his life was about to end. It was then he told me there had been a young woman. In Michigan. A very young woman. An actress. I've never forgotten her name. It was Eve. Eve Carson."

Edward leaned back in his chair, swallowing rapidly and holding his forehead. Ellie didn't move.

"Perhaps you can understand why I felt it was important never to speak of this to anyone. Edward, your father was a fine man." Margaret's voice trailed off as she turned to me and added, "He never knew . . ."

I tilted my head, wanting to grasp what I had just heard. "Are you saying he didn't know my mother got pregnant? He didn't know about me?"

Margaret drew in another breath for strength. "I can tell you this with absolute certainty. If my husband had known he had fathered another child, regardless of the circumstances, he would have searched day and night until he found you."

I swallowed the next wave of tears, dearly wanting to believe her words were true. The longing of my entire life was addressed in what this woman was saying to me—this woman who, of all the women in the world, had every reason to despise me.

With wobbling arms, Margaret pushed back her chair from the table. Edward rose quickly and strode across the room to help, but she was standing already. "If you will excuse me, I am going to lie down for a while."

"I'll walk with you to your room, Mother." Edward glanced over his shoulder at me before leaving the dining room. It seemed he wanted to say something, but he didn't. I didn't expect him to. Not yet. His expression made it clear he was processing all of this as best he could. In the meantime, his earlier request that I leave his house now seemed to be revoked.

Ellie and I sat across from each other, both speechless. I had the sense the two of us were cushioned together in a sort of soft, gauze-like silence.

Mark appeared in the doorway just then, announcing that he had come to see about the Christmas pudding. "It was Julia's idea, really. She wanted me to tell you she's ready."

"It will be a few more minutes, love. Tell the others for me, will you?"

Mark scampered off, and Ellie reached her hand across the table. I didn't know if she meant for me to reach for it or not, but I timidly stretched out my arm. She immediately gave my hand a squeeze.

I squeezed back.

Her smile floated across the table, making room for me in her heart the same way she had made room for me in her home.

"I feel so awful," I whispered.

"Oh, but you mustn't. It's going to be all right. You'll see. Give them—give all of us—a little time. That's all we need. A little time for this unexpected news to settle in. We'll come around."

I nodded hopefully.

"I knew there was something about you when I saw you last night. Now I know what it is. You have his eyes. Did you know that? You have your father's eyes. As clear as a blue sky on a spring morning."

Now it was Julia who burst into the dining room. "Mummy, Mark said I'm not allowed any pud because I didn't finish eating all my turkey!"

"You shall have your Christmas pudding, little love. Your brother is only putting you on. You just ignore him."

With a fist on her hip Julia declared, "But, Mummy, how can I ignore him? He's part of this family, you know?"

Ellie and I exchanged grins. "Well, Julia, he's not the only one who is part of this family, now is he? Every one of us has a place here."

I drew in the sweet implication of Ellie's words and held her blessing close. I was accepted. I, too, was part of this family. I belonged here.

"Mummy, will you please come and tell Mark that I get to have my Christmas pud?"

"Yes, yes, I'll come." Turning to me she added, "You will excuse me, won't you? I'll be back shortly."

"That's okay. I can start clearing the table."

"That would be lovely."

Julia grinned contentedly. Just before she left the dining room with her mother, she held up her hand to me with a twinkling grin. She wiggled her fingers so I would notice she was wearing the pink diamond ring I had given her from my Christmas cracker. I knew our friendship was sealed.

As I organized the plates and prepared to clear the table, my thoughts touched on all that had happened since I blew into Carlton Heath with the north wind on my heels. The sweetest impression that rested on me was that I was no longer alone. And not just because of the connection I now had with the Whitcombe family.

The attachment I sensed was larger than that. Something profound and abiding had happened in me at the heart level with Almighty God. He was the center of this celebration—the Father of Christmas past, present, and future. He had made himself accessible to me, to all of his children. I had responded, and now I belonged.

Reaching for one of the silly paper crowns, I placed it on my head and grinned at my reflection in the thick glass that covered the painting on the wall. I noticed in the reflection that someone else had entered the dining room. Turning toward the doorway I expected to see Ellie.

A new guest had arrived. A man about my age with a strong jawline and softly questioning eyes stood in front of me. He was wearing a tweed blazer over a black turtleneck. His light brown hair had a windblown look as if he had just arrived in a sports car.

"You must be Miranda," he said, rolling the "r" with the same Scottish twist that was so evident every time his father said my name.

I quickly pulled the paper crown off my head. "And you must be Andrew's son."

"Ian," he said.

"Ian," I repeated.

"So." He gave his earlobe a tug. "I heard you wanted to meet me."

"Really? The way I heard it, you're the one who wanted to meet me."

He smiled.

I smiled.

Both of us seemed to be turning a bit rosy.

I noticed Andrew standing just off to the side in the hallway. The jolly ole elf caught my eye and raised an eyebrow. I knew he was checking to make sure I liked the final gift he had just delivered on his rounds this year.

My answer to him was a great big bashful grin. I think he got the message. Ian certainly did.

That's when I realized the unimagined had happened. In my heart and in my life, it finally was Christmas.

Reading Group Guide

1. Do you know any women like Miranda who grew up without a father? How have these women filled the empty space in their lives?
2. What do you think of Miranda's decision to go searching for her birth father?
3. How did Doralee's spiritual experience affect Miranda in the long run?
4. Why do you think Miranda preferred to think of herself as an accident of nature rather than someone created by God?
5. Miranda liked accounting because the numbers could be "counted on" to always act in certain ways. What or who do you rely on to be stable when the rest of life seems to be on shifting sand?
6. How would you feel if you found yourself depending on the kindness of strangers at Christmastime?
7. What roles did the image of Father Christmas play in the book? In what ways was this "character" like God? In what ways was Father Christmas different from God?
8. Read Genesis 21:8-21. Ishmael was the son of a slave and of the slave's owner, Abraham. Early in life Ishmael was separated

from his father and raised by his mother. How do you think Ishmael felt about his father as Ishmael grew up? What do you think Hagar told her son about his father? Do you think she portrayed Abraham sympathetically or unkindly? What does this story tell us about fathers and mothers? What does it tell us about God as our heavenly Father?

9. Was there ever a time you felt your parents withheld important information from you, including possibly leading you to believe in Santa? How did you feel about your parents when you found out the truth?
10. Miranda was concerned that God might be like a one-eyed dragon on the other end of the swimming pool. Can you recount a time you thought of God as potentially dangerous? Did you, like Miranda, run away, or did you respond differently?
11. How did God win Miranda's heart? What does this tell us about him?
12. Can you recall a time someone beckoned you, like Christmas Present called to Miranda, "Come in, and know me better"? How did that make you feel?
13. What do you think of the way Miranda told the Whitcombes about her possible relationship to them? Do you think she handled the situation fairly for all involved?
14. What does the last paragraph of the book tell us has occurred in Miranda spiritually and emotionally?
15. Identify a time when you felt you were experiencing Christmas after a long winter in your life. How did that make you feel about God?

Engaging Father Christmas

"For I know the plans I have for you," declares the
LORD, "plans to prosper you and not to harm you,
plans to give you hope and a future."

Jeremiah 29:11

Chapter One

Around me swarms of Londoners rushed by, intent on their destinations and sure of their plans. My destination was the small town of Carlton Heath, and my plans revolved around a certain Scotsman who was now officially late.

I tried to call Ian again. His voice mail picked up for the third time. "It's me again," I said to the phone. "I'm here at Paddington station and—"

Before I finished the message, my phone beeped, and the screen showed me it was Ian.

"Hi! I was just leaving you another message." I brushed back my shoulder-length brown hair and stood a little straighter, just as I would have if Ian were standing in front of me.

"You made it to the station, then?"

"Yes. Although I was about to put on a pair of red rain boots and a tag on my coat that read, 'Please look after this bear.' " I was pretty sure Ian would catch my reference to the original

Paddington Bear in the floppy hat since that was what he had given to my niece, Julia, for Christmas last year.

"Don't go hangin' any tags on your coat," Ian said with an unmistakable grin in his voice. "I'm nearly there. The shops were crammed this morning, and traffic is awful. I should have taken the tube, but I'm in a taxi now. I'll be there in fifteen minutes tops. Maybe less if I get out and run the last few blocks."

"Don't run. I'll wait. It's only been, what? Seven weeks and three days since we were last together? What's another fifteen minutes?"

"I'll tell you what another fifteen minutes is. It's just about the longest fifteen minutes of my life."

"Mine too." I felt my face warming.

"You're at track five, then, as we planned?"

"Yes. Track five."

"Good. No troubles coming in from the airport?"

"No. Everything went fine at Heathrow. The fog delayed my flight when we left San Francisco, but the pilot somehow managed to make up time in the air. We landed on schedule."

"Let's hope my cabbie can find the same tailwind your pilot did and deliver me to the station on schedule."

I looked up at the large electronic schedule board overhead, just to make sure my watch was in sync with local time. "We have about twenty minutes before the 1:37 train leaves for Carlton Heath. I think we can still make it."

"I have no doubt. Looks like we have a break in the traffic jam at the moment. Don't go anywhere, Miranda. I'll be there as soon as I can."

"I'll be here."

I closed my phone and smiled. Whenever Ian said my name, with a rolling of the *r*, he promptly melted my heart. Every single time. His native Scottish accent had become distilled during the past decade as a result of his two years of grad school in Canada and working in an architect office with coworkers from around the world. But Ian knew how to put on the "heather in the highlands" lilt whenever he wanted. And I loved it, just as I loved everything about this indomitable man.

I looked around the landing between the train tracks for an open seat on one of the benches. Since none were available, I moved closer to the nearest bench just in case someone decided to leave.

Balancing my large, wheeled suitcase against a pole so it wouldn't tip over, I carefully leaned my second bag next to the beast. This was my third trip to England since my visit last Christmas and the first time I had come with two suitcases. This time I needed an extra bag for all the gifts I had with me, wrapped and ready to go under the Christmas tree at the Whitcombe manor.

Last Christmas and for many Christmases before that, the only gift I bought and gave was the one expected for the exchange at the accounting office where I worked in downtown San Francisco. Up until last Christmas I had no family to speak of—no parents, no siblings, no roommate. I didn't even have a cat. My life had fallen into a steady, predictable rhythm of work and weekends alone, which is probably why I found the courage to make that first trip to Carlton Heath last December. In those brief, snow-kissed, extraordinary few days,

I was gifted with blood relatives, new friends, and sweetest of all, Ian.

Christmas shopping this year had been a new experience. While my coworkers complained about the crowds and hassle, I quietly reveled in the thought that I actually had someone—many someones—in my life to go gift hunting for.

I had a feeling some last-minute shopping was the reason Ian was late. He told me yesterday he had a final gift to pick up this morning on his way to the station. He hadn't explained what the gift was or whom it was for. His silence on the matter led me to wonder as I wandered along a familiar path in my imagination. That path led straight to my heart, and along that path I saw nothing but hope for our future together—hope and maybe a little something shiny that came in a small box and fit on a certain rather available finger on my left hand.

Before my mind could sufficiently detour to the happy land of "What's next?", I heard someone call my name. It was a familiar male voice, but not Ian's.

I looked into the passing stream of travelers, and there he stood, only a few feet away. Josh. The last person I ever expected to see again. Especially in England.

"Miranda, I thought that was you! Hey, how are you?" With a large travel bag strapped over his shoulder, Josh gave me an awkward, clunking and bumping sort of hug. His glasses smashed against the side of my head. He quickly introduced me as his "old girlfriend" to the three guys with him.

"What are you doing here?" He unstrapped the bag and dropped it at his feet.

One of the guys tagged his shoulder and said, "We'll be at the sandwich stand over there."

"Okay. I'll be there in a few minutes." Josh turned back to me. "You look great. What's been happening with you?"

"I'm good," I said. "What about you? What are you doing here?" I was still too flustered at the unexpected encounter to jump right into a catch-up sort of conversation after the almost three-year gap.

"Just returned from a ski trip to Austria with a group from work. Incredible trip. I'm in a counseling practice now. Child psychologist. I don't know if you knew that."

"No. That's great, Josh. I know that's what you wanted to do."

"Yes, it's going well so far." He seemed at ease. None of the stiltedness that had been there right after I broke up with him came across in his voice or demeanor.

"And what about you? What are you doing in England?"

Before I could put together an answer, Josh snapped his fingers. "Wait! Are you here because you're looking for your birth father?"

"You remembered." Once again he surprised me.

"Of course I remembered. You had that picture of some guy dressed as Father Christmas, and it had the name of the photography studio on the back. That was your only clue."

I nodded.

"So? What happened?"

"I followed the clue last Christmas, and it led me here, to my birth father, just like you thought it would."

"No way! Did it really?"

I nodded, knowing Josh would appreciate this next part of the story. "The man in the photo dressed like Father Christmas was my father. And the boy on his lap is my brother, or I guess I should say my half brother, Edward."

"Incredible," Josh said with a satisfied, Sherlock Holmes expression on his unshaven face. "What happened when you met him?"

I hesitated. Having not repeated this story to anyone since it all unfolded a year ago, I didn't realize how much the answer to Josh's question would catch in my spirit and feel sharply painful when it was spoken aloud.

"I didn't meet him. He passed away a few years ago."

"Oh." Josh's expression softened.

"You know, Josh, I always wanted to thank you for the way you urged me to follow that one small clue. I've wished more than once that I would have come to England when you first suggested it four years ago. He was still alive then. That's what I should have done."

"And I should have gone with you," he said in a low voice.

"Why do you say that?"

Josh's eyebrows furrowed, his counselor mode kicking in. "I felt you needed that piece in your life. By that I mean the paternal piece of your life puzzle. I didn't like you being so alone in the world. I wish you could have met him."

"I do, too, but I actually think things turned out better this way. It's less complicated that I didn't meet him while he was still alive."

"Why do you say that?" Josh asked.

I hesitated before giving Josh the next piece of information.

In an odd way, it felt as if he needed the final piece of the puzzle the same way I had.

"It's less complicated this way because my father was..." I lowered my voice and looked at him so he could read the truth in my clear blue eyes. "My father was Sir James Whitcombe."

Chapter Two

Josh slowly leaned back, stunned. He raised an eyebrow and let out a low whistle. "I can see what you mean about its being complicated. No one will want to believe Sir James had a child outside of his reportedly idyllic marriage. Except the tabloids, of course. He was an incredible actor, you know."

"Yes, I know."

I realized we were in a noisy, crowded train terminal, but I still didn't want to take any chance of being overheard. Leaning closer and lowering my voice I said, "Only a few people know, so please don't say anything to anyone."

"I understand. Don't worry. Holding onto confidences is what I do for a living." Josh reached over and gave my shoulder a squeeze.

"I really mean it, Josh. If the truth got out, it would damage the lives of some people I really care about."

"I hear what you're saying. You can trust me, Miranda. I

think you know that. But in my experience as a counselor, I've found that truth has a way of rising to the surface. Sometimes you must wait for the truth to float to the top. Other times you must go to it, take it by the hand, and pull it up with all your might."

Josh's summary statement was typical of the way many of our conversations went when we were together. To me, he often sounded as if he had read one too many motivational books on inner healing.

An older gentleman who had been sitting on the bench behind me stepped around to the side and said, "Pardon me." He turned his cell phone away from his ear, and stepping closer he pointed at the open seat and said, "Were you waiting for a place to sit?"

"Yes. Thank you."

He tipped his cap and walked away.

"I'd better go." Josh glanced to where his friends had congregated, waiting for him. "Listen, here's my card. Call me if you want. Any time. I'd like to keep in touch."

"Thanks."

"Do you live here now?" Josh picked up his heavy bag and threw it over his shoulder. "In England, I mean."

"No. Not yet. I hope to move here when . . . well, soon."

"My e-mail is on the card too. Merry Christmas, and again, Miranda, I'm really glad you connected with your family. You needed that." He leaned over and gave me a kiss on the cheek.

I was watching Josh walk away when I heard another familiar male voice behind me. This voice was the one I heard in my dreams. All the good dreams that included a white wedding dress and a cottage in the glen.

My Scotsman had arrived.

"So, that's how it is, is it?" Ian MacGregor stood there with his fists on his hips. "I ask you to wait on me for a quarter of an hour, and you take to giving out kisses to the first man in a ski cap who comes your way. What was he peddling? Mistletoe, was it?"

I turned to Ian slowly, enjoying the chance to play along with his teasing. "Those are the chances you take when you leave a woman waiting, you know."

Ian's eyes lit up at the sight of me. His light brown hair looked windblown, and his handsome face had a ruddy glow. I tumbled into his arms and gave him the kiss I'd been saving for seven weeks and three days. Then he gave me the kiss he had been saving for seven weeks and three days. It was the best Christmas gift exchange ever.

I think we might have kept kissing, except our train had arrived and passengers were boarding. As we drew apart from our tight embrace, my watch caught on the strap of the messenger bag Ian used in lieu of a briefcase. I pulled it off his arm.

In the fumble to untangle ourselves, the bag tipped open, spilling his car keys, cell phone, and an old-fashioned, ivory jewelry box just large enough for a diamond ring.

Ian knelt down to gather up the items, and I knelt right along with him, trying to unclasp my wristwatch. Our faces were inches apart as he hurriedly tucked the jewelry box in his coat pocket and turned with a shy expression as if to see if I'd noticed.

Of course I'd noticed. What should I say?

Without hesitation, the truest impulse on my heart strode

right to the edge of my lips and did a lovely swan dive into the deep end as I said, "Yes?"

Ian gave me one of his fake growls. "I haven't asked you yet, woman."

"Asked me what?" I said, equal to his mock naiveté.

He kissed me soundly. "I believe you and I have a train to catch."

Chapter Three

I love the train ride to Carlton Heath. But I loved it more that afternoon because I was cozied up next to Ian, and both of us were smiling. I'm sure that to observers our grins were sophomoric and comical. I don't know about Ian, but I couldn't make my face behave seriously.

Neither of us spoke for the first little while as the train rolled out of the station. We sat close and settled in, remembering how it felt to have our arms linked and our fingers laced together. I leaned my head on Ian's broad shoulder and released a contented sigh. He kissed the top of my head.

His cell phone rang. He let it go unanswered.

"I'm ready to hear your confession," Ian mumbled in my ear.

"My confession?" I sat up and looked at him. "Do you mean you want to know who the mistletoe peddler was in the ski cap?"

"Yes. Go on."

"That was Josh. My old boyfriend. I've told you about him."

"And what was he doing at Paddington? He doesn't live here, does he?"

"No. He was on a ski trip to Austria."

"Is that it?"

"You mean is that all I have to say?"

"Yes. Is that it?"

"Yes. That's it, Ian. If you had arrived a few minutes earlier, I would have introduced you to each other."

"And if I had arrived a few minutes earlier, I would have—"

Before Ian could issue me a benediction of constant protection, his cell phone rang. Once again he ignored it. I had a feeling that was because his phone was in his coat pocket along with "the box." He seemed intent on ignoring the box for the moment.

"Actually, I do have one more thing to say about seeing Josh."

"So, there is more," Ian said.

"Not much more. What I wanted to add is that, even though it was strange seeing Josh after all these years, I'm glad I did. It always felt as if that relationship needed the final dots connected."

"And are they connected now?"

I smiled at him and nodded. "Yes."

His phone rang a third time. Ian gingerly pulled it from his coat pocket without also extracting "the box" and looked at the screen. "It's Katharine. I'll put her to rest and let her know we're on our way."

Katharine, the tall, gentle-spirited woman who married Ian's father, Andrew, two years ago, had been a kind friend to me on my first visit to Carlton Heath. She and Andrew ran a small place called the Tea Cosy. That's where I first entered the circle of friends I now called my own.

"Hello, Katharine. I'm with Miranda now, and we're on the train."

As he listened to her response, Ian pulled away from our relaxed position and sat up straight.

"Katharine, your voice cut out for a moment. Did you say heart attack?"

He listened carefully and checked his watch. "My car is at the station, so we'll go directly to hospital. Tell him we're on our way."

Ian closed his phone and turned to me with a stunned expression.

"Your dad?"

He nodded.

"What did Katharine say?"

"The doctor is referring to it as an 'episode.' They've run tests and are waiting for results."

Ian rose and said, "Wait here."

With determined strides he went to the automatic door that opened between the train cars and headed toward the front of the train. I knew that, if it were at all possible, he would convince the conductor to break a speed record in reaching Carlton Heath.

I felt my heart pounding as I checked my cell phone and saw that I had two missed calls from Katharine. My phone must have been temporarily out of range when she tried to reach us. She hadn't left a message, so I didn't have any further details. My first response was to try calling her back, but when I did, she didn't pick up.

I sat with my phone in my lap, blinking and trying to sort out the implications of this unwanted news. *Please don't take him, God. Not now. Not at Christmas. Not this Christmas. We need Andrew in this world.*

I fixed my numbed gaze on a box held protectively in the lap of a woman the next aisle over. The picture on the box was of a nativity scene. All the key players were present: Mary, Joseph, baby Jesus, three wise men, two shepherds, a lamb, and a donkey. The fully set stage reminded me of my mother, and instantly thoughts of her bombarded me.

My mother, who always referred to herself as "Eve Carson the Actress," was big on curtain calls. She loved it when all the key players were on stage together, ready for their accolades. Her curtain call on life came far too soon, and there definitely was no applause at her passing. I was her only daughter, and she was my gypsy mother.

I remember exactly where I was sitting the moment one of the stagehands in Salinas came to tell me of her fall at the dress rehearsal for *The Merchant of Venice.* I was eleven years old, and my favorite place to make myself invisible was backstage in the wardrobe room. I could always find a trunk to use as a couch and an unused coat to fold into a pillow. My companion in that private boudoir was always a book.

Sometimes I'd fall asleep there. Other times the seamstress would slip me peppermints she had lifted from the supply set aside for the actors to help clear their throats before performances.

My mother knew where to find me, as did most of the others involved in the various theatrical performances. And I knew well enough to stay out of their way if I wanted to keep coming back to my hideaway.

On the afternoon of my mother's accident, my perch wasn't on a self-made sofa but on a folding director's chair in the corner by the rack of dresses. Each costume held a pungent fragrance of perfume, lotion, stage makeup, and perspiration. When they were all gathered together on the rack in a colorful assortment, the scent was exotic and strangely intoxicating. I knew that a bit of my mother's scent was mixed into that wild bouquet. So in my logically illogical preadolescent mind, I was somehow close to her.

I had settled in the director's chair reading *A Wrinkle in Time* and was at the part where the starfish grows back one of its appendages.

A panicked stagehand, dressed all in black, burst into the wardrobe and motioned for me to come with him. He said only three words: "It's your mother."

I read the truth in his face. I could see it all right there between the deeply creased lines radiating from his pinched eyes. She who had been to me all I knew of my past, present, and future was about to be severed from my life. I remember thinking in that micromoment that I would never be able to grow another Eve Carson the Actress to replace her.

As the train chugged on toward Carlton Heath, my tears came like quiet rain, remembering my mother and staring at the nativity scene on the box. Christmas was about birth, new life, and celebrating Christ. Last year all of that had been true. This year... I blew my nose and prayed that today would not be the day Ian would experience the severing of Andrew MacGregor from his life.

Chapter Four

Jan returned to his seat on the train carrying two insulated cups of hot tea. I knew he had been as far as he could get to the engine room, but I let him think I believed he had only been as far as the snack car.

"Twelve minutes," he said. "Twelve minutes before we arrive in Carlton Heath. My car is parked on the west end of the lot. We might have to put the top down to fit everything in. Is that your warmest coat?"

I nodded. It was the only coat I'd brought with me.

"The hospital is about ten kilometers from the station. Do you think you'll be warm enough?"

"I'll be fine. I have a scarf."

"Good." He sipped his tea. I could tell by his expression that it was too hot. Holding onto my cup, I waited for it to cool. A faintly cheering sense of familiarity came into view as I looked out the window and watched the red brick row houses with their slanted roofs and smoking chimney pots. I had looked forward to this day for so long. Never did I expect the ominous news that would run to meet us before we entered the village of Carlton Heath.

We didn't talk the rest of the way, but we did make good use of our nonverbal communication skills. Being in a long distance relationship for the past year, Ian and I had learned a variety of ways to communicate our affection, even though we were thousands of miles apart. On the train it felt like a luxury to squeeze his arm and offer him a comforting look. I knew he was taking in all my unspoken messages.

I'm not so sure he was able to read my unspoken messages once we arrived at the train station though. Ian smashed my small suitcase into the nearly nonexistent trunk of his Austin-Healy sports car, and I drew in a sharp breath through my closed teeth. He was in his "make it happen" mode for good reason. I was in the "save the presents" mode for equally good reason. I chose not to use that moment to communicate anything either verbally or nonverbally.

Drawing in the crisp winter air, I looked up at the clear sky and watched my breath form airy snowballs that instantly evaporated. This, I remembered. This moist, chilled air. This feeble covering of the ancient trees. This shade of pale blue above with hints of green and earthy brown below. The beauty of this small corner of England at this time of year was the beauty of lacy frost on the windows at first light and of long, willowy shadows at dusk.

Even in the midst of everything that was happening, I felt privileged to be here.

Crawling into the sports car on what still felt like it should be the driver's side, I buckled up before we took off for the hospital. I'd been with Ian before when he opened up on the country roads of Kent. We had gone for a picnic in the country last August when I was in England visiting him. I knew his "baby" could hum, and hum she did, all the way to the hospital. My ears froze, and my nose dripped from the cold, but my feet, tucked up under the heating vent, were nice and toasty.

Ian parked, pulled out my large suitcase, and quickly put the car's top in place. He took off for the hospital entrance with my suitcase bumping along over the uneven pavement of the parking lot.

As I trotted to keep up, a beautiful thought broke through my concern for Andrew and my growing exasperation with Ian. If I were the one lying in the hospital bed, Ian would race to my side just as he was racing to his father's side. Not since the loss of my mother did I have anyone in my life who would care and come for me in that way.

We found Andrew's room, and tall, graceful Katharine met us with hugs.

"How is he?" Ian marched past Katharine and went to his father's bedside.

"He's sedated," Katharine said in a soft voice. "The doctor should be around in a moment to talk with us about the test results." She reached for my hand and gave it a squeeze. "I'm so glad you're here, Miranda."

"I'm glad too." I squeezed her hand back.

"Dad, how are you feeling? Miranda and I are here now."

The sleeping giant only gave a twitch of his mouth in response, causing his snowy white beard to move slightly.

I slipped my hand into Andrew's where it rested on his

great, barreled chest. I couldn't imagine the world without this man.

You must heal, Andrew MacGregor. Do you hear me? Heal and mend. Get strong. You are so deeply loved by many. You can't leave us now. You can't. You have to stay with us.

"Are you comfortable, Dad? I can bring you another pillow if you like."

Andrew's only response was the steady rise and fall of his chest.

The doctor entered before Ian managed to extract a response from his father, which was probably a small kindness for the sedated man.

"What can you tell us?" Ian asked the doctor.

The doctor dove into an overview of what had happened to Andrew, what procedures had been followed, and how the test results had come back indicating no need for further concern.

"I have every reason to believe your father is going to pull through this. What he needs is lots of rest and some recommended adjustments to his diet and exercise. You'll receive the information when we release him."

"Does that mean he's able to go home now?" Ian asked.

"No, I'd like to keep him here for observation overnight to see how he responds to the medication I've started him on. If he has no adverse reactions, I'll provide you with that prescription. He's a strong man, and I anticipate a full recovery."

"What a relief," I said softly.

"Have you any further questions for me?" the doctor asked.

Ian glanced at Katharine and me and then back at the doctor. "No. This is better news than we had hoped for. Keep on giving him your best care. That's all I ask."

"That is the plan, Mr. MacGregor," he said.

I knew Ian would like his answer. Ian liked having a plan.

The doctor left, and Ian pressed his chin against the top of my head, kissing me on the crown. "This is good news," he said. "Very good news. If you need to go for a bit, Katharine, I'll look after things here."

"Well," Katharine lowered herself into the chair next to the bed and said, "I was planning to stay. But since you're here, I should check in at the Tea Cosy. I left Ellie in charge of serving the expected holiday guests, and it is close to teatime."

"What about the Christmas play tonight?" I asked.

For the past forty years the Carlton Heath Theatre Guild had carried on a tradition of performing Charles Dickens's *A Christmas Carol* at Grey Hall. I knew this was the first year the Guild had an all-children cast—except for Andrew. He was playing the showstopper role of Father Christmas.

I remembered going to the production last Christmas Eve and watching Andrew take on the role of Christmas Present. Before Andrew created his own adaptation of the Father Christmas character in the Christmas Present scene, the part had belonged to my father.

Ellie, my half brother's wife, had told me many stories of how Sir James Whitcombe took to the stage each year and embodied the role. He was Father Christmas to all the children in the village of Carlton Heath. He visited their homes and schools with gifts and good cheer, and when he passed away, the town mourned the loss longer than any of his devoted fans with their blogs and Web sites.

In some ways the town still was mourning. This year was

only their third Christmas without Sir James. Andrew had given the role a worthy run, but now he was unable to don the hooded Father Christmas costume and bring hope and cheer to the stage and to the people of Carlton Heath.

"I'm waiting to hear from the Guild director," Katharine said. "He is considering postponing tonight's performance in light of Andrew's situation. If they do postpone, we'll have a performance on Christmas Eve. We hadn't planned on that since we felt the children should be home on the night before Christmas."

"Do you think Andrew will be well enough to resume his role by tomorrow night?" I asked optimistically.

A low rumble sounded from Andrew's chest. "I'm not dead yet. Or had none of you noticed that?"

"There he is!" Ian leaned over his father. "Ready to give out orders again, are you?"

Ian looked at me and smiled. The room seemed to have suddenly become more spacious.

"What have they done to me, son?" Andrew's eyelids fluttered open and then closed again.

"You had a mild heart attack, Dad."

"Feels more like a Saxon attack."

The three of us smiled.

"What day is it?" Andrew asked, still not opening his eyes.

"It's December twenty-third." I slipped my hand into Andrew's large paw.

"And whose soft hand is this?"

"It's Miranda's, Dad. We're all here for you."

"Where's my Katharine?"

"I'm right here." Katharine rose and kissed his forehead. "You're on the mend, Andrew. The doctor said we're not to worry. You need to rest now."

"How can a man be expected to sleep when he's flanked by his son and two beautiful women?" Andrew's closed eyelids fluttered as if they were just too heavy to open. A smooth expression came over his rugged face. The three of us watched as his mouth drooped, and his breathing returned to the steady rhythm of sleep.

"Go on, then," Ian whispered to Katharine. "I'll stay with him. I'm sure he's going to be sleeping for the next while."

Katharine nodded, as if she finally agreed leaving might be the best choice. Turning to me she said, "Is there a chance you might want to come with me?"

"Sure. Do you need some help?"

"I wouldn't mind some. I left everything in such shambles."

"Of course. I can go to the Tea Cosy with you now, if that would help."

"Yes, that would be best. Ian, are you all right with that plan?"

"Yes. I can manage here. Miranda, don't make any commitments for dinner though. Particularly with men in ski caps." He gave me a wink. "I'll meet you at the Cosy at seven o'clock sharp."

"I'll be ready," I said.

"And I'll be ready too," Andrew mumbled without opening his eyes.

"No, you'll be sleeping, Dad, if you know what's good for you."

"Being with all of you, that's what's good for me. That and maybe a kiss or two."

Andrew rumbled right into a slurred and paraphrased version of a poem I'd heard him quote a number of times. The name of the kiss-giver seemed to change according to whom he was trying to coerce at the moment. This afternoon it was me.

"Say I'm weary, say I'm sad;

"Say that health and wealth have missed me;

"Say I'm growing old, but add—

"Miranda kissed me!"

In response, I planted a nice, warm kiss on his whiskered cheek and whispered my own paraphrased version of one of my favorite quotes from Shakespeare's *Much Ado About Nothing*. I had many lines memorized from my mother's performances, which I heard over and over. "Serve God, love well, and mend."

Chapter Five

"Are you sure you're not too tired to do this?" Katharine asked once we were in her car and on our way back into town.

She had a good point. Usually this was when my jet lag kicked in. "No, I'm wide awake. I think the scare with Andrew had something to do with that. All that adrenaline."

"Che-che-che," Katharine responded in soothing agreement. The funny sound she made reminded me of the indistinct call a person made to attract a squirrel or a flock of birds. During the past year her "che-che-che" had come to mean many things to me, including the sense of comfort she was bestowing on both of us now.

That's how it was with Katharine. Her husband had just suffered a heart attack, and yet she was asking about me, making sure I wasn't too tired. I loved Katharine. I loved Andrew, and without a doubt I loved Ian. I was more than ready for our everyday lives to intersect the way they were now. But a few items needed to be resolved to pull all the pieces together. My hopes for this trip included settling those issues.

Just as my thoughts went to one of those unresolved concerns, Katharine inadvertently brought up the topic. "I thought you should know that Margaret plans to come to the Tea Cosy this afternoon."

Katharine turned off the main road and took the shortcut to Bexley Lane where her tea shop was located.

"Oh good," I said. But I could tell my enthusiasm level wasn't convincing by the look on Katharine's face as she glanced at me.

Unlike my mother, I couldn't act well. I could pretend, however. And ever since I had entered the scene with the Whitcombe family here in Carlton Heath, I had pretended that Margaret would one day accept me. She didn't have to like me, but I imagined all sorts of ways she could receive me into the clan.

Margaret was the matriarch of the Whitcombe family now that my father was dead. She was my father's only wife. Understandably, my sudden appearance along with the evidence I produced to verify my place in the Whitcombe lineage was distressing to her, which is why I had done everything I could to keep my identity quiet.

This was a small village. The Whitcombes and MacGregors were close friends. As much as I wanted the awkwardness to magically go away between all of us, I knew it would probably be like this for a long time.

Even so, I liked to imagine all would be well. Ian and I would marry. We would move to Carlton Heath. Margaret would accept me, and I would at long last be "home." I would finally belong somewhere. And I would be part of a family.

Katharine was halfway down the bumpy, narrow back road that I called the "romantic route" because it went past the ivy-covered church with the old cemetery, the magnificent trees with their gnarled trunks, and a collection of stone cottages with trimmed hedges. One of the cottages held a special memory for me, and I was eager to see it again.

Katharine came upon what I had dubbed "Forgotten Rose Cottage" because of the surplus of neglected rosebushes that grew up both sides of the stone dwelling. She slowed the car and veered around a pothole.

"I love that little place," I said.

"Lovely, isn't it?" Katharine offered me a soft smile.

The long-neglected stone cottage looked different than it had last summer. Someone had done a significant amount of cleanup.

"Did someone buy the cottage?"

"It's possible."

My heart sank. I had dreams about that little, fairy-tale house. I dreamed of one day acquiring the place with Ian. I could see us working side by side in our jeans and sweatshirts, painting and decorating and making the long-neglected cottage into a home. Our home.

But that would never be if someone else had snatched up the Forgotten Rose Cottage and decided to make it their dream.

A chest-tightening sadness came over me, and I felt an urge to fight for the house. "Is there a way to find out if someone has bought it?"

"I'm sure there is. You should ask Ian. He has ways of finding out such things quickly."

I crossed my arms in front of me and thought of the many things Ian and I needed to discuss this week. Maybe I should have stayed at the hospital with him instead of stepping right into seeing Margaret my first few hours in Carlton Heath.

Glancing at Katharine, I realized I'd been so wrapped up in my own world that I hadn't asked how she was doing with the fright of Andrew and his trip to the hospital. For the rest of the short drive to the Tea Cosy, I put my attention on Katharine.

And in her Katharine way, she put twice as much love and attention right back on me.

As she turned her car onto Bexley Lane, the long awaited sight didn't disappoint. Every lamppost on this beautiful stretch of road was adorned with a large evergreen wreath. Long garlands of evergreen and ivy dotted with red berries hung from one lamppost to the next. The wreaths as well as the swaying garlands were trimmed in twinkling lights and pert, red ribbons.

Even though it was only dusk, all the lights were lit, turning this street into a twinkling fairyland that looked like a Victorian Christmas card. Of all the places of business on Bexley Lane, the Tea Cosy exuded the most charm. The building was one of the oldest in Carlton Heath; made of rock and limestone, it hinted at being a well-aged, diminutive castle. The sign that hung on the lamppost adjacent to the shop was in the shape of a teapot.

As Katharine and I approached the front door, I stepped ahead of her just for the personal delight of being the one to reach for the oddly-shaped metal latch and to open the heavy, wooden door. The string of merry silver bells jumped and jingled, and once again I stepped over the timber threshold and entered one of my favorite places in the world, the Tea Cosy.

A warm, amber fire burned in the ancient hearth of the permanently soot-covered fireplace. Along the mantel and at each table small red votive candles flickered contentedly.

I took a quick look around and spotted Margaret. She was seated in the far corner in a tall chair with her back to the door.

"Shall we?" Katharine asked.

I knew she was asking if we should go and greet Margaret. With a nod, I followed Katharine across the uneven wooden floor. She spoke in her buttery smooth way. "Hallo, Margaret. We've good news on Andrew. Did you hear?"

"No. Only that he had gone to hospital. How is he?" With a sideways glance at me, Margaret added, "Welcome back, Miranda."

She was a round and rosy woman with fair skin, white hair, and wire-rimmed glasses. Not the sort of looks one imagines for the wife of such a distinguished film star, but Margaret carried herself with a regal air.

"It's good to be back." I reached for Margaret in preparation to greet her with a hug or at least a handshake. When she didn't respond in kind, I ended up giving her arm an awkward pat.

Ellie, my half brother's petite, sparkling wife, must have heard Katharine and me because she flitted out of the kitchen in her white apron with a tray of warm scones in her hands. On her head perched a headband with felt reindeer antlers.

Ellie loved life. She loved people. As soon as she saw me, she put the scones on the table for Margaret and threw her arms around me in a welcoming hug.

"You're here! This is perfect. Julia has been counting the days until her Auntie Miranda arrives. She's at the house, hoping you'll go there first. I suppose you've been to hospital, though, isn't that right? How is Andrew? We've all been so concerned, haven't we?"

"Yes," Margaret said. "What is the news of Andrew?"

Katharine gave the good report and added, "We don't anticipate any complications or further problems. It's the best report we could have received, really."

Ellie clapped her hands together. "Wonderful news!"

"I'm so pleased to hear such a report," Margaret said. "What a relief that must be for all of you."

"Yes, it's a blessed relief. Miranda and I have come back to do some baking that went by the wayside this morning. Before I get everything ready in the kitchen, would you care for more tea?"

"Yes, that would be lovely. Miranda, would you care to join me?"

I looked at Katharine and back at Margaret. Had I been set up for this meeting? I didn't think so. Arranging this meeting would have been a challenge, given all the details that hadn't gone according to schedule so far that day.

"If you don't mind, Katharine," Ellie said, untying the strings on her apron, "I must go on a quick errand. Your timing is perfect, really. I need to make a dash."

"Of course. I appreciate all you did today."

"It was a pleasure." Reaching for my arm as I lowered myself into the chair across from Margaret, Ellie said, "I'll see you back here in less than an hour."

"I'll be here."

As Katharine and Ellie left me alone at the table with Margaret, I noted that I had the same feeling I'd experienced on my first job interview. As much as I wanted Margaret to accept me, I still didn't like sitting there, not knowing what the outcome of our meeting was going to be.

"How fortunate that you and I have this opportunity to speak with each other privately before the holiday festivities begin," Margaret said.

I nodded, waiting.

"I have wanted to tell you how much I have appreciated your discretion this past year. Edward and I were speaking not long ago of the unique situation between you and our family. Edward reminded me of how you are to be commended for your maturity and prudence." Margaret paused as if waiting for my response.

The only words that came to mind were, "Thank you."

Margaret seemed like the sort of woman who did a lot of thinking on a subject before letting her opinions be known. I couldn't tell if she had expressed all that was on her mind. A weighted "however" statement seemed as if it might follow, and I waited for it in bone-dry silence.

But apparently Margaret had said all she intended to. At least at this point.

She reached for her china teacup and took a small sip. I leaned back and felt as if the adrenaline-delayed jet lag had come over me all at once.

"I should probably see if I can help Katharine with the tea," I said.

"Yes, of course."

Feeling officially dismissed, I got up and was almost to the curtain that separated the small kitchen from the dining area when the sound of the cheery jingle bells on the front door announced that someone else had entered.

I turned to see who it was, and for the second time that day I saw the last person I expected.

Chapter Six

"How about that?" Josh sported a victorious grin as soon as he saw me. "The guy at the train station said this might be the place."

All eyes were on Josh as he dropped his heavy bag off his shoulder and bumped the chair of one of the guests closest to the door.

"Oh, sorry. Pardon me." He nodded at the ruffled woman. She raised her gaze to his ski cap, and he immediately removed it. Unfortunately, his uncombed and most likely unwashed hair looked worse than the ski beanie.

I tried to direct him back, preferably out the door, but at least away from the guests. So far, on all my visits to Carlton Heath, none of the busybodies seemed to find my connection to their town or to the Whitcombes or MacGregors out of the ordinary. That was because Ian and I were such an item of interest. I was sure our names had been discussed more than once over the chubby china teapots positioned between the ladies who loved to gather at the Tea Cosy for a good chat.

This scene with Josh was guaranteed to be a teatime tale for many weeks if I didn't find a way to redirect this inconvenient American out the door and on his way.

I tried to make it appear as if I were simply addressing a wayward tourist and not someone I knew when I said in a low voice, "I'm not sure this is where you want to be right now."

"Why? Is a private party going on here?" Josh wasn't catching any of my subtle hints, conveyed through a variety of facial expressions.

"No, but..."

"Then would it be okay if I ordered something to eat?"

I knew how determined Josh could be once he put his mind to something. If he wasn't going to leave, the path of least disruption would be to tuck him into a corner and try to keep him quiet. At least until most of the curious women went on their way.

Putting on my hostess demeanor, I said, "Go ahead and take a seat. I'll bring you some tea."

I started to head for the kitchen when out of the corner of my eye I saw that Josh was making a beeline for an empty table in the far back corner—the table next to Margaret's.

"Actually," I said quickly intervening, "I think you would be better off at the table over here by the kitchen. There is more room for your baggage."

Boy, was that an understatement. If there were any way I could tuck him *inside* the kitchen, then our mutual baggage would be less obvious to everyone. *This is not good. I wish I'd insisted he leave instead of making a place for him.*

Ducking into the tiny kitchen and pulling the curtain shut behind me, I closed my eyes and tried to think. I could feel myself panting.

"What is it?" Katharine asked.

I put my finger to my lips, hopeful that nothing we said could be heard beyond the curtain. Yet I knew all too well how easily sound carried in this place.

In a low whisper, I pointed to the other side of the wall. "My old boyfriend! I ran into him at the train station in London. I told him about Carlton Heath. I never thought he would come here!"

Katharine, in her serene way, handed me a pot of fresh tea. "Please tell our guest the scones will be ready shortly."

If I hadn't counted Katharine as a close friend as well as my (hopefully) soon-to-be mother-in-law, I would have protested.

Exiting the kitchen with the pot of tea in one hand and a china cup and saucer in the other, I was aware that every eye in the room was on Josh. Some of the women stared from adjusted positions and postures that weren't exactly covert. Flora, who owned the Bexley Lane Gifts and Curios Shoppe, had been preparing to leave her table at the Tea Cosy when I first arrived.

She now had joined another table, and all three women had positioned their chairs so they faced the kitchen. As soon as I entered the dining area, I felt the curious gazes shift from Josh to their tea and scones, as if I were a teacher who had stepped out in the middle of an exam and returned before the naughty students had finished copying each other's answers.

Katharine followed me out of the kitchen and took another fresh pot of tea to Margaret. I appreciated her going to Margaret. Katharine would know what to say.

As I placed the tea and cup in front of Josh, he said in a low voice, "Hey, I just realized this might be awkward for you."

I was sure he caught onto that brilliant insight as soon as he noticed the attention he was receiving from the curious audience.

"It could be awkward for you, as well," I whispered.

"Is there someplace else we can go? Just for a few minutes?"

I shook my head. "This is a very small village."

"So it seems. It's great, though, isn't it? Bexley Lane, just like the address printed on the back of the photo. I had no problem finding my way here. I can see why you like it so much."

"Josh, is there a reason you came here?" I knew if we kept our voices low, we might not be heard. This table by the kitchen was the most isolated, which is why few guests ever chose to sit there. It also helped if I stood because the way the table was angled, my back would block Josh from his audience.

"I came because I was curious to see this place. My flight was overbooked, so when free tickets were offered in exchange for seats, I was the first one at the counter. My rescheduled flight goes out at midnight, and I thought, 'Who knows when I'll be in England again? Why not go to Carlton Heath?' And here I am."

"But how did you know you would find me here at the Tea Cosy?"

"That was easy. When I described you to the guy at the train station, he said you had gone off with someone named Ian in his Austin-Healy. He said Ian is related to the owner of this place."

I felt myself relaxing slightly. His explanations made sense.

This was his idea of a diversion. A little adventure. He would drink a cup of tea, leave, and tell all his associates about his train ride to the English countryside between his flights.

I poured the first cup of tea for him in an effort to appear to have a reason for lingering at his table.

Josh smiled up at me. And that's when I knew I was in trouble. It was his flirty, how-you-doin' smile, not his good-to-see-you-but-I-gotta-go smile.

"So, I have a question for you," he said, trying to come across casually. I could tell he was nervous though.

"What's your question?"

He cleared his throat. "I realize I'm putting myself way out there, but after seeing you at Paddington station, I had to ask. Are you with anyone now?"

"Yes, I am with someone."

Josh seemed to slump in his chair. "I thought that's what you might say. By any chance, is it the guy with the Austin-Healy?"

I nodded.

"Well, at least I can say he has good taste in cars and women."

I tried to offer a friendly, consolation prize sort of smile, but one thing puzzled me.

In my lowest of low voices, I asked, "Did I give you any signal, any indication at all, at the train station that I was available?"

"No." Josh shook his head. "You just look amazing and I was... well, a guy can hope, can't he?"

I knew all about hoping. For the past year I'd begun to hope about many things, including the fanciful wish that I might one day live in the Forgotten Rose Cottage, even though no indication had ever been given to me that it might be available. That small flit of a thought gave me enough compassion to excuse Josh's impulsive decision to seek me out. He was, after all, one of the few people in my life with whom I'd had a close relationship at one time.

"Listen." Josh aligned himself so that my standing position more thoroughly blocked him from the ladies. I was sure by now the ones with hearing aids had their devices turned up all the way.

"There is one more thing I wanted to say to you. Do you remember my brother?"

I nodded.

"He's a lawyer now, and I thought you should know, in case you need representation for..."

I gave Josh a determined look that fortunately silenced him. I knew where he was going. If I was the daughter of Sir James, certainly someone needed to assist me in fighting for my rightful portion of his inheritance. I'd been over this road already, and my choice had been to let it go. I never went in search of my birth father with the anticipation of financial gain. All I wanted was information and hopefully a relationship. I had received what I went after. I never wanted to jeopardize my fledgling family relationships by going up against Edward or Margaret with a claim to anything. End of discussion.

"I take it you have all that covered," he said, reading my not-so-subliminal message.

"Yes. It's covered. And I want to tell you again how glad I am that you regard information with complete confidentiality. As a professional, I mean."

"Got it." He obviously understood my masked message that I was counting on him to keep silent about my identity.

Leaning back and looking at the cup of tea in front of him, he said, "So, I guess I should try some of this English tea before I leave."

"Yes, you should." I was referring to the "should leave" part more than the "try the tea" part. But at the same time, I knew I would never forget my first visit to the Tea Cosy and my first pot of proper British tea and plate of Katharine's scones. I did want him to enjoy the fruit of his adventurous trek from Heathrow.

"I need to get back to the kitchen," I said.

"I understand. Really, I do."

I could tell Josh was now the one sending the cryptic message. He never had been one to overstay his welcome.

"You seem to fit in here," he said almost as an afterthought. "But, you know, if things don't work out with...whatever, you know how to contact me."

In an effort to keep our parting light and breezy and as uncomplicated as possible, I said, "Well, you know, if that counseling practice of yours doesn't work out, you can always try detective work."

Josh smiled.

"I'll see about the scones to go with your tea."

As if we were a well-orchestrated team, Katharine came up next to me just then and offered Josh a plate of warm scones along with clotted cream and jam. She explained how to open the scone and spread the jam first, leaving the clotted cream for the dollop on top. While she extended her hospitality, I headed back into the kitchen.

With a quick glance to the back of the room, I saw Margaret directing a quick glance our way.

Whatever your perception is about all this, Margaret, please don't jump to any conclusions. I don't care what the other women here think. I do care immensely, though, about what you think.

Chapter Seven

From the kitchen, I could hear everything being said as it seeped through the curtain. Flora apparently had decided to take her leave but found it necessary to shuffle over to Josh's table to greet Katharine before making her departure.

After exchanging pleasantries about how Andrew was improving in hospital, Flora spoke to Josh in a timbre loud enough for most of the room to hear. "I do hope you're enjoying your tea and scones. We're all quite fond of Katharine's baking here. A little too fond, some of us are, I should think."

"I can see why you'd feel that way," Josh said in what I recognized to be his counselor sort of response.

"It's not often that we see visitors in our little village. We're not exactly a tourist destination, are we?"

"It's a charming place," Josh said politely.

"Our resident royalty seemed to think so," a second woman's voice chimed in. "One of the charms of Carlton Heath, of course, is the quiet. At least that's how things have been since his passing."

"She means Sir James, of course," Flora added.

"I see." Again, Josh seemed to be using his counselor responses to keep engaged in the conversation, yet remain aloof and noncommittal as to how much he actually knew.

I realized at that moment that Josh's expert "engaged yet noncommittal" demeanor had been a hallmark of our relationship. Even though we connected on a number of levels while we dated, we never had melded at the heart level the way Ian and I had almost instantly. My relationship with Margaret as well as with my half brother, Edward, bore the same characteristics as my relationship with Josh. We were connected or "engaged," as it were, in many areas. Yet aloofness was what marked the relationship.

Since Josh didn't seem to be snapping at any of the bait thrown into the conversation about Carlton Heath's most famous resident, Flora tried once more with a subdued announcement that Sir James's widow was in their presence. "She's the one in the corner there. A lovely woman, really. Rather given to her own company though. Not that anyone could blame her. We all understand why, don't we? After living in her husband's shadow all those years, the dear has spent most of her time trying to stay out of the limelight. She's become rather accomplished at being amongst us yet staying invisible, if you will."

My heart suddenly went out to Margaret. She and I were more alike than I had ever thought. I, too, was acquainted with the art of making myself invisible. I knew all too well the loneliness that incubated in such places as backstage wardrobe rooms and back tables in busy tea shops.

"I'm rather curious," Flora said. "If you don't mind my asking, what does one manage to cart around in such a large duffel bag?"

Josh's mumbled response must have been meant to be heard only by Flora because I couldn't make out what he said.

Flora certainly heard his answer. Her "Oh my!" response echoed off the kitchen walls. I could hear a faint twittering throughout the Cosy, as if each of the observers was checking with the others to see if anyone had heard what he said.

The bells on the door jingled, suggesting that Flora was making a hasty exit. Katharine appeared in the kitchen with her cheeks rosy and her lips upturned.

"What did he say to her?" I whispered.

Katharine cupped her hand to my ear. "He told her his duffel bag was large enough to carry his dead aunt."

Covering my mouth, I muffled my laugh. I'd forgotten all about Josh's morose sense of humor. I knew he *really* needed to get out of town now.

The diversion he had just created was a gift to me, whether he meant it as such or not. The topic of the day would now be about Josh and the speculations on his poor auntie instead of whether he and I were somehow connected. I owed him for that one.

Rummaging in my purse for a slip of paper, I wrote Josh a quick note.

Thank you! I hope all goes well for you.
(And your unfortunate auntie!)

Returning to the dining area, I planned to slip him the note as if it were the bill, even though I knew Katharine wouldn't charge him since he was a special guest.

When I stepped past the curtain, nearly everyone was already gone, including Josh. Margaret was gone as well. It didn't surprise me that a number of the women had ducked out, no doubt with the objective of bustling to the nearest phone to start the alert.

I could picture Josh trekking to the train station down Bexley Lane with his duffel bag over his shoulder. A number of certain residents between here and the station would be, at this very moment, answering their hotly ringing phones and hurrying to their windows to have a look as he passed by.

With all the excitement over, a friendly calm returned to the Cosy. I put more wood on the fire, cleared the tables, and went to work washing dishes. Last August I'd helped out here one afternoon while Katharine went for a hair appointment and Ian and Andrew repaired the plumbing in the apartment upstairs. Even though the building was old, Andrew had managed to do an impressive job of updating the four-room apartment space where he and Katharine lived.

I experienced a calming and unexpected contentment last August while carrying out the simple domestic tasks that accompanied the running of a tea shop. When Katharine returned from her hair appointment, I told her I preferred the work I'd put my hands to that afternoon over the tedious work I'd done at a large accounting firm in San Francisco for almost ten years.

When I tried to explain to Katharine that this was a place of peace for me, she said, "You are a woman drawn to home and hearth. Never doubt the happiness such simplicity can bring you."

From that moment, I knew I had a place here. It was as if my internal compass had reset and would now always point to the Tea Cosy and to Katharine, the woman who filled this small space with so much love and grace.

The timer on the stove gave a dull buzz. I put on an oven mitt and pulled out two trays of Katharine's warm, fragrant shortbread Christmas cookies. I'd tasted these cookies on previous visits, and the sight and scent of them started my mouth watering. Katharine called these cookies "Andrew's Scottish shortbread biscuits" and had confided to me that her secret ingredient was Madagascar vanilla bean.

Usually Katharine used a round cookie cutter on the thickly rolled-out dough. This time the cookies cooling on the trays were cut in the shape of stars. Christmas stars.

I looked at the plumped-up stars and once again thought of the imagery of the five-armed starfish from *A Wrinkle in Time* and how it related to the loss of my mother. She was the missing part of me, the part that had so defined who I was and what I would become.

Reaching for a spatula, I slipped it under one of the Christmas star cookies and lifted it so I could touch the warm star, my finger gently tapping on each of the five appendages.

Just then Katharine entered the kitchen. I looked up at her, and I knew. I just knew. The broken star of my life had been made whole through the gift of her friendship. The part I thought I would go through life without had grown back when I wasn't watching.

Chapter Eight

Sometimes when revelations come, they must be spoken aloud to become fully vested. Those breakthrough moments of understanding, accepting, and receiving are validated and affirmed in the presence of another.

That had been the case for me last Christmas when I sensed a constant, gentle presence throughout my time in Carlton Heath. At the church where I sat beside Ellie on Christmas morning, studying the Christ figure portrayed in the stained glass windows, I was compelled to believe in God.

I didn't know it at the time, but two things were happening at once. As I was trying to find a way to enter into what I knew would be a life-changing conversation with Edward and Margaret, God's Spirit seemed to be closing in on me with the same objective. On the one hand, I wanted to reveal to the Whitcombes that, because of Sir James, I was related to them by blood. On the other hand, God was trying to reveal to me that because of His Son and because of His blood, I could enter God's family.

I still don't know how to describe what happened that day in such a simple, quiet way except to say that I believed. I went from not belonging to God and His kingdom to being accepted and belonging to Him and His eternal family. I understood that my connection to Him came because of Christ's blood. It was that simple and that impossibly complex all at the same time.

With Edward and Margaret, it seemed to be still mostly complex. I was related to them—or at least to Edward—by blood. Yet I still was waiting to be fully accepted into their family.

Last Christmas Katharine had been the first one to whom I had entrusted the story of what seemed to me mysterious, ancient, and true. The story of how I had been pursued by God, and now I was changed. I belonged to Christ.

When I spoke my revelation to her, the truth was sealed. I was a believer of infantile status, but a Christian nonetheless. I was a fledgling follower of Christ, and I knew she was someone who had followed close to Him for many years.

The foundation of our friendship began to grow that day, I think. And now, a year later, as I held the Christmas star cookie in my hand, I saw what had grown in my life where for a long time all that had existed was great loss.

I put down the cookie and stepped over to Katharine in that small kitchen space. Wrapping my arms around her, I whispered in her ear, "I love you."

"I love you too, Miranda." She stroked my hair and released a breathy "che-che-che" sound, as if she were calming a small bird.

Aside from my mother and Ian, Katharine was the only

other person on this planet to whom I had said, "I love you." I think she knew that.

We pulled apart. Not awkwardly, but like two dancers. I hadn't hugged Katharine exactly like that before, but it instantly felt like a familiar motion, as if we were well acquainted with the ways of all close mothers and daughters.

She smiled at me and spoke a single word filled with hope. "Soon."

I nodded. I knew what she meant. Ian took Katharine into his confidences as well. I'm sure she knew about the small box he had picked up that morning in London. She undoubtedly knew what was in the box. And she was probably feeling a similar anticipation, waiting for what we both knew would be one of Ian's well-planned moments when the box was opened.

Katharine slid two more cookie sheets of shortbread into the oven, and the two of us went about the kitchen duties as if this were the next act in the ancient, domestic ballet of women.

We had nearly finished all the cleanup from the afternoon teatime when the jolly jingle bells let us know someone else had entered the Cosy. We didn't need to step out of the kitchen to see who it was. The merry voices let us know right away that Ellie had returned with her observant thirteen-year-old son, Mark, and precocious six-year-old daughter, Julia.

"Auntie Miranda!" Julia sang out her greeting. "Auntie Katharine! Where are you?"

"In the kitchen," Katharine called out in a matching, sing-song voice.

Brown-haired Julia burst through the curtain and entered the kitchen with a squeal. She wrapped her arms around my middle and hug, hug, hugged me.

"How's my favorite little girl?" I asked, kissing the top of her head.

"Your favorite little girl is happy you are finally here! Have you seen it yet?"

"Have I seen what?"

Katharine intervened. "Julia, it's not yet Christmas. We have to keep a few things secret until then."

Julia placed both hands over her mouth, and I gave Katharine a raised eyebrow look. Katharine, the one who didn't make it a practice to keep secrets, was directing young Julia to do just that. Well, well, well!

Peeking around my middle, Julia eyed the cookies. "Are those biscuits for anyone special?"

"Julia!" Ellie spouted, entering the kitchen and catching her little beggar in the act.

Julia turned her innocent eyes to Katharine, and a Christmas star was in her hand before Ellie had another opportunity to protest.

"Only one," Ellie said. "And see if your brother would like one as well."

"Markie!"

"Please don't screech like that, Julia. Go ask your brother politely and in an inside voice," Ellie said.

"Here." Katharine handed over another biscuit. "I have a feeling his answer will be yes."

Julia trotted out with a plump star in each hand.

"Have you heard the news about tonight's performance?" Ellie asked.

"We understood the Guild was considering canceling," I said.

"Not so," Ellie said gleefully. "The Theatre Guild has decided not to cancel the performance tonight. The curtain will go up as scheduled, and guess who will be donning the robes of Father Christmas?"

"Certainly not Andrew," Katharine said.

"No, not Andrew. Have you another guess?"

Neither Katharine nor I could come up with an obvious choice. Ellie's husband, Edward, would be the next logical Father Christmas since he was Sir James's son and therefore would be immediately received by the townspeople since Andrew wasn't available. However, Edward wasn't the sort to ever appear onstage. He stayed far away from his father's footsteps. In this regard, he and I shared a common goal.

"I will give you a hint," Ellie said. "We were just at Grey Hall and saw the new Father Christmas having a costume fitting, and Mavis was telling him he was quite a catch. But he told her he already was taken."

"Ian?" Katharine and I said in unison.

"Ohh. Did I give too much of a clue?" Ellie looked disappointed at our deductions. Had she forgotten what a small village this was?

Just then my cell phone rang with the customized tune that told me Ian was calling. "Speaking of the jolly ole elf..."

"Ho, ho, ho," I answered.

"Madam, you seem to have mistaken me for my American counterpart."

"Then should I have said, 'Hee, hee, hee?' I heard the news."

"So you did. Ellie is there now, I take it?"

"Yes, she's here with the kids. How's your dad?"

"Much improved and sleeping soundly. Listen, you and I will have to reschedule our dinner plans."

"Well, that's a good thing because it just so happens I have a play to attend tonight. I'm hoping to get a good seat right up front."

"I'll be looking for you there. How is Mark?"

"Fine, I guess. I haven't seen him yet. Why?"

"He'll be onstage tonight as well."

I knew Mark was an understudy for Scrooge in this all-children performance of Dickens's classic play. Apparently Andrew wasn't the only one who wasn't well enough to carry on that evening.

As soon as Ian and I said our "see you laters," I left Ellie and Katharine and went to check on Mark. The two women had stepped up the biscuit production now that the treats were definitely needed for that evening's refreshment table at intermission.

I found Mark seated beside the hearth about to make the last bite of cookie disappear. Julia was pretending she was the tearoom hostess, flitting from table to table with an imaginary pot of tea and chattering with her invisible friends.

Mark greeted me politely, and I pulled up a chair next to him by the waning fire. "I heard you have the leading role tonight."

"Yes, I do." His thin lips pulled tight in a squiggly line. Bits of shortbread crumbs dotted the corners.

"You're going to do a great job. I'm just sure of it."

Mark didn't look convinced, but he thanked me all the same.

"Are you feeling nervous?"

He shrugged bravely.

"I'll tell you a little trick that might help. My mother used to tell herself every opening night that it was only a dress rehearsal. She said she never got the jitters."

"Was your mother in a lot of performances?"

"Yes, she was."

"Did she go to a lot of parties?"

"A lot of parties? I don't know. I suppose she went to some. She went to cast parties with the other actors."

"What did they do at those parties?"

"Same sort of things you do at the cast parties here. Eat and talk about the performance."

Mark reached for the iron poker and taunted the roasted logs into bursting into what looked like a thousand escaping fireflies. He seemed to be pondering my answer rather intensely.

"Did that answer your question, Mark?"

"Sort of."

"What is it you wanted to know?"

"I wanted to know..." he hesitated, breaking the depleted log in half by hitting it directly in its hollowed center.

"What?" I wanted him to know he had my full attention.

"Did your mother kiss a lot of men?"

I drew back and tried to read Mark's expression. "Why did you ask that?"

Mark shrugged.

I didn't leave his comment alone. "What prompted you to ask that question?"

Mark looked down at his feet. "It's because I know."

"Because you know what?"

Without looking up he said in a low voice, "I know who your father was."

Chapter Nine

I let out a slow, steady breath. "Did someone tell you about my mother, Mark?"

"No. No one told me. I heard my grandmother talking to my father. The parts they didn't say, I figured out."

I thought a moment. "Have you told anyone what you heard?"

"No." He adamantly shook his head.

"I think you should tell your parents and your grandmother. They would like to know what you heard."

"But I wasn't trying to listen in on them."

"I know. But since you did hear them talking, I think you should tell them what you heard."

"Is it true then?"

For a moment I considered dodging the question. I knew I could think of a way to avoid telling Mark the truth. That's what my mother did. She spun many fanciful tales in response to my challenging questions and managed to effortlessly enchant me right out of reality and into the realm where I could pretend that life was something other than what it was. For a moment I wondered if that was the best approach to take with Mark.

Then I thought of Katharine and her penchant for not hiding truth once it was revealed. Even Josh the psychologist, with his comments on how truth always rises to the surface, would tell me to be honest with Mark. What was it Josh had said about how sometimes you must wait for truth to surface and other times you must go to it, take it by the hand, and pull with all your might?

Mark had bravely taken truth by the hand and now was pulling with all his might. He could end up carrying my response with him the rest of his life.

I reached over and put my hand on Mark's shoulder. "Yes, it's true. My father was Sir James."

Mark didn't reply. In the hardening lines around his eyes, I instantly saw the reason my mother told fairytales instead of truths. Her lies were a misplaced sort of kindness, I suppose, in that it was her way of protecting my sensitive, young spirit. Perhaps my quirky mother and the bohemian lifestyle she imposed on me was her attempt to do the best she could with what she had. Don't all mothers do that? What my mother had was a wealth of fantasy.

Mark's dark hair fell across his forehead as he looked down at his hands. "Why do you think she did it?" he asked in a low voice.

I wasn't sure what he meant, so I asked him to expand his question.

"Why do you think your mother...you know...did what she did with my grandfather?"

I had no immediate response for him.

"I know how babies are born," Mark said with a muffled fierceness. "You don't need to pretend I don't know anything like Julia." Backing down he added, "If I shouldn't be asking this sort of question, then..."

"No, it's okay. The answer is, I don't know. I think my mother loved your grandfather. I really do. I think they probably both felt something meaningful and real toward each other when they met. Your grandparents were separated at the time..."

"I know," Mark said quickly.

"So when your grandparents got back together, my mother chose not to tell him she was expecting me. She raised me by herself, and we just went on."

An airy stretch of silence fashioned invisible bonds between my astute nephew and me. I reached over and gave his hand a small squeeze. His fingers were cold. He looked up with a softened expression that reminded me of Ellie. He definitely had his father's sharp, analytical mind, but he also had his mother's tender spirit toward all living creatures.

"Thanks for talking to me about it," he said in an adult-sounding voice.

"You're welcome."

His wobbly, thin-line smile returned. "Whenever I call you Aunt Miranda, everyone else will think it's still because you're a family friend. But I'll know who you really are."

I leaned over and pressed a motherly kiss on the side of his head. In a whisper I said, "And I will always know who you are, Mark Whitcombe. You are my amazing nephew. And I will always love you."

My unexpected declaration embarrassed Mark, but I decided that was okay. I didn't have much experience in being around young children or finding ways to express what I felt in my heart. My first attempts were bound to be clumsy.

Ever since Ian started to shower me with love, affection, and hope, I felt eager to spill that love out whenever I had the chance. Now that I was finally back in Carlton Heath where the few people in this world that I truly loved resided, I wanted to show them that love, even if the moments turned awkward.

I held onto that thought as I helped finish up the cookies. It was easy to feel and express love for Ellie, Katharine, and Julia. Especially Julia. She kept giving me hugs and saying things like, "I can't wait until you live here all the time, Auntie Miranda."

Once the cookies were done, I had to peel myself away from a clapping game Julia had started. Ellie had sent Mark to Katharine's car for my luggage. She had him transfer it to her car since I'd be staying with them that night. But I intercepted Mark and pulled from my suitcase the items I would need to dress up for the performance later that evening.

As soon as everyone left—Katharine to the hospital and Ellie and the kids home to dress for the play—I took a quick shower and an even quicker ten-minute nap. Then I changed into the special dress I had brought for the performance that evening.

Last year when I attended the play, Ellie was dressed as a Sugar Plum Fairy. I still had sparkles from her ensemble on my peacoat. Katharine had been adorned as a regal lady of the theater. All my clothes were waiting for me in a London hotel room last year, so I attended in my crumpled travel clothes.

This year I couldn't wait to join the merriment by dressing up in my new cheery-cherry-swishy-merry red Christmas dress. I returned to the kitchen for some soup Katharine had left for me on the stove. A note on the kitchen counter reminded me that the Whitcombe family driver would come for me at 6:40.

I had just finished the soup when I heard the door bells jingle.

"I'll be right there!" I called out, placing my soup bowl in the sink.

Heavy-booted footsteps crossed the uneven wooden floor coming toward the kitchen. Apparently the Whitcombe's driver hadn't heard me so I called out again, "You didn't have to come get me!"

The kitchen curtain parted and a magnificent, deep voice rumbled, "Oh yes I did." In front of me in all his white-haired, velvet-robed glory stood Father Christmas.

Chapter Ten

For the briefest of moments, it seemed I was looking at *the* Father Christmas. Tilting my head and studying the eyes, I said, "Ian?"

"Ian to you. Father Christmas to all the wee girls and boys." With a pause he opened his palms and asked, "What do you think? Other than that I must be daft to have agreed to do this."

"No, not at all. You look fantastic! Very convincing. The beard is so believable. Does it itch?"

"I think you would be the one to best answer that question." Ian drew me close and kissed me good. "Well? What's your answer, woman?"

"My answer?"

"Does the beard itch?"

"Oh." I quickly put away the flitting thought that he was asking for an "answer" because he had included a proposal somewhere in the kiss, but I had been too swept up to hear it.

"Actually," I said, regaining my coy composure, "I'm not sure. You better try the kiss test one more time."

Ian willingly obliged.

We drew apart, and I said, "I'm still not quite sure..."

Another kiss came to me as visions of spending the rest of my life with this man danced in my head.

Margaret's driver found Ian and me in the middle of test kiss number four. Neither of us had heard him enter the Tea Cosy. We untangled from our hug and hid our smiles.

Ian addressed the driver somberly. "I'll be taking Miranda to the theatre. Sorry you didn't get the update."

The chauffer tipped his black cap and left us to our kitchen canoodling. Our kiss was short and sweet, followed by a tiny kiss on the end of my nose.

Reaching for my hands and standing back to look at me at arm's length, all Ian said was, "Miranda, you..."

"You like my new dress?"

"The dress is lovely, but it's the beautiful woman wearing the dress I'm in love with."

We paused a moment, standing hand in hand, making mushy eyes at each other, and then I laughed.

"What?" Ian seemed to have forgotten he was dressed as Father Christmas.

"Your outfit is equally ravishing," I said. "But it's the amazing, handsome man wearing the Father Christmas costume I'm in love with."

"So it's not a one-sided crush I'm having on you then, is it?" Ian sneaked in another kiss on the cheek.

I giggled. "Now that one tickled. And the answer to your question is the crush is terminal and highly mutual."

"We'd better get out of here then. Where's your coat?"

I strolled with Father Christmas to his Austin-Healy parked

in front of the Tea Cosy. We zigged down the narrow lane and parked in back of Grey Hall.

Last Christmas I had walked to Grey Hall from the train station and approached the Victorian-style building on a wide walkway lit by eight metal shepherd's hooks. A lantern hung from each hook, twinkling in the dark night. Before me, decked out in long garlands of evergreen boughs, was the theater my father had built during the late 1980s in a style reminiscent of Dickens.

As memorable as that arrival had been, this year with Ian, slipping in through the back entrance was memorable for other reasons. This time the only "décor" I noticed were the faces of the young performers as they watched Father Christmas swoosh past them and head for center stage behind the thick, blue curtain.

Ian pulled out a stack of index cards and stood on his mark, concentrating on getting the lines down. In less than twenty minutes those curtains would part and he would be "it"—the opening performer. All eyes would be on Ian, my Ian, and he would convince them he was Father Christmas.

I knew he could do it.

I blew him a kiss and wiggled my way through the maze of props backstage. If I wanted to, I could find the side door that would take me out to the front of the auditorium. But it seemed more fitting to go out the way we had come in, walk around to the front of Grey Hall, and promenade up the wide path lit with the hanging lanterns on the shepherd's hooks. In a way, I was giving tribute to my father for the theater he had built, as well as giving tribute to my mother who always let me sneak around backstage with her before a performance.

What a difference I felt over the way I had approached this theater last Christmas. I had made peace with the thought that my mother loved the theater as much as she loved me. I had come to appreciate the generosity of Sir James to this community, and in a clandestine way, I felt proud to be his daughter.

Entering the bustling lobby, I inched over to the coat check counter. Around me dozens of proud parents chatted with friends, checked their coats, shook hands, and made merry. Ellie was one of the coat checkers this year, which was a little silly due to her petite size. When I stepped up to the window, she was holding three coats and nearly drowned in all the woolen thickness.

"I'll wait until after you hang those up," I said.

"Miranda, look at you! What a beautiful dress. You look absolutely gorgeous! Ian is going to be gobsmacked for certain."

"Gobsmacked?" I repeated with a laugh. "Let me see your outfit."

She handed the stack of coats to her coworker, a tall man in a black top hat and tails, and opened her arms to reveal her surprise ensemble.

"I'm a snowflake," she said. "Can you tell? Someone thought I was trying to be the White Witch of Narnia. I think I may have gotten it all wrong this year."

"Oh, no. You definitely look like a snowflake. I would have guessed snowflake right away."

Her short gown was white with shimmering, pearl-shaded sequins. The sleeves and hem were cut in fanciful, straight-lined snips and clips the way a child cuts a folded-up piece of paper before opening it to reveal a snowflake. She wore white tights, white boots, a sprinkling of iridescent sparkles across her fair skin, and a wreath of white stars around her head.

"Do you think so, really?"

"Definitely. You make a darling snowflake."

"Thank you, Miranda. Have you seen Edward yet? He and Margaret might already be seated. Head toward the front on the left side, and you'll see them. I'll be there shortly."

The usher, dressed in a Nutcracker uniform, handed me a program, and I entered the darkened theater. Fresh boughs of evergreen shaped into huge Christmas wreaths hung from each of the Victorian-style lighting sconces. The ceiling glowed in the amber light, reflecting the inlaid plaster frescos with their repeating oval patterns of soft white-on-white. The dark blue velvet stage curtains were trimmed across the top with golden tassels from which bright red Christmas balls had been hung like holly berries.

Tender memories of my visit last year returned. I think the scent of the pine boughs started the feeling of having come full circle.

When I had reluctantly entered this place a year ago, I still was harboring a deep anger against my mother. Her offense was that the theater was her other love. Acting was her life. And a fall from a faulty balcony on a Venetian set took her life—not only from her but also from me.

After my mother's death, I was raised by Doralee, a bald woman with seven cats named after Egyptian pharaohs. Doralee was one of my mother's theater friends who lived in Santa Cruz where she bravely fought cancer and lost. The incongruous part of it all to me was that she lost with victorious words of heaven on her lips. Doralee was the first Christian I had met and possibly the most peculiar.

My adolescent years in her home fostered an independence that aided me as I faked my age after her death to obtain a job in San Francisco. My strength and independence of the past decade were born out of my silent rebellion against the theater. In some crazy belief birthed in my preteen years and fostered by the vacuum left in my mother's departure from this earth, I thought I could "get back" at the theater if I ignored the place that had been my mother's home and heart.

So I never went to the theater. Nor did I think of it or give it any regard in conversations. This was a challenge while I lived in San Francisco, a place where going to the theater was as much a part of life as going to a restaurant. But I was up to the challenge and remained a devoted boycotter.

Until last Christmas.

I had entered Grey Hall to gain information about my father. But that decision turned out to be the gift I "gave" my mother last Christmas. I said an important good-bye to her that night as I watched vigorous Andrew stride across the stage. I took a first step toward peace inside this theater, which I later discovered had been funded by my father.

Now, a year later, the love of my life was waiting center stage in this same theater, and I entered unencumbered. A nice, round, full circle of peace with the theater encased me in the same way the evergreen wreaths encircled the Victorian-style sconces along the side walls.

I drew in a breath for courage as I walked to the front and stood at the end of the row where Edward and his mother were seated. Seeing them reminded me that I may have made my peace with the theater, but with the two of them, I was walking into a broken circle that I had little hope of repairing. Yet here I was, available. Hopeful. And feeling a little sick to my stomach.

I should have waited for Ellie.

Edward stood in his tall, stiff, professor-like stance and looked at me through the lower portion of his rectangular glasses. Offering his hand, he said, "Good evening, Miranda."

"Good evening, Edward. Good evening, Margaret." I offered my hand to her and let it dangle in the space between us just in case she chose to reach for it. She didn't. Margaret had lightly touched my fingers with a gloved hand when we first met, before she knew who I was. Since then I had been with her half a dozen times, but she had never touched me again. Not once.

Instead of a handshake, Margaret offered me a regal nod. She seemed to be taking in my red dress from top to hem as I stood in the aisle, waiting to be allowed entrance to the Whitcombe row.

I glanced around the quickly filling auditorium in case I would need to find a seat in another row.

Edward, in his usual gentlemanly form, said, "Would you care to sit with us, Miranda?"

"Yes. Thank you."

I slid past Edward and Margaret and was about to leave the seat beside her empty for Ellie when I decided I would attempt to move closer to Margaret both figuratively and literally. I reminded myself of how she had complimented me on my discretion at the Tea Cosy. I also remembered how the other women at the Tea Cosy whispered about her aloofness. From much experience, I understood the art of trying to remain invisible; I recognized the symptoms in Margaret's demeanor.

I hadn't arrived at a sense of earnest sympathy or genuine compassion for her. But I did understand. And maybe that was enough of a first step, even if Margaret never responded to me in kind.

Which she didn't.

Margaret shifted in her seat and exhaled a disagreeable sound that in the past might have been enough to make me get up and move. This night I was determined in this place of full circles to do everything I could to inch this disconnected ring closer to peace and settled completeness.

When Ellie swished down the aisle a few moments later, she motioned for me to move over one seat. I made the change. As Ellie settled into her seat like a bird in a nest, I leaned back, feeling as if I had at least inched closer to Margaret.

The lights inside the theater flickered on and off, indicating the performance was about to begin. The audience hushed. The lights dimmed. The blue velvet curtains parted.

There stood Ian—my Ian—strong and bold and stunning in his flowing white hair, beard, and fur-lined Father Christmas robe. A wreath of holly now circled his head.

In his left hand he held a staff. He raised his right hand to the audience, allowing the wide velvet sleeve to slide down his brawny forearm. Ian's commanding presence was magnificent.

Andrew would have loved seeing this. I wish he and Katharine were here.

"He's so like Sir James!" Ellie whispered to me.

A tender sweetness came over my heart as I realized that my father wore that same robe and stood on this same stage only a few years ago. I had missed seeing him in this role just as Andrew and Katharine were missing Ian now.

Time and distance seemed to fade. I smiled at Ian the way I used to sit in the front row and smile at my mother.

With a quick glance at Margaret, I wondered if she had a special smile she pulled out for my father every time it was opening night for him. Or did she harbor her own unremitting grudge against the theater?

Oh, Margaret, if only you knew how similar we are. If only you would give me a chance.

Chapter Eleven

Ian's booming voice rode over the audience like a tidal wave as he delivered the opening line. "Marley was dead. As dead as a doornail."

Ellie reached over and gave my hand a happy squeeze. I squeezed hers back. The play was afoot, and all my attention was center stage. Ian completed his short monologue, stepped to the side, and gave a sweeping gesture to mark the commencement of the first scene. The cast of characters filed on stage beginning with Mark in his Scrooge business suit costume. He launched his first line by yelling at two of the bookkeepers, telling them to work faster.

"You are sorely mistaken if you think I will be giving you the day off for Christmas!" Poor Mark, his preadolescent voice cracked on "sorely mistaken" and "Christmas."

The audience muffled a collective chuckle. I turned to Ellie and saw that she was making a motherly wince. "Keep going, Markie," she whispered.

Mark went right on, undaunted by the wobbly opening. Within minutes he had the audience in the palm of his hand and showed no signs of stage fright. I felt so proud of him. His sense of timing and deadpan expressions proved quickly that he wasn't just the stand-in understudy. He was a natural. He was unmistakably the grandson of Sir James Whitcombe.

By the time the intermission lights came on, it was clear I wasn't the only one bursting with excitement and pride over Mark's performance.

"Your son is brilliant," the woman behind us said, patting Ellie on the shoulder.

"He's doing quite well, isn't he?" Ellie was all smiles. "A bit of vocal range lurch there at the beginning, but he pulled it off, wouldn't you say?"

Edward adjusted his glasses and nodded. I wondered how he really felt about his son's success.

A woman behind Margaret said, "It takes only one such performance to set a course for a lifetime. I dare say your grandson has revived the talent of our own Sir James this evening. Why has the young man not performed before?"

"It was his choice," Edward said firmly.

I had a feeling it might have been a choice strongly influenced by Edward. His affection for the theater and all that came with the life of an actor was as low as mine had been last year.

"Shall we go to the lobby for a bit of a sweet?" Ellie rose from her seat.

Edward and I both went to the lobby with Ellie while Margaret stayed behind. We were soon caught up in the crush of people gathered around the refreshment table. It was fun hearing all the comments about young Mark and his performance.

The good people of Carlton Heath had all come to the same conclusion. Mark was destined to follow in his grandfather's footsteps across the golden stage. Each of them seemed to enjoy announcing that acting was "in his blood," as if they were the first one to arrive at that conclusion.

One woman even had the boldness to say, "The talent obviously didn't fall to you, Edward—no offense meant."

"None taken," he said.

"The talent skipped a generation and has fallen on Mark, wouldn't you say?"

With the audience high on the speculations of young Mark's future on the stage, we returned to our seats and settled in for act two.

The curtains parted and six extras, including Julia, entered dressed as waifs, all wearing nightgowns and sleeping caps that looked like puffed-up muffin tops.

Instead of staying with the pack while Scrooge and the Spirit of Christmas Present visited the workhouse, Julia stepped to the side of the stage and gave a little wave to her mum and dad. Ellie waved back.

Pleased with the ruffle of giggles her antics produced, Miss Julia favored us with a six- year-old, ballerina-style spin around. Her costume filled with air and puffed out. She spun a second time, and Ellie whispered, "Oh dear, she knows better than to be showing off like that."

Pointing her finger at Julia and inching it in the air like a little worm, Ellie silently directed the free-spirited waif back to where she belonged on stage.

Clever Mark ad-libbed the obvious interruption with a quick quip. He glared at his sister with his hand on his hip and said, "Oh, Spirit of Christmas Present, it seems you're not the only spirit sent to torment me this night."

The crowd laughed. Mark broke character just long enough to turn to his mum and dad and offer a shrug. He squared his shoulders and went on with his next line without missing a beat.

Julia, not having caught the implication, looked at the audience with a grand smile, as if she were the source of all the merriment. As soon as she was offstage, she found her way through the back of the hall and came to our aisle. Margaret held out her arms for Julia to sit on her lap.

Julia demurely slid past her grandmother. I was surprised since Julia and her grandmother shared a close and sweet relationship. But Julia was definitely "mummy's girl," so when she edged her way past her grandmother, I thought she was going to cuddle up with Ellie.

Instead, Julia headed straight for me. She invited herself up into my lap and settled in as if this were the only place in the world she wanted to be.

Julia whispered to her mother and me, asking if we saw her spinning on stage.

"Yes, darling," Elli whispered to her overeager thespian. "Now hush. We mustn't talk until the play is over."

I glanced at Margaret. If she was miffed that Julia had come to me instead of her, she didn't show it in her expression. The rest of the play I tried not to think of Margaret but instead concentrated on enjoying the delight of having my cuddly niece on my lap and my clever nephew on the stage.

Before the fall of the curtain, Ian returned to his mark, center stage. With grand, Father Christmas hand motions, he had a final word for the merry audience.

"I charge you, gentlefolk, far and wide,
Heed this tale as told you this night.
Whenever you happen upon those in need,
Look to your heart and do a good deed.
Gather close this Christmastide,
All your loved ones by your side.
Mother, father, daughter, son,
May God bless us, everyone!"

The crowd erupted in applause. A standing ovation followed as the entire cast assembled onstage. Julia apparently had forgotten she would be given this additional chance to be in the spotlight.

She couldn't scamper off my lap quickly enough and charged up the narrow side steps in her flowing waif nightclothes. She joined her brother in the lineup. Mark did an admirable job of sharing his big moment with his little sister.

The houselights went up, and Ian fixed his gentle gaze on me. I blew him a kiss. He stayed in character and simply gave me a nod of his snowy head. I couldn't wait to see the magic that I knew would happen in the lobby when the little children would have a chance to sit on his lap and have their photos taken.

As we filed out of the row, I sidled up to Edward. "Was it

here that you had the photo taken on your father's lap when he was dressed as Father Christmas?"

"I don't recall where the infamous Christmas photo was taken. It was quite some time ago. Do you remember, Mother?"

Margaret needed for Edward to repeat the question to her. She thought a moment and then shook her head. "No, the doors to my memory on such details seem to have lost a few of their keys."

I smiled at Margaret in response to her comment and gave her a warm and open gaze. I wanted her to see that my hope for the door that had been unlocked between us earlier at the Tea Cosy would remain unlocked.

She didn't smile back. She looked the other way, and when we arrived in the lobby, Edward arranged for the driver to take her home.

The rest of the lobby was humming with activity. Parents on all sides were congratulating each other for their children's performances. Buoyant cast members were taking advantage of the table spread.

I watched Mark as he stood tall and straight, receiving a steady stream of handshakes and accolades.

Making my way to the other side of the lobby, I joined the parents and children who had stepped into a line, instinctively forming a queue to have a chat or a photo with Father Christmas. Ian was seated on a high-backed chair that was trimmed with evergreen and red ribbons.

I stood to the side, trying to suppress my grin as I watched Ian with the children. He poured on the charm, holding babies, letting them pull on his beard, or leaning over to listen to toddlers as they whispered in his ear.

He *was* Father Christmas.

For fun, I got in line too. Ian looked up and noticed where I was standing. He winked at me, and I understood I didn't have to wait in line. Ian already knew what I wanted for Christmas. As a matter of fact, I had a pretty good feeling my wish was at the top of his list.

Chapter Twelve

"We're thinking of going to hospital," Ellie said, coming up beside me after most of the hubbub in the lobby had calmed down. "Edward hasn't paid a visit to Andrew yet. We thought we might all pop over instead of going directly home. Do you and Ian have plans for a trip to hospital as well?"

"I'm not sure what we're going to do. Should I call you after Ian is finished here?"

"No need. We're not ready to leave just yet. The children are enjoying their moment of glory. A bit too much, Edward thinks, but how often will such an event occur?"

Ellie flitted off to finish her obligations in the coat room while I strolled over to the refreshment table to see if I could do anything to help clean up.

A woman dressed in a hilarious penguin costume, complete with a long beak, said, "Oh, no, we have it all covered, dear, but thanks ever so for offering. You're the friend of the Whitcombes, aren't you?"

"Yes. I'm Miranda."

"We think your beau did a lovely job as Father Christmas."

"I'll tell him you said so. Your costume is . . ." I hadn't selected my descriptive word ahead of time and nearly couldn't find the right one. " . . . charming."

"I'm the Christmas penguin, you see."

I didn't know any stories about Christmas penguins, so I apologized for my lack of familiarity with British Christmas tales and asked her to explain.

"Oh, there's no explanation, really. This was the only costume I had!"

I laughed with her, and we joked about how she could start a new tradition.

Flora from the Tea Cosy stepped close and entered into the conversation as if she had been with us from the beginning and, having stepped away for a moment, she now had returned. She had quite a talent for slicing into conversations that way.

"My, that was an interesting young man at the Cosy this afternoon, wasn't he?" Flora looked at me through her large, round glasses.

I gave her a noncommittal nod.

"The bag he carried was altogether ominous, though, wouldn't you agree?"

I nodded again.

"I understand he carried it with him to the train station, got on the 3:22 for London, and who knows what he's up to now. Good riddance, I say."

Clearly Flora's sources were on the job that afternoon, all the way to the train station, to give her a full report.

"We don't need his sort around here, do we? No one quite

seems to know why he came here. You wouldn't happen to know, would you?"

My wonderful knight in shining velvet robes came to my rescue at just the right moment. He greeted the women, received their compliments, and politely asked if he might steal me from their company.

The Christmas penguin was agreeable, but Flora made it clear she had hoped for a longer visit.

As Ian and I stepped away from the ladies, I said, "You came at just the right time."

"Did I now? You weren't getting uncomfortable talking about Josh, were you?"

I looked up at him. "You heard."

"Of course I heard." With a twinkle in his eye, he added, "Christmas wishes weren't the only secrets whispered in my ear once I put on these robes."

"What did you hear?"

"Only that the menacing, ski-cap stalker followed you here, engaged you in a brief conversation, had some tea and scones—with jam and cream, by the way—and left on the next train to London."

I laughed at his rundown. "You got it all straight then. Except for one addition."

"What's that?"

"Josh wanted to know if I was taken."

Ian raised one of his stage-makeup, white, bushy eyebrows. "And what did you tell him?"

"I told him I was practically engaged to Father Christmas, and if he didn't get out of town, you would run him over with your reindeer."

"Did you, now?"

Nudging Ian to the side of the lobby, as far away from any possible eavesdroppers as possible, I said, "I told Josh something else, and I need you to know about it."

Ian's bushy eyebrows dipped, expressing his concentration in what I was about to say but exaggerating the expression in such a way that made the moment seem more dramatic than I thought it should be.

In a whisper, I said, "I told Josh who my father was."

Now Ian's eyebrows lifted in an equally exaggerated fashion, almost causing me to laugh. I knew what I was telling him wasn't a laughing matter.

"I felt I could tell him since he was the one who first urged me to come to Carlton Heath after seeing the photo of my dad dressed as Father Christmas. I trust Josh to keep the confidence."

"Are you sure you can trust him?"

"Yes. He's a psychologist. He keeps confidences for a living. I just wanted you to know. And as far as his visit to the Tea Cosy, I'm convinced it was more about satisfying his curiosity concerning Carlton Heath and the chance to add a few more hours of adventure to his ski trip than it was about me. That's how he is."

"You're sure, then, that I don't need to hunt him down and make it clear he doesn't have a chance to reconcile with you?"

"You don't need to hunt him down. We don't have any reconciling to do. All is settled."

"You're sure?"

I nodded. "I'm sure."

I never had a brave defender like Ian in my life before. I kind of liked his expressions of eagerness to protect me. His valor seemed a little more believable, though, when he wasn't looking at me with two snow-white caterpillars appearing as if they were doing push-ups on his eyebrows.

Mark dashed up to us at that moment, his face flushed with the rush of the sudden glory. "Are we leaving soon?"

"We're ready if you are," Ian said.

"Mark, you did such a fantastic job. I'm so proud of you."

"Thank you, Aunt Miranda." He seemed to emphasize the "Aunt" just enough for me to catch his meaning.

I smiled, and he smiled back. The lump in my throat didn't go down easily.

"Mark and I will bring the car round to the front," Ian said.

"Okay. I'll meet you out there in a few minutes." I returned to pick up my coat from among the few left hanging in the coatroom and then stepped out into the chilly night air.

A jolly sight greeted me. Father Christmas was behind the wheel of his convertible sports car with the top down. Mark was perched on the top like a celebrity in a parade, ready to wave to loyal fans as he passed by at two miles per hour. Both men were once again receiving the accolades due after such memorable debuts.

I slipped in on the passenger's side only after excusing my way through the final circle of adoring fans. This gathering of merry-eyed girls in the preteen bracket gazed at Mark with unalterable admiration. His life in this small village would never be the same.

"Will you sign my program?" one of the girls asked.

I pulled a pen from my purse and watched Mark enjoy his moment in the moonlight.

Once the giggling flock scattered, Ian started the engine. As soon as it began to rumble, Ian waved his hand so that the wide sleeve of his brocaded robe flapped like a great bird.

"Good night, Father Christmas!" one of the preteens called out, igniting another round of giggles from her chums.

"Happy Christmas to you all," he called, as we drove out of sight.

The cool, rushing breeze chilled me instantly even though Ian had the car's heater going. Mark was full of glee over his newly acquired fame and found happiness in scrunching into the narrow storage space behind the seats, lifting both hands in the air, and shouting, "Whoo-hoo!" for the first two blocks.

Ian and I exchanged smiles. Watching Mark was too fun to tell him to stop. Every child should feel that happy, that free.

Ian leaned over. "I'll take a dozen. Just like him."

With a cunning grin I replied, "I think you'll need a bigger car."

Ian laughed his deep-hearted laugh, and our merry mobile headed over a ridge. We turned on the cutoff road that led toward the old church.

From behind a stately rise of the unaltered medieval forest, we saw it, all at the same moment. The golden moon. That eternal orb, broken in half, teetering in the velvet night like a crown cast at the foot of a throne.

Ian stopped the car. The engine purred. The three of us stared without speaking.

Mark sat up straight in his seat of honor and quietly sang in Latin. I have never heard anything so piercingly beautiful.

His boys' choir voice wasn't cooperative on the high notes,

but it didn't matter. Mark wasn't performing now. It was just us—Ian, me, Father God, and all the hosts of heaven bending down to listen to a song that rose from a true heart.

Ian took my hand, and a line from a Christmas carol rode over the top of Mark's canticle, blending perfectly. *Let heaven and nature sing....*

At that moment, I felt as if I were experiencing a snapshot of heaven. The glorious beauty and sense of perfection and wonder felt like a glimpse of that which is true and lasting. It was as if I were viewing a wallet-sized photo of eternity.

For so many years I had gazed at the snapshot of my father. The photo, in all its curious wonder, was still only a flat, frozen image of a real person I had never met. The photo carried with it a clue about a place called "Carlton Heath."

Now here I was, experiencing the immenseness of Carlton Heath in all of its beauty. It was far beyond the sketchy speculations that had risen in my imagination from the one simple photo.

As Mark's voice rose into the night air, I wondered, was everything around us more or less a fixed snapshot that alluded to a greater beauty? A deeper mystery? A hint of what was to come? How many unknown layers were there to life—to the eternal life that was hidden in Christ? What glorious surprises awaited us in the real land of which this earth was only a snapshot?

Let heaven and nature sing....

Mark's song ended on a note that he sustained much longer than I would have thought possible. Then all was silent except for the low rumble of the car's engine.

Without any of us trying to define what had just taken

place, Ian edged the car back on the road and continued our short journey to the hospital.

I watched the moon as we drove down the lane and thought of how the upturned golden curve of light resembled a smile. I liked the imagery that Father God was pleased with our spontaneous worship and was smiling down on us.

Keep smiling, Father God. Keep smiling on us, I pray.

Mark scooted down into the narrow space behind the bucket seats and bundled up in a plaid wool blanket Ian earlier had pulled from the trunk. My guess was that Ian made the blanket available just in case Mark came down from his high and needed more than his fame to warm him.

The blanket was the MacGregor tartan, of course. I remembered the blanket fondly from a picnic Ian and I had last summer. We took off with plans to spend the day on the coast of southern England. I wanted to picnic beneath the fabulous White Cliffs of Dover. However, we only made it as far as Windsor before the car began to sputter. Ian found a repair service, and we spent the day strolling around the castle grounds, waiting for the fuel line to be replaced.

Ellie had packed us a picnic lunch, which we carried along with the MacGregor plaid blanket to a grassy knoll on the public grounds of Windsor Castle. There, within view of the British guards with their tall fur hats strapped under their chins, I learned about the MacGregor crest and the clan motto, "Royal is my race."

As Ian turned the steering wheel and headed for the hospital on this cold winter night, it did indeed seem as if he was part of a "royal race." His white hair and beard shone in the moonlight. All the gold and silver trimming on his robe stood out with regal shimmers. His jaw was set. His face directed straight ahead. The Scottish warrior was on his way to see his father.

All was calm. All was bright.

Oh, how I wanted to believe this was how life was going to be. Once I had a few significant pieces of the plans for my future lined up, I could nestle into this place of beauty and hope. Carlton Heath was not yet fully my home, but I wanted it to be—soon.

Chapter Thirteen

The hospital staff at the front desk had big smiles and hellos for us when we entered and they saw Ian in full costume.

"What did you bring us, Father Christmas?" the admitting nurse asked.

"Good cheer and merry greetings," he said in a robust voice. Some of the faithful employees seemed to be looking behind Ian for his sack of gifts. A childlike shadow of disappointment crossed their faces when they didn't see a bag slung over his shoulder filled with goodies.

"We do have biscuits left over from the play tonight," Mark said. "My mum is bringing them."

A few minutes after Mark announced the biscuits, Ellie, Edward, and Julia entered the hospital carrying the promised goodies.

The lobby suddenly became cheerier. Night staff appeared from behind swinging doors and file cabinets.

"We're going to visit my father," Ian said to the head nurse. "You won't mind if we're above the limit for visitors, will you?"

Ellie held out the bag of cookies as potential bribe material.

"We'll look the other way this time." She reached for one of the shortbread stars. "Katharine is already in there."

Ian led the way down the hall of the quiet hospital. Mark looked up at the sign that read Children's Ward over the doorway of the first wing we passed. As we kept walking, Mark asked Ian, "Are children staying in there, in the children's ward, tonight?"

"I would imagine so."

"Will they be going home for Christmas?"

"Perhaps. If they're too ill, though, they will be staying here."

Julia, who had been holding my hand as we made our way down the hall, asked, "If the children don't go home for Christmas, how will they get any presents?"

"I'm sure they receive their presents here," Ellie said in her optimistic voice.

Mark stopped walking. "How many children are in the children's ward?"

"Hard to say," Ian said.

"We need to find out how many children there are, and we need to bring them some presents," Mark said decisively.

"That's very considerate of you, Mark," Ellie said. "It's a lovely idea. First, we must pay a visit to Uncle Andrew, though. Shall we do that? We can check on the children's ward on our way out."

Mark picked up his feet, still deep in thought. All six of us entered Andrew's room quietly. As soon as weary Katharine saw us, she motioned for us to enter and come closer.

"How's the patient?" Ian asked.

Andrew's distinct voice rose from the bed. "The patient is growing impatient. That's how the patient is."

We gathered around, all saying our hellos at once. The rhythmic drips and beeps of the machines seemed as hypnotizing as a swinging pocket watch. Andrew's deep-chested breathing carried the steady ruffles of air flowing in and out at a comforting pace.

"You're looking more yourself than you did earlier," Ellie said.

"Am I, now?" Andrew smiled weakly.

He looked up at Ian in the convincing costume and added, "What's this? A visit from the man himself?"

"It's really Uncle Ian," Julia said with a twinkling grin.

"Is that so? Well, I was convinced he was Father Christmas himself."

Julia giggled.

"The role is only temporary," Ian said. "You do know that you're expected to pick up where you left off next Christmas, don't you? I was only a fill-in."

"Aye, you've been talking to Katharine, haven't you? She refuses to accept my resignation."

"Good for her," I said.

"The play went off wonderfully well," Ellie said. "But you were missed."

"Mark was the star of the show," I said. "And Julia was superb."

Both children beamed in the light of the praise as Andrew added, "Good job, you two."

His eyelids drooped. Apparently he had used up all his personal visiting hours and was ready to sleep some more and heal.

"You are getting better, aren't you?" Julia patted Andrew's shoulder.

"Yes, Uncle Andrew is getting better," Ellie answered. "We should let him rest. He's had a very long day."

We said our good-byes to a sleepy-eyed Andrew and made our way out of the room.

"Father," Mark reached for Edward's arm as soon as we were out the door. "May we go for a visit in the children's ward now?"

Edward and Ellie looked surprised that Mark hadn't forgotten his request on the way in and dropped the subject.

"We really should be on our way home," Ellie said. "It's been a long day. And tomorrow is Christmas Eve, after all."

"Yes, but, Mummy, what about the children here at hospital? Tomorrow is Christmas Eve for them as well. Not all of them will be going home for Christmas, though, will they?"

"Possibly they will," Ellie said hopefully.

"I think we should visit them the way we visited Uncle Andrew. It won't take long."

The rest of us looked at each other, trying to gauge our collective thoughts on the possibility. I hadn't realized Mark was a young man of such compassion.

"Look," Mark continued as firmly as a diplomat, "Uncle Ian is already dressed like Father Christmas. Why could he not take some gifts to the children tonight?"

"Yes, Mummy!" Julia tugged on Ellie's hand. "Can we do it, please?"

Edward was facing Katharine. "I would imagine Father Christmas already has made his rounds for this year in the children's ward."

Katharine shook her head. No alternate Father Christmas had come. Since my father had played that role in years past, it seemed no replacement had picked up the part.

"Well," Ellie said brightly, "how about if next Christmas we make a visit to the children's ward as a family project? We'll have time to pick lots of presents. And we'll bake lots and lots of biscuits. Won't that be lovely?"

"We can't wait for next Christmas," Mark said firmly. "Not all the children in there will get better, will they? This might be their last Christmas."

Mark's evaluation seemed to hit all of us in the same soft spot in our hearts.

Edward remained the voice of reason. "We aren't prepared this year, though, Mark. We don't have gifts for the children. If we plan for next year, we can arrange to have lots of gifts. That would be better, wouldn't it?"

Julia gave a little wiggle-hop. "Mummy, you can give the children my presents. I don't need any new toys." Her sincere expression was enough to melt any heart.

The first heart it apparently melted was her daddy's. "I suppose..."

"The children can have all of my gifts as well," Mark added.

Edward appeared too choked up at the moment to respond.

Clearing his throat, he said, "Ian, would you mind keeping the costume on a bit longer?"

"Not at all," Ian said robustly.

"Right, then. It looks as if we'll be back shortly with some gifts to distribute."

Chapter Fourteen

By the time the Whitcombe clan returned to the hospital with all the gifts and a round of rosy cheeks, it was after ten. The excitement had kept the children going. Ellie had managed to tuck two dozen gifts into a large laundry sack. Edward looked more invigorated than I had ever seen him. I was seeing an entirely new view of my half brother and finding he wasn't as stodgy as I had thought.

I knew his father—our father—convincingly carried out the role of Father Christmas right up until he passed away. Locals told tender stories of how they had whispered their Christmas wish into Father Christmas's ear when they were tiny and how, magically, their wishes always came true.

Now it was Ian's turn. He adjusted his beard and the holly wreath on his head. Ellie brushed off the lint from his brocaded velvet robe, and Ian slung the laundry sack over his broad shoulders. Mark and Julia flanked his sides, and the rest of us trailed him as an unconventional group of elves.

"I've brought my camera," Ellie said with a sugarplum twinkle in her eye. "Might be a lovely gift for the parents, don't you think? Snapshots of the look on their children's faces when they see Father Christmas."

"What a great idea, Ellie."

A gathering of night nurses and a doctor stood waiting for us at the door that opened to the children's ward. They ushered us in, and Ian's deep, golden voice called out into the dimly lit hallway, "Happy Christmas, one and all!"

A nurse adjusted the light switch so that the ward glowed with a Christmas morning sort of brightness. Through the doors we could see the children rubbing their eyes and trying to see what was going on. One of them, a little girl in a neck brace, was the first to get a full view of Ian. Her squeal alerted the entire ward as she called out, "It's Father Christmas!"

Ellie snapped pictures. Edward hung back, his eyes looking tenderer than I had ever seen. I wondered if in his childhood he had been like Mark, accompanying Sir James in his Father Christmas robe. Was Christmas a time of tender memories for my half brother?

Ian and Julia strode over to the bedside of the delighted little girl in the neck brace. Ellie kept snapping pictures. Mark assisted Father Christmas by looking for a gift inside the sack.

"That one." Julia pointed to a present wrapped in paper that was dotted with silver stars and tied with a pink ribbon.

The little girl's eyes were wide as she stared at Father Christmas. "I hoped you would come. I was afraid you wouldn't know where I was."

"I've come indeed. And I have a gift for you," he said.

"Open it!" excited Julia said.

The dazzled little sweetheart didn't seem to be able to overcome her amazement enough to tear the wrapping paper from the box. "May I hold it for a while?"

"You may hold it as long as you like." Ian placed his hand on the girl's forehead and said, "God bless you this day, dear child. You are His special gift. May He hold you ever close to His heart."

She closed her eyes and eagerly received the blessing. As we left her room, the darling was still hugging the silvery box with her eyes closed and her lips pressed into an endearing smile.

We went from room to room down the hall and watched Julia and Mark as they assisted Ian in distributing gifts. Ellie snapped dozens of photos. Ian placed his hand on each child and blessed each one. Every child responded differently, but all of them seemed mesmerized and delighted. Even the older children.

In one of the last rooms we entered, a boy who looked to be about ten years old stared at the doorway. The pillow behind him seemed to be swallowing his bald head. His mother sat beside him, holding his hand and telling him what was happening. "He's come into your room now, Bobby. It's Father Christmas! Do you see him? He's come to see you! It's Father Christmas!"

The young boy was too weak to respond with more than a slight rising of his upper lip. Ian went to his side.

"Happy Christmas, young Bobby. My helpers and I have brought you a gift."

"Can you see his white beard, Bobby?" the mother said. "And the wreath of holly on his head. Do you want to feel his robe? Here. Look at the velvet trim stitched in gold. Very regal, isn't it?"

The little boy's hand lifted and rested on Ian's arm. A brightness appeared in his eyes. I wondered if the weakened state of this poor child would be too much for Mark and Julia to handle, but both of them moved closer instead of shrinking back.

Ellie continued snapping pictures. The tenderhearted mother, with her face glowing in the diffused light, leaned over her son and helped him engage with Father Christmas.

"Father Christmas has brought you a gift," Mark said. "Shall I help you open it?"

The boy nodded weakly. His delighted expression was fixed. Mark opened the gift, and I saw him hesitate as if this was the one item he had wished for and now it was going to this frail child.

"It's a junior microscope." Mark held up the box.

The boy's chest quavered, and he released breathy, happy sounds and reached for the box.

His mother looked up at Ian and the rest of us. With a stunned expression she said, "How did you know? You couldn't possibly have known. That's all he's wanted for months. How did you know?"

"We didn't know," Julia said plainly.

All of us tried very hard to keep our wobbling lips from giving away how surprised and touched we were.

I felt as I had when we watched the moon in Ian's car. Leaning closer to the mother, I said, "This is the part of Christmas when we can hear heaven and nature sing."

She nodded. "Bobby, tell Father Christmas what you want to be when you grow up."

With an expansive exhale, Bobby wheezed, "A doctor."

I looked at Ian and saw two glistening tears race down his ruddy cheeks, dampening his beard. All of us, except perhaps Julia, realized it would take a miracle for Bobby to win the battle against whatever it was that had invaded his young body. The chances were slim that he would live long enough to become a doctor.

Katharine drew close to Bobby's mother and placed her calm hand on the woman's shoulders. This was what Katharine did best. She was a comforter. This mother's Christmas gift was having Katharine there with her at this moment to support her.

Ian reached out his hand and placed it on Bobby's forehead. He blessed the young boy and continued with a prayer, asking the Lord to heal his body and to fulfill all His purposes for Bobby's life.

Edward stepped out of the room, and I wasn't far behind him. I felt a reservoir of tears building up, and I wasn't sure I could contain them. Sniffing and swallowing in the corner, I saw Edward speaking with one of the doctors. He was handing over his business card. I heard him say, "Whatever expenses this family doesn't have taken care of, I would like to cover. Anonymously."

"Yes, of course," the doctor said. "I did this often for your father. I know how to proceed."

At that point, all I wanted to do was crumble into a chair and weep.

But Ian and the children were on the move. We had one

more patient to visit. Her name was Molly. When she saw Julia, the two recognized each other.

"What happened to you, Molly?" Julia asked.

"I had my index taken out two days ago. Do you want to see the bandage?" Molly pulled back the covers and revealed a large gauze patch on her side where her appendix apparently had been removed.

"Did it hurt?" Julia asked.

Molly nodded.

"Do you feel better now?"

"A little."

"Good because we brought Father Christmas to see you." Julia pointed at Ian as if Molly hadn't noticed the larger-than-life figure standing behind her. "And we brought you a present, too."

Molly smiled at Ian. "I know who you are," she said in a whisper.

He put his finger to his lips and indicated that she should keep her voice low. "You will keep our secret, won't you?"

Molly nodded.

Mark pulled a gift from the sack for Molly. "Happy Christmas."

"Happy Christmas to you too. Thank you for the present." She tore off the wrapping paper and gave a small "ohh!" of glee when she saw the picture on the outside of the box. "It's the singing teapot! I wanted one of these very badly."

By the expression on Julia's face, it was clear that, just like her brother, she had given away the gift she had hoped for. With a quavering lower lip, she said, "I always wanted one too." She looked to her mother, and Ellie gave her a pacifying expression.

I quelled a happy smile because I had purchased the exact same singing teapot for Julia in San Francisco. It was in my suitcase now and would be under the tree at Ellie and Edward's by tomorrow. Julia would have her singing teapot after all.

Ian stepped over to the bed and placed his hand on Molly to give her the final Christmas blessing in the children's ward. Ellie snapped the picture and then our entourage made its way back to the lobby. A chorus of "Thank you," "Happy Christmas," and "Good-bye, Father Christmas" followed us to the door. The night staff added their expressions of appreciation with smiles and tears.

"Well, we best be on our way," Ellie said. "What a night, for all of us!"

A bit dazed, we all filed into our cars. Ian had put the top up on his, and when I climbed into the passenger's seat, I pulled the plaid blanket over me. "I'm going to close my eyes for just a minute," I announced as I felt the jet lag settle into my bones.

The next thing I remembered was the back of Ian's rough hand tenderly stroking my cheek and his deep voice saying, "Miranda, we're here."

Chapter Fifteen

I barely remember Ian ushering me into the Whitcombe manor late that night and carrying my luggage up to the guest room. I do remember Ian's warm kiss good night, his whisper in my ear and how it was filled with promise. He said he would see me in the morning. That in itself was a dream. We were together on the same side of the globe and would be only a hop and a skip away from each other. Not an ocean away.

My dreams that night in the comfy guest bed Ellie had made ready for me must have been the sort of dreams I had rehearsed many times over during the past year. I floated from one happiness to another and sank deeply into the kind of rest that restores and renews.

I found out later that poor little Julia was beside herself by ten thirty the next morning. She had waited so patiently for me to wake up, and I was fast asleep every time she checked.

When I finally awoke, I went to the thick-paned window and

looked out at a gray, dark world that made it seem much earlier in the morning than it was. Grumpy old clouds bundled in their heavy winter coats bumped into each other and crowded the sky, stubbornly refusing to let the sun peek through.

I stretched and felt luxuriously rested but chilled.

Dashing back to bed, I heard a tap on my door.

"Who is it?"

"It's Ju-lee-ah," my favorite niece sang out. She must have heard me rustling about. When I told her she could come in, she peeked around the door with a hopeful grin. I held out my arms and smiled. She jumped up on the bed while I admired her freshly combed hair, pulled back with a red ribbon on the side. Her sweater was also red with a row of little Christmas trees around the cuffs and collar.

"Don't you look cute this morning?"

"This is my Christmas Eve Day sweater. I have a different one for Christmas Day to wear with my new Christmas skirt. What are you wearing for today and for Christmas?"

"I'm not sure yet. Something warm. It's cold, isn't it?"

"Yes. Cold and rainy. We've had our breakfast already, Auntie Miranda. You were the sleepyhead, weren't you? Mummy said we may do whatever we wish because Uncle Ian called, and he's not ready yet so you must stay with us until he's ready."

"Is that so?"

"Would you like to have your breakfast in bed? Because Mummy said if you want to eat in bed, Natasha can bring up a tray, and I can have tea with you."

"Who is Natasha?"

"She's our new helper. She has red shoes, and she wears

them even when it isn't Christmas. Have you seen our beautiful Christmas tree yet? It's the biggest tree we've ever had. Daddy and Markie and I went to the forest, and we were supposed to cut down our Christmas tree last week, but when we got into the forest, I started to cry."

"Why? What happened?"

"I didn't want to cut any of the trees down, so we left without one. And do you know what Mummy did the next day?"

"Let me guess. Your mom went to the forest and cut down a tree all by herself and dragged it home to surprise all of you."

"No, silly! My mummy couldn't do all that."

I wouldn't it put it past Ellie.

"Mummy went to a store where they have pretend trees that look even more real than real trees. She bought the very biggest one they had, and now every year we get to have the same very big tree for Christmas. And I put the star on the top. Do you want to come see it now? It's the most beautiful tree in the whole world."

"The most beautiful tree in the *whole* world?"

"Yes." Julia giggled and gave a resolute nod of her head. "It is the most beautiful tree in the whole world. Do you want to come see it?"

"First, I have something very important to do."

"What?"

"I must give you your morning tickle. Come here." I wrapped my arms around my favorite little chatter bug, and before I commenced with the tickling, I said, "I love you, Julia-Bean. I love you, love you, love you."

"I'm not a bean."

"Yes you are. You're my little Julia-Bean. Whenever one of your little Julia-Bean giggles gets planted in my heart, it grows and grows and grows until it's so big that everywhere I look all I see is happiness!"

She seemed surprised at my silliness and expressions of affection, but she received them by glibly offering her soft cheek to me so that I might plant the expected kiss on her smooth, pink skin. Instead of one kiss, I tickle-kissed her with a dozen kisses all over her head, cheek, and neck, and so the morning tickle fest began.

Julia squealed gleefully and tried to tickle me back under my chin. Her pudgy little fingers moved like a harpist and made me laugh even though it didn't really tickle.

We called a truce, and she gave me a kiss right on the end of my nose to seal our peace pact. I thought of how Ian had kissed the tip of my nose last night in the Tea Cosy's kitchen, and I realized I had received more kisses, hugs, and snuggles in the past year than I had since my mother died.

I thought of how much my mother would have loved all this. This house, this bed, the sight and sounds of me tickling my niece on Christmas Eve morn. But these riches of Sir James's had not come to her. All she received from her brief love affair with him was me. And now I had managed to slide in and enjoy so much of the goodness of this family.

But for how long?

With our tickle fest over, Julia asked, "What about the tree? When will you come see the tree?"

"How about if get cleaned up first? You can go tell your mom and Natasha that Princess Miranda and Princess Julia would indeed like to take their tea in bed this morning, and Princess Miranda would also like some toast with marmalade."

"Oh yes, I want toast too. With marmalade." Julia slid off the bed. "I'll go tell them. Do you want an egg? We have new Christmas eggcups."

"Well yes, if you have new eggcups, of course I want an egg for breakfast."

"And baked beans and bacon? That's what I had for breakfast."

"Why not?" I said.

Julia was on her way to order what I had come to learn was a typical English breakfast. The first time I saw the baked beans and grilled tomato slices on the breakfast plate next to my over easy eggs and wide strips of lean bacon, I thought it was a joke. Who eats baked beans for breakfast? Well, now I do. Every time I come to Carlton Heath.

Half an hour later, even though Julia and I were both dressed and ready for the day, we slipped back under the puffy comforter in our stockinged feet and stacked up the pillows behind us so we would be nice and comfy. We waited like two little princesses with our hands folded on top of the comforter as timid Natasha entered the room with a heavy tray laden with our breakfast delights.

Once she saw that Julia and I were in the silliest of moods, she smiled and helped me balance the tray on my lap before quietly exiting and leaving Julia and me to our feast. We had a stack of well-toasted bread that required marmalading. We had a steaming teapot wrapped in a quilted tea cozy and ready to be tipped over and poured into our waiting china cups.

Marvelously and perhaps miraculously, we managed all the finer details of our feast without a single spill or drip of orange marmalade on the bed.

Our voices were low as we talked, tucked away in the warm bed in that spacious bedroom in the Whitcombe manor. Mostly Julia talked, and I listened. She had much to tell me about the Christmas gifts she had helped wrap, the vase she and Daddy bought for Ellie, and how she knew where Mummy had hidden the Christmas crackers this year.

Memories of my sparse Christmas mornings with my mother came to mind. She and I also cuddled up in bed and talked softly. I suppose I thought I was a princess then too. My mother and I certainly had no maid to bring us toast on a silver tray. We mostly lived in budget motels during my formative years. The blankets were thin, and the sheets were cold and rough and smelled of bleach.

I remembered how I would find ways to wrap up the tiny soaps and shampoos allotted to us in the nicer budget motels. Those were my gifts to my mother on Christmas morning as we curled up together in bed. She always responded with such surprise and pleasure when she opened the soaps and shampoo as if I had given her something of great worth that she actually wanted or needed.

My mother always had a box of chocolates for us at Christmas. I don't know if the chocolates were given to her or if she bought them, but that's what we ate for breakfast. As many decadent bonbons as our stomachs could hold.

Being with Julia, I realized the delight of such a moment was the same whether we were dining on second-rate chocolates or full English breakfasts. These two moments carried the same weight in value because of the gift of being close to someone I loved. I would give anything to have one more Christmas morning with my mother and our little soaps and box of chocolate. Oh how I would love to hear her ethereal, lilting laughter one more time.

Since that wasn't possible, I felt as if God were giving me a special gift on this Christmas Eve morning. He gave me breakfast in bed with my niece.

I finished the last sip of cooled tea in my china teacup and whispered a secret thank-you to Gracious God, who always seemed close whenever I was in this room.

Julia watched me drain the last drop. "Good. Now may we pleeeease go downstairs and see the beautiful tree?"

I laughed at her tenacity. "Yes, let's go see the most beautiful tree in the whole, wide world."

I took her hand as we headed down the ornate staircase. I hoped Margaret was staying in the rooms she occupied in the east wing of the manor. I knew from previous visits that she didn't usually wander far from her quarters.

What bothered me was that this was Margaret's home, and in that respect, I was her guest. The last thing I wanted to do was cause this glad time of celebrating to be strained or tense for anyone under this roof. Unfortunately, from past experience I knew that tension was the unnamed ambiance whenever Margaret and I were present in the same room.

Chapter Sixteen

For a day that began so leisurely, everything stepped up its pace as soon as Julia and I went downstairs. Ellie was busy in the kitchen alongside Natasha preparing all sorts of wonderful Christmas feast goodies. She had presents yet to wrap, as did I, and she wanted to pull together a meal for Katharine, who had gone back to the hospital to be with Andrew for the day.

I took in all the details, prepared to help out any way I could, and felt a slight sort of guilt for playing the princess for so long that morning. Ellie didn't mind. She was floating along on her usual river of grace.

"Julia said you heard from Ian. Is that right?" I reached for one of the grapes in a beautiful glass bowl on the marble countertop in Ellie's renovated kitchen.

"Yes! Oh, did you not get that message? We're to keep you occupied today until he's ready."

"Ready for what?"

Julia giggled and covered her mouth. Ellie stopped chopping celery and froze as if she had forgotten something. Or maybe she was trying to remember something.

"We're to keep you occupied until he's ready for Christmas," Ellie said brightly. "That's it. You can imagine how his plans have been upset, what with the unexpected news of Andrew and the visits to hospital, not to mention the last-minute role he played as Father Christmas last night. He has a few things to do today."

"Okay."

I wasn't worried about Ian's readjusted schedule even though Ellie seemed flustered. I knew I would see Ian soon, and that was all that mattered.

Tugging on my hand, Julia said, "May we go now to see the Christmas tree, please?"

"Yes, let's go. Then I'll wrap gifts for your mom."

The largest room in the Whitcombes' beautiful home was referred to as the drawing room. Located at the front of the manor, it boasted the largest windows in the home, with a magnificent view of the tall, ancient trees that stood guard around the circular driveway.

Ellie loved to decorate and had gone all out again this year with her snowflake theme, incorporating touches of sparkly, dangling snowflakes hung from the ceiling on fishing wire. Swags of greenery were looped over the mantel of the enormous fireplace as well as across the doorframe and the front windows. Tiny white lights were woven into each garland. On this gray day, the lights twinkled cheerfully and made the room merry and bright.

The ceilings were high, so Julia's eager voice echoed in the large, open area as she said, "Do you see it? Do you see how big it is? It's the best Christmas tree ever, and we get to have it every year."

"It *is* the best Christmas tree ever." I drew close and stood beside her to admire the commanding beauty of the artificial wonder where it stood in front of the center window. "It's the most wonderful Christmas tree in all the world!"

"I know. I told you it was."

The tree reached at least ten feet, with the lit star at the top adding another foot of dazzle. The white lights that circled the tree were accompanied by a delightful assortment of every type of ornament and dangling prettiness Ellie had collected over the years. Around the base were a dozen or so gifts. More gifts for the children had been clustered around the tree the day before, but at least a dozen of those presents were now cheering up the children in the hospital. Even with those generously offered gifts gone, the Whitcombe children would have an abundant and merry Christmas.

I thought of all the times over the years when I had heard people say Christmas was too commercial and materialistic. They were right, of course. I couldn't disagree. But if any one of those bah-humbug, Christmas Scrooges had lived my life, if they had come from where I came from, with motel soaps and shampoos and never a Christmas tree to fill a room with cheer and wonder, I think they would have softened their railings. If they could feel what I felt at this moment, gazing at the Christmas tree with wide-eyed Julia, they would say that tradition, decorations, and gifts were a beautiful way to celebrate Christ's birth.

"We'd better get to work on those few things your mother asked me to do," I said.

Julia was happy to help. She stayed close most of the day while Mark seemed to find things to do that didn't fall into the chore category. The house hummed with merry-making activity. The kitchen exhaled a stream of wonderful fragrances. Christmas music floated through the house. The lineup of tunes included everything from "I'm Dreaming of a White Christmas" to a variety of boys' choir canticles sung as Mark had sung them, in soul-stirring Latin.

Edward kept to his desk in the library most of the day, but his door remained open. I was aware that Mark and Julia regularly ran in and out to tell their dad this or that about the activities.

At one point in the late afternoon, as I walked past the library on my way to the drawing room with freshly wrapped presents in my arms, I paused by the open door and smiled at Edward. He smiled at me. I could picture my father seated behind that desk and wondered if this home was filled with the same warmth and happiness when Sir James was the head of the household.

I found my opinion of Edward elevating. He was available to his children. They had free access to come into his presence at any time.

Gazing past the library down the long hall that led to Margaret's quarters, I wondered what it would take for Margaret to open her door to me. If that door ever did open, would it remain open?

After the final gifts were deposited under the tree, I returned to the kitchen and admired the assortment of wonderful foods spread across the counter. In one corner Ellie had placed two large wicker picnic hampers. The tops were open, and she was filling them with freshly baked breads, wedges of imported cheese, and a big, fat, wrapped-up ham.

"That's quite a lot of food for Katharine," I observed. "What a feast!"

Ellie jumped and nearly dropped the ham.

"Oh, I didn't see you come in; you startled me. Yes, so, how is everything going with the gift wrapping?"

"It's all finished. The gifts are under the tree. Julia and Mark are both upstairs, and I was about to clean up the mess I made in the dining room with all the wrapping paper."

"Oh, don't fuss with that. It's almost time for you to go. You should get ready."

"Go where?"

"With Ian. He's coming by to pick you up. Did Julia not tell you? Oh, me-me-me, oh my. I knew I should have told you myself."

"That's okay. I should have put my cell phone in my pocket so he could call me. Did he say where we're going?"

Ellie tilted her head like a little bird and looked at me strangely, as if my question were an odd one.

"I'm trying to decide what to wear," I went on. "If we're going out to a nice place for dinner, I don't want to be in jeans when he arrives."

"Oh, yes. Of course. I would say..." Ellie made a funny humming sound as she pursed her lips together and thought. "Something lovely would best fit the occasion, but it should be something comfortable that you love to wear. I think the red dress you wore last night would be perfect for an encore performance."

"Are you sure?"

"Oh, yes! Because you can wear it with the black cashmere sweater, and it will look absolutely elegant."

"I don't have a black cashmere sweater."

Ellie slapped her hand over her mouth. "Oh me. Me-me-me. I certainly am atwitter! I can barely remember what I'm supposed to say and not supposed to say. Come. Come, come, come!"

Ellie wiped her hands on her apron and propelled her short legs at an impressive pace out of the kitchen and into the drawing room. I kept up with her, and when we stopped in front of the tree, she looked around at all the gift boxes that had been rearranged by Julia.

"This one." She reached for a rectangular box tied with a wide, silver ribbon. "Open it now. It's okay. You'll see."

I hugged Ellie before I tore off the wrapping. "Thank you for the cashmere sweater."

She feigned surprise and blinked her eyes. "Why, Miranda! How ever did you guess what I was giving you this year?"

"I'll open it upstairs," I said. "Just so the children don't think I've started something they would like to finish."

"Good idea. And if it doesn't fit, or if you don't like it, it's not a problem to return or exchange. Although, we won't be able to do so today since Ian will be here in fifteen minutes. You really should get going, Miranda!"

I smiled at my willy-nilly sister-in-law and dashed up the stairs. Behind my closed door, I opened the box and pulled out a beautiful—and I was sure very expensive—black cashmere sweater. The fitted, classic sweater went perfectly with the cheery-cherry-merry red dress and made me feel elegant. It transformed and completed the outfit.

I added my fun sparkly necklace and earrings. They weren't expensive, but they added a final glimmery touch, and since I hadn't worn them last night, it felt as if I really were wearing a different outfit.

I didn't have enough time to pay extra attention to my hair, but Ian said he liked it when I wore it down so that it skimmed my shoulders and could easily be, as he said, "tussled by the breeze."

I tried not to think about the obvious fact that everyone else seemed to know this was going to be a "special" evening with Ian. I knew what that meant. How could I not see all the clues?

A little coaching seemed in order so I told myself, *Whatever you do, Miranda, when he pulls out "the box," try to act surprised.*

When I heard loud voices downstairs echoing up the stairway, I knew Ian had arrived. With one last look in the mirror, I thought of how much this felt like a long-buried, youthful wish that never had come true. I never had gone to a high school prom or even a dance where I dressed up and made a grand entrance.

The day had begun with my playing the princess role, and so it continued as I opened my guest room door and promenaded down the fantastic staircase. I was just at the window seat in the landing when Ian came into view in the wide entryway. He was flanked by Mark, Julia, Edward, Ellie, and…

Oh, Ian!

He was wearing his dress kilt.

Chapter Seventeen

"There she is!" Julia announced my descent with a happy squeal.

All eyes were on me as I carefully made my way down the polished wood stairs. The only eyes I cared about were Ian's, and his eyes definitely were shining with all the affection and admiration a woman could ever dream of receiving.

He placed his hands behind his back and stood tall, as if he were ready for me to inspect him in his formal white shirt, bow tie, jacket, MacGregor plaid kilt, and knee socks held up by elastic bands that we had found in a shop last summer in Windsor.

I smiled my immense approval, and he smiled back the same. Offering me his arm, Ian said, "See you later" to our small audience and led me to the front door.

"Your coat, Miranda!" Ellie rushed to hand me my coat. "I put it in the pocket, just in case."

"Okay," I said, having no idea what she was talking about.

Ian helped me with my coat, and we stepped out the front door under the motto for the Whitcombe manor that was engraved over the entrance, "Grace and Peace Reside Here."

I slipped my hand in the coat pocket and smiled. Ellie had put a handkerchief into my pocket. That was her "just in case" gift. I knew it wasn't just any handkerchief. As I fingered the edges, I could tell it was one of Margaret's handkerchiefs, with her defining touch of a tiny pink rosebud she embroidered in the corner.

I felt squeamish about having one of Margaret's hankies with me. Ellie was free with her gifts for others, but Margaret only gave her embroidered handkerchiefs to those who were closest to her. On several occasions during the past year, Margaret had opportunities to give me one of her unique works of art, but she hadn't done so. What would she think if she knew Ellie had given me one of the rosebud hankies?

Then it occurred to me how much time I spent fretting over what Margaret thought of me. Margaret wasn't coming with us this evening. This was my time to be with Ian. I turned all my focus on him.

Ian opened the car door for me and there, waiting on my seat, was a single red rosebud. The deep merlot fragrance tickled my nose as I gave the rose a twirl across my lips. Apparently the pink rosebud on the edge of the handkerchief wasn't the only rose that would lace this enchanting evening.

"Thank you." I looked into Ian's set expression.

He took my face in his hands and kissed me tenderly on the lips. We shared another kiss before Ian got in the driver's side and headed around the circular driveway and through the open gated entrance.

"How's your dad doing?" I still twirled the rosebud and drew in the scent.

"Much improved."

"That's good news. Katharine must be relieved."

"That she is."

"So, will he be able to come home for Christmas?"

"Yes, definitely."

"Do we need to help Katharine get him at the hospital?"

"Not at the moment."

The car rumbled down the familiar country lane, and I looked at Ian. He was being unusually brief with his answers. But he looked happy. I had the feeling that, in the same way I had put away thoughts of Margaret for our evening together, Ian was setting aside the concerns he had over his dad.

This was our time at last. A contented smile settled on my lips.

The car ambled along, and the slowly setting sun peeked out from behind the gray clouds for the first time that day. As if elated for the chance to finally break through the gloom, the sun shot stunning beams of light that pierced the dormant winter landscape like shafts of translucent hope.

We drove past a row of narrow birch trees lining the road, and the determined sunlight played a flitting game of hide-and-seek between the birches. Elongated strips of light and dark flashed across the lane, producing a strobe light effect. Ian cut through the pulsating lines of sun and shadow and came into an open place in the road where he stopped and let the car roar a moment before making a turn.

We were fully in the sunlight for the briefest of moments, and then the precocious ball of waning fire found her way into the pocket of a waiting woolen cloud. In that brief, sunlit moment, I looked at Ian and smiled. I saw flecks of winter gold reflected in his eyes.

"You're glowing," he said to me.

I could imagine how the slipping sunlight behind me had cast one last fling of radiant amber lights to the ends of my tussled hair.

God, in all His glory, seemed to have sent His golden blessing to lightly touch us both in the closing of the day.

Ian smiled. I smiled back. Then he turned left.

I expected him to turn right. The high road was the most direct way to reach any one of the neighboring towns that had restaurants that would be open on Christmas Eve. Nothing in Carlton Heath would be open.

"Where are we going?"

Ian only smiled.

His low-to-the-ground sports car bumped along the road, and I contented myself to settle into his secret. Maybe we were going to the train station. I kept watch out the window in the twilight to get a glimpse of the Forgotten Rose Cottage.

I felt a wave of the same sadness I had felt the day before when I had realized someone else had stepped up to that small dream of mine and taken the Forgotten Rose Cottage for his own.

The first time I had seen the cottage was last Christmas. I had walked past it on my way to find the Tea Cosy and had noted that it appeared no one lived there.

A few days later, after I had met Ian, the two of us went for a stroll. I was about to return to San Francisco, and the time had come for us to talk about where our relationship might be headed. We were walking past the cottage when Ian stopped, squared his shoulders, and said, "I don't think we're done yet, Miranda." His simple declaration began to topple the fortress that had long protected my untrusting heart.

My response to him that day had been, "I don't think we are either."

Then we kissed for the first time. It was the most natural, mutual, perfectly timed and perfectly executed kiss ever. When I opened my eyes, there was Ian's strong and handsome face. And in the background, behind Ian, was the stone cottage.

That image seared itself into my heart and mind and had kept me hoping and dreaming for the past year.

Resolving not to be sad about the Forgotten Rose Cottage as we approached, I saw a warm, amber light glowing from the two front windows. Curls of smoke rose from the chimney. The front walkway was lined with lanterns on shepherd's hooks just like the ones that lined the entrance to Grey Hall.

The revived cottage looked like something from a fairy tale.

A small "oh" escaped from my lips. Forgotten Rose Cottage looked exactly as I had dreamed it could look. In my fanciful imaginings of what might happen with some strategic renovations to the property, this was what I had seen.

Ian pulled the car to the side of the road and cut the engine.

Memories of our outing at Windsor last summer came back. "Is something wrong with the car?"

"The car is fine. Come with me."

"What's going on?" I asked.

"You'll see."

We walked up the lit pathway past the well-groomed shrubs. I tried to see inside the windows, but they were covered with shades.

"Did someone buy this place and turn it into a restaurant?"

"It's not a restaurant." Ian walked to the front welcome mat and glibly motioned toward the door. Another single red rose was tucked through the ring of the lion's head brass door knocker.

I looked at Ian for an explanation. His face was ruddy. His grin jubilant.

"For you." He handed me the rose. Then reaching for the latch, he said, "And also for you."

He opened the front door of the Forgotten Rose Cottage. "Welcome home, Miranda."

Chapter Eighteen

I couldn't move.

"Come." Ian held out his hand to me and invited me over the threshold.

The cottage was lit by firelight and by the flickering amber hope of a dozen votives strategically placed in the sparsely furnished room.

The long stem rose in my hand shook.

"Ian, how . . . ?"

"I'll tell you everything soon enough. Just drink in the moment, Miranda."

In front of us, an earnest stack of logs burned golden in the hearth. The only furniture I saw was a table with four chairs inside the kitchen area and a plush leather loveseat positioned in front of the fire.

On the polished wood floor I noticed a trail of rose petals. As my eyes adjusted to the soft light, I saw that the rose petals led to a Christmas tree in the corner. Ian flipped a light switch by the door, and the tree lit up.

"Ian, it's a Christmas tree!"

"That it is."

"Ian, you got me a Christmas tree."

"That I did."

I followed the rose petal trail to the medium-sized, stout tree. It looked magical in its covering of starry lights. I imagined it had, no doubt, been hewn by Ian and carted here in his convertible. I now understood Ellie's earlier message about Ian not being "ready." The man had been busy today.

As I approached, I noticed something besides the tiny white lights was attached to every branch. And then I saw what it was.

Roses.

Red roses. Dozens and dozens of red rosebuds. They hung like ornaments and nestled in the branches like birds' nests.

The sight was beautiful beyond words. I stood, stared, blinked, and cried a little as I tried to take it in.

"Did you do all this?"

"I had a little help from Katharine."

Ian knew I never had had a Christmas tree. My mother and I never had one. Doralee didn't believe in them. And once I was on my own in an apartment, it seemed silly to pay for a tree when I had no ornaments to decorate it. To the occasional friend or office associate who visited me at Christmastime and remarked about the absence of a tree, I always said I was doing my part to help the environment.

When Ian had found out last Christmas that I never had put up a tree, he said, "One day you'll have your tree, and it will bloom in roses just for you."

At the time, I had thought he was trying to unveil to me his poetic side. I had no idea this romantic man of mine was making plans. Plans that were being unfurled tonight. This was my Christmas tree, and it was covered with roses.

Ian wrapped his arms around me and kissed the side of my neck. "You are my rose, Miranda. And you are forgotten no more."

My tears fell lightly on his arms as he held me secure.

"And this place is no longer 'Forgotten Rose Cottage.' We'll give it a new name." He kissed my shoulder and then my neck. I drew in the fragrant scent of the evergreen tree.

"Ian, I can't believe all this."

"Believe it."

"How did you...?"

"Come and sit." He led me to the loveseat.

"Explain all this to me," I said.

"The cottage is yours, Miranda."

"How? Did you buy it?"

"No."

"Then who? How...?"

Ian got up, walked to the fire, and placed another log on the stack. Leaning against the mantel, he said, "Your father bought the cottage twelve years ago."

"My father?"

"Yes. Sir James, I've been told, was as taken with the property as you were when you first saw it. He bought it without many people knowing because he wanted to use it as his painting studio. That's his table in the kitchen, and the sofa you're sitting on was his as well."

My hand instantly went to the dark brown leather and smoothed over the surface. *My father sat here by this fire. This was his cottage.*

"I knew how much you loved this place, so I made some inquiries last August. When I found out it belonged to Sir James, I went to Edward to see if I might either purchase the property from the estate or lease it from him. He deliberated for some time with the barristers. Last week, at Edward's request and by his hand, the papers were drawn up to give the property to you as part of your inheritance."

My jaw went slack.

"The cottage is yours."

"If Edward did that, it means he had to tell the lawyers who I am."

Ian nodded.

"Did Margaret agree to all this?"

"As far as she needed to for Edward to make the arrangements."

I leaned back and let the implication of this news sink in. Margaret might not approve of me, but Edward agreed to this. He acknowledged the blood relationship between us.

"Edward has papers for you to sign, of course, and there will be time for meetings with the barristers next week to settle all the fine points. The place needs fixing up, but it's yours."

"I can't believe this."

"Believe it. It's true."

The dancing flames in the hearth warmed the smoky, sand-colored stones of the fireplace. Above, on the thick, carved wood mantel, my eye went to a single, long-stemmed red rose that lay rested on the wood beam. Next to the rose was a box. A familiar little white box.

I tried to hide my delight, but the discovery must have

shone in my eyes because Ian cleared his throat and shifted his position.

None of the clever lines that flitted through my thoughts came to rest on my lips. I wanted to tease him, but this didn't seem the moment for that. I would wait for Ian to speak. My answer was ready, as I'm sure he already knew.

"Miranda." Ian gathered up the box and the rose and moved closer to me.

I felt my pulse beat faster.

"You know my heart toward you. It has not wavered from the first. I have set my affections on you and you alone."

Holding out the rose to me, Ian lowered to one knee and took my hand in his. With his soft hazel-brown eyes fixed on mine, he dipped his chin. "Miranda, will you have me for your husband?"

I heard the answer in my heart before it danced off my lips. "Yes. With all my heart, yes."

Ian took the ring from the box and slipped it on my finger. The dainty, platinum ring bumped over my knuckle and settled in its new home. I held out my hand and blinked back the tears.

"The ring belonged to my mother," he said.

"It's beautiful."

"Do you like it, then?"

"I love it." The firelight twinkled in the simple, classic setting. "If I were to pick out a ring, this is what I would have chosen."

Ian settled in beside me and told me how his father, as a young man, had saved his money for years before he could buy

Ian's mother this beautiful ring. "When they married she had a simple, thin band, but my dad always wanted her to have a diamond. When I was a boy, I remember him telling her that every time she looked at the ring she was to remember that she was of great value to him and deeply loved."

I held my hand closer and admired the sparkling diamond and the simple curves of the setting.

"Before my mom died, she took off the ring and gave it to me. She told me to save it because she was sure one day I would meet the right woman. And when I did, she said this ring would whisper to that woman that she is of great value to me and that I loved her deeply."

We drew close for a lingering kiss, and then we kissed again.

"I love you," I whispered.

"And I love you."

Ian drew back. "So, the next question is, when?"

"When what?"

"When will you make good on your promise to marry me?"

"Soon."

"Yes, but when?"

"I was thinking springtime might be nice. It would be pretty here then, wouldn't it? We could have our reception in the garden."

"It might rain, but we know how to adapt to a little rain."

"I would like the service to be at the old church in Carlton Heath."

"Of course."

"In front of the stained glass window."

"Whatever you wish."

"And I'd like to move to Carlton Heath before the spring. The sooner the better."

"It's your home."

"It's our home," I said. "This will be our home."

I had no words after that. Only a few slow tears and a full heart.

Resting my head on Ian's shoulder, I looked at the fire and then closed my eyes. I thought I should say something. Nothing came. Only peace. A deep, abiding peace.

We kissed again, and Ian murmured in my ear, "Are you sure you want to wait all the way until spring? What if I went out and found us an agreeable minister and brought him back here this evening?"

I laughed. "On Christmas Eve?"

Before Ian could press his idea of hunting down a minister, we heard noise coming from outside. It seemed to be coming from the walkway.

"Were you expecting someone?" I asked.

"Ahh!" Ian checked his watch. "They're early. I should have guessed they would be early."

"Who's early?"

Just then we heard the clear, true notes of Mark and Julia's voices as they began singing on our doorstep.

"It's our Christmas Eve supper via special delivery," Ian said. "And from the sounds of it, I'm guessing it's our evening entertainment as well."

Chapter Nineteen

Together Ian and I went to the front door to welcome the Whitcombe family. Ellie and Edward were each holding one of the beautifully decorated picnic hampers I had seen Ellie filling earlier in her kitchen. Julia jitter-wiggled her way right over the threshold and wrapped her arms around my middle.

"Did you know?" Julia asked. "I tried very hard to keep the secret, but Mummy said you might have guessed."

"No, I didn't guess a thing about the cottage." I looked up at Edward with an intense gaze of gratitude and said, "Thank you, Edward. Thank you so much."

"What about the tree?" Julia asked. "Aunt Katharine told me about the tree, but she said I mustn't tell. Do you like it?"

"Yes. Very, very much."

"What about the proposal?" Ellie asked. Then opening her eyes wide and slapping her hand over her mouth, she said in a small voice, "He has asked you already, hasn't he? We did give you enough time, Ian, did we not?"

"Plenty of time." Ian took the heavy basket from Ellie. "I asked her, and she said yes. There's not much to tell."

I swatted playfully at his arm for the way he had so quickly downplayed the intensely emotional last thirty minutes of our lives.

"Of course she said yes." Ellie gave me a hug and reached for my hand to see the beautiful ring.

Everyone admired it appropriately, and Ellie said, "Did you need the hanky?"

I realized everything had happened so fast that I hadn't thought to reach for the hanky. I also realized I still had on my coat. Unfastening the clasps, I removed my coat and slipped into the role of hostess of the "No Longer Forgotten Rose Cottage."

I said, "May I take your coats?"

"We might have hangers in the bedroom closet," Ian said. "I haven't checked."

I gathered all the coats the way Ellie had in the cloakroom at Grey Hall and went to the back of the cottage to the bedroom. It was empty except for two blank canvases propped against the wall and a collapsed easel beside them.

My father's unfinished paintings.

In a way, I was also one of his unfinished paintings. The canvas of my life and Ian's from here on out were blank and ready to be painted. This was a place of new beginnings for us.

The closet was empty and void of hangers, so I stacked the coats on the floor and turned to join the others. However, Mark had stepped into the bedroom and was standing nearby as if he had something to say.

"I wanted you to know that I did what you said." Mark looked solemn.

I wasn't sure what he meant.

"I told my grandmother what I had overheard her saying to my father about you."

"Oh. Good. That was good, Mark. What did she say?"

"She was not pleased, I will tell you that. She said I should keep the information to myself."

I nodded my agreement.

"I thought you should know."

"Thank you, Mark." I smiled at him, hoping to put him more at ease. "You did the right thing."

"You did the right thing as well." He was sounding awfully mature. "I was glad you told me the truth. I'm not as young as they all think I am. I know much more than they think I do."

"What about also telling your parents? I think they would like to know what you heard and what you know at this point."

"I don't think my parents would understand."

"You might be surprised. Talking to them would be a good thing for all of you."

I knew Ellie and Edward would appreciate the gift of their teenage son opening up to them. He had gone to Margaret on his own. Perhaps the rest would come without my nudging.

I put my hand on Mark's shoulder and said in my most sincere voice, "I love you, Mark. I want you to know that."

"I know." He looked away.

Without prolonging the moment, I said, "Good. Now let's go see what your mom brought in those baskets."

Mark and I joined the others as Ellie finished laying out

her abundant Christmas Eve dinner spread. She had thought of everything for our picnic by the fire. We had sliced cold ham and four different sorts of cheese with stone-ground wheat bread. The gourmet assortment of mustards, pickles, and olives gave us an exceptional variety to choose from. There also was a creamy pasta salad with peas.

I had just finished helping Ellie put out an assortment of little cakes when she instructed everyone on where to begin with all the goodies. She had spread out a blanket for the children to sit on the floor since the number of seats was limited.

Out of the corner of my eye, I caught Mark's disgruntled acceptance of his being one of the "children" who would have to sit on the lowly blanket.

I didn't think it would be humanly possible to feel any happier than I did at that moment. The only person missing was Margaret. I concluded that her absence was her choice and an indication of how things would be from here on out. Some things might not be mendable. I had every piece of the family puzzle except the Margaret piece.

I focused back on the moment and the circle of people who were making this Christmas Eve picnic a festive celebration of our engagement. The laughter and words of praise for Ellie's culinary delights were punctuated by a subtle vibrating sound followed by a beep. The source of the buzz and bing was Edward's cell phone.

He ignored it each time, but due to the frequency of the prompts, Ellie finally said, "You really should have a listen. It could be something amiss with your mother."

Edward stepped into the vacant bedroom while the rest of

us carried on our merriment. A moment later he returned to the living room with a grave expression on his face. Everyone looked at him, waiting for an explanation. All he did was motion for me to join him in the other room.

"Is everything okay?" I asked, once we were around the corner from the others.

"I thought you should see this." Edward held out his phone so I could view the picture displayed on the small screen.

I squinted until the image became clear.

All the air seemed to siphon out of the room. My hand went to my mouth as I whispered, "Oh no."

Chapter Twenty

Is that me?" I asked Edward, hoping it wasn't but knowing it was. "Is that a picture of me?"

"Apparently it is. Can you read the headlines?"

"Yes."

"This hit the newsstands in London an hour ago."

"How did the press find out? How did they get my picture?"

"I thought you might be able to tell me."

I shook my head and felt my fingers go numb.

Ian stepped into the room just then, and reading the expression on my face, he came to my side. "What's happened? What is it?"

Edward showed him the picture. I was facing the camera, but I had no particular expression.

"I can't make out the headline," Ian said.

In an emotionless voice, Edward repeated the news line header. " 'Sir James Had a Love Child.' "

Ian ran his fingers through his hair. "We have to quench this before it goes any further."

"It's already on the Internet," Edward said. "And syndicated press. My assistant has been monitoring the situation. Miranda, who knows about your identity? Who do you think might have leaked this?"

Mark was the first person who came to mind. Mark was upset, true, but he was only thirteen. He wouldn't release such information to the press. Or would he?

Then I remembered who else knew. And so did Ian.

He punched his right fist into the palm of his left hand. "It was your old boyfriend, wasn't it? He sold you out to the tabloids."

"I can't imagine Josh would do that." I looked at the picture again on Edward's phone, trying to make out the background to understand where I had been when the picture was taken. "That's the sweater I wore when I arrived in London. So it is a recent photo."

I looked up at Ian. "I don't want to believe it was Josh, but..."

"Where's your phone?" Ian asked. "You have his number, don't you? Is he still in London?"

"I don't know. I think I have his card in my coat pocket but—"

Ian was across the room in one swift motion. He pulled out Josh's business card and punched the number into my phone.

I rubbed the tightening muscles on the back of my neck. "If that's his business number, he probably won't be there since it's Christmas Eve."

Ian couldn't hear me, so he held the phone to the side of his ear with the screen facing me. When he turned the phone that way, an instant memory came back to me.

"Paddington station," I said. "The guy at Paddington station who offered me his seat. He's the one who took the photo of me. He took it with his cell phone."

"Are you sure?" Ian asked.

"I'm pretty sure. It makes sense. The man was close enough to overhear me talking to Josh. When he offered me a seat, it seemed a little odd, but I didn't think much of it at the time."

"Let me understand this." Edward's expression stiffened. "You're saying you told a stranger at Paddington your connection to us?"

"No. Josh isn't a stranger. He's my old boyfriend. A number of years ago I showed Josh the Father Christmas photograph with you and your dad... I mean, our dad...." I felt awkward changing the words to "our dad," but that was the truth.

Ian closed my phone, disconnecting the call to Josh.

"I didn't expect to see Josh at Paddington. It was a coincidence, and it just seemed right to tell him why I was here since..."

Ian took up my defense. "Josh was the one who urged Miranda to come to Carlton Heath in the first place."

"That's right. And he's a professional counselor, so I would like to think I can trust him to maintain confidentiality. I didn't think anyone could hear me when I was talking to him; it was so noisy at the station. But then this man got up from the bench behind us and held his cell phone the way Ian just did, and I think he took my picture with his phone."

"Well then, that's it." Edward reached for his phone and pressed some numbers. "I have calls to make."

I felt my chest compress. I suddenly understood much more clearly why Margaret and Edward had appeared so devastated last Christmas when I had revealed my identity to them. As a family, they had finally experienced a short break from all the media attention after Sir James passed away. My appearance meant it was only a matter of time before they ceased being a private family once more. And now that day had come.

I felt sick to my stomach about it all. "I wish this hadn't happened."

"Well, it has," Ian said in a comforting voice. "So we go on from here."

Edward's demeanor was as reserved and steady as ever as he finished his phone call and turned to Ian and me with direction. "I've conferred with our legal counsel. We had a plan in place for when this might happen. I've made the necessary calls, and now all the steps will be put in motion."

"What steps exactly?" I asked.

"We've put out a call for a press conference the day after tomorrow. Better to air our side of the story on Boxing Day than on Christmas. I can assist you in preparing your remarks. I will go on camera, but Mother will not."

"Wait, Edward. I'm not following you. What do you mean a press conference? Aren't we trying to avoid the press?"

"We have a system. This was routine when my father was alive. The press wants a story. We want peace and quiet. If we don't give them a story, they create their own. Therefore, we control the story through our network of publicists and reporters. All you'll need to do is go on camera for thirty seconds, ninety at the most. You'll deliver a prepared statement. It's best if you can do it without notes."

I felt as if the room had tilted. Ian put his strong arm around me.

Edward looked at his watch. "I've alerted our security service. They'll be at the gate when we return to the house tonight in case the paparazzi are waiting. It would be best if you rode back with us rather than in Ian's car."

"Edward, I'm so, so sorry."

"We all supposed this day would come," Edward said matter-of-factly.

"I just hate that it did," I said. "I don't like thinking about what this will do to Margaret. It's going to change what everyone thinks of her and what they think of Sir James."

Edward looked at me with what could almost be considered a softening in his expression. "Miranda, this is going to change how people view you as well. Have you thought about that?"

No, I hadn't thought about that. My eyes welled with tears, but I refused to let them fall.

Ian drew me close. "Calm yourself, Miranda. We'll work this out together."

Edward exited the room. I could hear him giving an abbreviated summary to the adults in the other room. When Ian and I entered, I noticed that Ellie had taken Julia into the kitchen to distract her young ears.

Mark, however, sat with the adults. "You needn't speak in code, Father. I already know."

I couldn't tell if Mark's announcement startled Edward. What I did know was that Mark was trying his best to prove his place as an adult in the Whitcombe clan.

I knew I would do well to follow his example and be brave.

Chapter Twenty-one

As Edward predicted, a gathering of photographers awaited us as the town car with its darkened windows rolled up to the front gate of the Whitcombe manor. In all the times I'd come and gone from the house, I never had seen the gate closed or the security booth manned, which it was tonight.

"This is how it used to be," Mark said to me.

Ellie, in her eternally effervescent optimism, said, "Do you remember that, Markie? You liked the guard at the back garden post. What was his name? He had the big dog with the white spot on its nose."

"Raymond," Mark said. "The guard was Raymond, and his dog was Digger."

"That's right. Perhaps Raymond and Digger will be back at their post."

I tried to imagine how Ellie had carved out such a successful marriage and journeyed through motherhood with guards, dogs, and paparazzi as part of the everyday schedule.

We rolled through the open gate, and cameras flashed against the car's darkened windows. I looked down, just in case the cameras captured an image in spite of the shades. Edward and Ellie didn't flinch. They seemed confident in their anonymity inside the specially prepared car.

"You'll want to use this." Edward pulled a large, black umbrella out from under the seat. "With such advancements in telescopic lenses, it's best to exit with the umbrella between yourself and the front gate."

I followed Edward's instructions and opened the huge umbrella once I was outside the car and then used it as a covering for the six or so feet I crossed to the front door. The rest of the family used umbrellas as well and entered behind me. A tall man dressed all in black with a cord hanging from his right ear greeted me in the entryway and took the umbrella from me.

"Subject is clear," he said to whomever was at the other end of his sophisticated communication system.

I wasn't quite sure what to do, so I thanked him and looked to Edward for direction. This was all different from how things had been at the house a few hours ago. Yet Ellie and Edward acted as if the presence of all these people in their home were normal.

Edward was carrying a sleeping Julia in his arms. Ellie was ushering Mark forward. Ian was the last to enter. Behind him I could see the faint flash of cameras like distant lightning.

"Off to bed with you, Mark," Ellie said. "We have an early morning! When you wake up, it will be Christmas."

Mark looked sullen. He wasn't to be tempted off to bed with the promise of new toys in the morning. His serious, adult leanings were in full play tonight.

"I think I should be allowed to sit in on your meeting, Mum and Dad."

Edward and Ellie exchanged glances.

"I heard you, Father, when you were talking on the phone with Grandmother before we left the cottage. You said you plan to talk with everyone tonight. I should like to be included."

"All right then, Mark. You may sit with us. Let me put your sister into bed first. Ian, would you start a fire for us in the drawing room?"

"I can start the fire, Father." Mark spoke with a stubborn edge to his voice.

"That would be lovely, Mark," Ellie said, taking over directions for Edward. "While you and Uncle Ian start the fire, Miranda and I will get a pot of tea brewing."

I followed Ellie into the kitchen while Ian trailed Mark into the drawing room.

"How do you do this, Ellie?"

"Do what?"

"This life you guys have. Everyone is taking this alert status so calmly. I feel horrible that Edward had to call in security on Christmas Eve, of all nights. These men should be home with their families."

"They'll be home for Christmas. Edward has a sophisticated rotation plan. It's not as bad as it might seem. For any of us. We're used to it, Miranda. You'll get used to it too. Life will go back to normal quickly. You'll see. Today's news is always tomorrow's liner for the canary cage. That's what Sir James used to say."

Ellie put the teakettle on the stove and looked around the

clean kitchen. "Natasha did a lovely job cleaning up. I'm afraid I left her with quite a mess."

Glancing at me in my still unconvinced slump, she continued her cheer-up talk. "Now, don't worry, Miranda. This will blow over. These media explosions always do. It may seem like a mess now, but it will settle. You'll be old news before you know it."

Lowering myself onto one of the stools at the counter, I said, "I still want to apologize."

"For what?"

"For the inconvenience this breaking news is to you and your family, but especially to Margaret."

"You could always tell her that, couldn't you? I mean, it wouldn't hurt to say such things to her at this point. You're saying them from your heart, and that does make all the difference, doesn't it?"

I nodded, but instead of making an effort to face Margaret, I lingered in the kitchen. My excuse was that Ellie needed help to prepare a tea tray with six china teacups and saucers. We used the same silver tray from which Julia and I had been served our princess breakfast in bed. I had a feeling that this tea party would be anything but cozy and giggly, though.

Ellie carried the tray to the drawing room while I followed with another tray laden with grapes, cheese, cookies, and cream and sugar for the tea.

The long, low coffee table that sat in the center of the circled seating area was decorated with a small nativity scene in the middle. I remembered seeing the hand-carved figurines in Ellie's kitchen window last Christmas.

We lowered the two trays to either end of the coffee table, leaving the miniature nativity set unruffled in the center.

For some reason, that was important to me. It was, after all, Christmas Eve. Christ's birth, that generous gift to us from Father God, was the center of this holiday celebration. It was in this home a year ago that that truth was made real to me. I needed to know now, even if it was demonstrated in only this subtle way, that the nativity was still the focal point of this night and this home.

Margaret already was seated in the drawing room by the fire, but I avoided making eye contact with her. I was aware that all the window shades were drawn. The lights on the tree were lit, but they didn't seem to cast the same merry twinkle across the room as they had that morning. The furniture had been pulled around in a half circle facing the fire.

"Would everyone like tea then?" Ellie asked as, with expert ease, she poured from the silver teapot. I assisted by passing around the steaming cups of tea balanced on the saucers.

When I handed Margaret her cup, our eyes met for a flicker of a second. "I understand congratulations are in order," she said.

"Yes, thank you," I said.

Ian added, "Miranda agreed to be my wife. In spite of all the uproar, this is a very happy night for us."

"Indeed," Margaret said.

I wished the right words would come to me at that moment and I could say to Margaret what was on my heart. But I froze with a simplistic sort of smile sitting on my lips in a wavy line.

Edward picked up the conversation from there.

"I will start by giving everyone a summary of the current situation."

He went through the list of who had been contacted, where the security was in effect, and what was scheduled for the media interview the day after Christmas.

All of this seemed so un-American to me. Disaster was at our doorstep, and we were settled around a fire, drinking tea, planning our civilized counterattack.

Edward continued. "I was reminded by one of my advisors that this will pass quickly due to some of the other more scandalous happenings in the news at the moment."

I hadn't kept up on British or world news for the past few days, so I wasn't aware of what scandalous happenings were going on, but I did hold onto what Ellie had said in the kitchen about how this bit of news would pass quickly. I knew things would be intense for a few days and probably shaky for the rest of my stay. But then was it possible the big rush of the media would be over?

I hoped so.

As Edward concluded his update, I began to breathe a little more deeply and steadily. I was trying to muster up the courage to say something that would let Margaret know how much I regretted bringing this upon their home, especially at Christmas.

Before I could speak up, Mark said, "May I say something, Father?"

"Yes, Mark."

"A person should not be blamed for something that's not their fault. Isn't that right?"

"Yes." Edward was looking at Mark as if he wasn't sure where the conversation was headed.

"So a person like Aunt Miranda should not be blamed because of who her father was."

An odd hush settled on the gathering. If there was any doubt Mark understood what was going on, that doubt was now removed.

"There are a few more complications, son. It's not as easy as all that."

Margaret shifted in her chair. I had a feeling she was about to get up and leave.

Mark, who had been watching my expression, said, "I did not choose that you would be my father. Aunt Miranda did not choose who would be her father either. None of us can choose who his or her parents will be. Wouldn't you agree, Grandmother?"

Edward jumped in, deflecting the curved question Mark had tossed at Margaret. "We may not have our choice as to how we come in to the Whitcombe clan, Mark, but it is up to each of us how we choose to live with the Whitcombe burdens and blessings."

His statement seemed to settle equally on all of us in the room. My first thought went to how many blessings this family had received. My next thought was that I might very well be the burden each of them would have to bear.

Ian reached over and took my hand, giving it an encouraging squeeze.

"I propose," Edward continued, "the less said on this topic, the better for the time being."

"Right," Ellie agreed. Popping up, she reached for the silver serving tray. "What do you say we all turn in for the night? You know, Mark, we have lots of days ahead of us that we'll be together. We can always talk later, can't we? What if we all get some sleep? What do you say to that?"

Margaret was the first to rise and leave the room. Mark trailed her, with Ellie following him carrying one of the tea trays. Ian, Edward, and I were left by the waning fire.

For a few minutes none of us spoke. Ian was the one to break the silence. "I want you to know, Edward, that I appreciate how you've supported Miranda and me, especially the past few months. You have put a fine and noble effort out there for both of us, and I know your father would be pleased with how you've handled the blessing of being a Whitcombe."

"Not at all." Edward brushed off the comment as he stood up, preparing to leave the room. "I'll keep both of you informed should there be any changes in our plans or schedule. Ellie said she wants to prepare a family brunch for us at around ten o'clock tomorrow morning. We'll see you then, of course."

I looked down at my hands. The light from the fire reflected on my engagement ring and sparked in me a sweet glimmer of hope.

I held onto that glimmer through the night as I slept in the upstairs guest room. My sleep was restless. I would doze off for a few hours and then awaken with a horrible mixture of elation over remembering that Ian and I were engaged, quickly followed by the heaviness that stayed on me after Margaret left the drawing room.

When the filtered morning light finally entered my

chambers, bringing the details of the room into focus, an unexpected, faint signal seemed to go off in my head. The signal was telling me to leave. Run. Jump ship now. Go! Get far away from this place and these people.

Let this be your great closing scene on these relationships, Miranda. Now is your chance to prove how invisible you can be. Quietly gather your belongings right now and leave. No curtain call. Just go.

That's what my mother would have done. I knew where those thoughts were coming from. I knew the ancient fire from which they were forged.

But I was not a mirror image of my mother, just as I was not consciously reflective of my father. I was a unique blend of the two in the innermost parts of my makeup. But mostly I was myself. I was free to make my own decisions.

And my decision was to marry Ian and settle here in Carlton Heath.

Chapter Twenty-two

Due to my restless sleep, I stayed in bed and slept much later than I expected. It was after nine by the time I was up and dressed and on my way downstairs. Last Christmas jet lag had awakened me along with early riser Julia, and the two of us had quietly watched the snow fall.

This year she must have had instructions to leave me to my slumber because I wasn't aware that she had tried to wake me.

Making my way downstairs, I could hear voices coming from the drawing room around the tree. With a determined heart, I put on my best Christmas morning smile and stopped at the open door of the drawing room. Around the tree sat Ellie, Edward, Mark, and Julia. They were opening gifts and taking pictures. None of them noticed I was in the doorway.

I decided to pull back and not enter into their family gift exchange the way I had the previous year. Instead of being with the Whitcombe foursome, I faced what I had been avoiding all last night—that I needed to talk with the matriarch of the family. I needed to tell her from my heart, as Ellie had said, how sorry I was for the situation she was facing.

Since Margaret wasn't with the others around the tree, I assumed she was in her apartments at the end of the hall.

With each step down the long hallway, I felt my heart beat a little faster. I wished Ian were with me, but he was accompanying Katharine to the hospital this morning to take Andrew home. Besides, I knew this was a conversation I needed to have alone with Margaret.

I paused in the middle of the hallway. To the right was a series of small, rectangular windows positioned at eye level. Each window was painted with a small pink rosebud in the center. Margaret had painted the rosebuds, just as she had embroidered the handkerchiefs with rosebuds.

The irony of the symbol that seemed to represent so much to both of us settled on me as I looked out the window into the back garden. Just down the lane was a cottage—my cottage—with a Christmas tree—my Christmas tree—covered in red roses. Margaret and I were both women who had been romanced and loved and who carried with them tender images of the beauty of that love.

I hated being the living, breathing evidence that Sir James had at one moment been unfaithful to his love for Margaret. Yet Mark was so right when he said that wasn't my fault.

Pressing my feet forward toward Margaret's apartments, I tried to rehearse what I would say to her. None of the practice sentences cooperated nicely as I tried to line them up.

Standing for a moment before the closed door, I drew in a

deep breath. I still didn't know what I would say. But I did know that my heart toward Margaret was sympathetic and sincere. My feelings toward our complicated situation were simple. I wanted peace. Grace and peace and, just like the motto that was etched over the front door of this home.

My father was the one who put the motto over the door. Grace and Peace Reside Here.

Without realizing it, as I repeated the motto, my hand rose and covered my heart as if I were about to make a pledge. My whispered prayer right before I knocked on Margaret's door was, "May grace and peace reside here, in my heart, as well."

My hand rose and knocked four taps.

"Come." Margaret's voice from behind the door sounded strong.

I pressed open the door and saw her seated in one of the dark red chairs that flanked the fireplace in her spacious apartment. A warm fire glowed in the hearth. Soft Christmas carols played in the background. The window shades were down. A vanilla-scented candle flickered on the round table between the two chairs.

She didn't turn to see who it was, so I asked, "Margaret, would it be all right if I came in?"

"Yes." She still didn't turn to face me.

I never had been inside her quarters. As I approached the fireplace, I saw the morning newspaper on the floor beside her chair. My photo was there—front-page news. Seeing it so boldly displayed made me feel sick to my stomach.

She turned to look at me, and I could see her eyes were red and swollen. I stepped closer. Her stature seemed to diminish by the large chair. Her expression was that of a young child and not that of a fierce matriarch.

My lips seemed to stick together, and my throat felt as if it were swelling shut. The first words that peeped out before I could stop them were, "Margaret, I am so sorry."

Then more words tumbled out from my heart. "I want to apologize to you, Margaret. I've brought complications to your life. I hate that my existence has been a source of pain for you. I realize you have no reason to take me into your home, let alone into your heart. Especially now, with this on the front page of the newspaper and with reporters lining up at the gate. But I have to tell you that all I want is peace between us. Grace and peace."

Margaret motioned for me to sit in the chair across from her in front of the fire. Her gaze was on the fire, not on me. She took a long while before responding. I waited, practicing the same sort of grace and peace toward her that I was asking her to show to me.

When she spoke, it was in a low and weary voice. "I do believe that, if my husband were still here, he would have welcomed you into our home without reservation. He would not have hesitated to show you his love, his approval, and his kindness. He would have expressed great joy today to hear of your engagement."

Her words warmed me. But only for a moment.

"However, my husband is no longer here. And I am not my husband. It is up to me to choose, as my son said, how I will respond to the blessings and burdens that come with being a Whitcombe."

I nodded, waiting for her to continue.

"Mark was right, of course. It's not your fault you were born. Yet..." Lowering her chin, Margaret continued. "I heard something last evening at Grey Hall. I don't think the woman who said it realized I was within hearing distance."

I immediately thought of the way I had spoken too loudly at Paddington station. Was Margaret about to compare my mistake to the way one of the Carlton Heath busybodies had failed to exercise discretion?

Margaret apparently had another objective in mind. "One of the women asked who you were and why you were seated in our row. She wondered if you were a friend of Ellie's. The other woman stated that she had heard that you were the daughter of a homeless, unwed mother and that the Whitcombes had taken you in."

I couldn't argue with the description. It was true.

"Mark followed me to my rooms last evening," Margaret continued. "He was quite set on making his point clear to me. I tried to explain that he did not understand the implications of the scandal of your birth. He sat in that chair where you are sitting now, and he said to me, 'Grandmother, is Christmas not also about a scandalous birth?' I have been thinking on this for most of the night."

"I would never compare my mother with Mary," I said quickly.

"Nor I," Margaret echoed firmly. "Yet a few curious parallels are in play."

"I don't know about that, but I do accept what the woman said at Grey Hall. I am the daughter of an unwed woman, and yes, I think it could be said that she was homeless."

"That may be, Miranda." Margaret looked at me for the first time. "But you are also the daughter of a fine and noble man who had a well-established home. He would have wanted me to receive you as his own. I suppose I have gained an odd sort of sympathy for Joseph in this small drama we seem to be playing out in my home. Joseph chose to enter into the circumstances, as inconvenient as they were. He adopted the Christ child as his."

Once again, I wanted to dismantle the parallels Margaret was drawing between Jesus' family and the Whitcombe family. I didn't think I should be compared to Christ.

But, for some reason, the combination of Mark's words to her and the sympathies she felt toward Mary and Joseph's lives seemed to be the brick and mortar she was using to build a bridge toward me. I was ready to meet her halfway.

Margaret cleared her throat. "You asked a few moments ago if I might extend to you peace. Grace and peace. These are the words my husband had written over the doorpost of this home long ago. He often said those would be the qualities that would mark our family. I regret to say that, with you, I have not remained true to his wish."

With a deep breath, she said, "Miranda, I offer you peace within these walls. You are welcome in this home, in this village, and in this family. I choose to believe that you are not a burden to the Whitcombe family; you are a blessing."

I went to Margaret in one swift motion and offered her my open arms. She responded with surprise at my exuberance. Yet she received my hug, and there was no mistaking the intent of her heart or the intent of mine. Together we were marking a new beginning.

"Thank you," I whispered to her as we drew apart.

"May the Father's grace and peace remain over us," she said as a benediction. I knew she meant our heavenly Father. But for me, in that moment, the term also carried with it the blessing of my birth father.

And that was all I had ever longed for.

Chapter Twenty-three

I left Margaret's quarters a different person. The burden I had carried for the past year of trying to prove myself worthy of acceptance was gone. In its place was a calm assurance. It felt as if the "nativity scene" of my life was now balanced.

I wondered if Margaret had any idea of the immensity of the Christmas gift she had just given me. The week ahead would be one such as I had never experienced. But she had. This was a familiar path for her. Margaret had it within her power to guide me through the deep waters.

For the first time, I believed she would stand beside me through whatever lay ahead.

I was eager to go to the drawing room now, feeling like a different person than the one who had sat at the family meeting in that room the night before.

When I rounded the corner at the end of the long hall and walked into the wide entryway, a rush of cold air filled the open space. The security guard was holding the door as Ian entered with his arm around Andrew. Katharine was right behind them.

I rushed to meet them. Katharine gave me a kiss on my cheek from her chilled lips.

"Look at you!" I said to Andrew. "You're up and going strong. I'm so glad you're here!"

Andrew, the jolly ole elf, caught my eye and raised an eyebrow. He had looked at me that same way a year ago when he had "delivered" Ian to me as the last gift on his Father Christmas rounds. Fixing his expectant expression on mine, he said, "I hear there is news to be told."

"Yes, there is news to be told." I held out my hand. "Very good news."

I looked at Ian, and he winked at me. I winked back.

Returning my gaze to Andrew, I saw a rim of silver tears welled in his eyes.

"You said yes to the man, did ya?" Andrew asked, trying to sound gruff.

"I did."

"And did he go down on his knee?"

"He did."

"Well done." Andrew gave Ian a fatherly nod of approval.

"The ring is beautiful, Andrew. I love it. Thank you." I didn't know exactly what to say for such an extraordinary gift.

"She would have loved you as much as the rest of us." Andrew took my hand to his lips and gave the memory-filled ring a tender kiss. Then he looked up at me with an expression of tender affection.

I started to cry.

I hadn't realized that Margaret had left her apartment and was now part of our gathering in the entryway. Just as I was about to wipe my tears with the back of my hand, I felt a soft hand slip into mine. It was Margaret's. She was handing me a handkerchief. One of her rosebud handkerchiefs.

I looked her in the eye and smiled my appreciation for the small gift with the enormous significance.

The rest of the Whitcombe family joined us in the entryway. Mark looked at his grandmother, and then he looked at me. I made sure he could see that I was holding a pink rosebud handkerchief—Margaret's and my flag of truce. Mark lifted his chin the same way his father often did and gave me a slight nod of acknowledgment that he understood what I was communicating.

Julia wiggled up close to Andrew and was waiting for her chance to say her little hello to him.

"I'm glad you're better now, Uncle Andrew," she said.

"So am I, dear child. So am I."

"Did you see our beautiful Christmas tree? You must come see it." Julia reached for Andrew's hand and tugged for him to come with her to admire it.

"First, we've something important to do."

"What's that?" Julia asked.

"Miranda must make good on her promise and kiss the patient man."

I took two eager steps toward Ian and met his lips, giving him a full kiss. Julia giggled softly.

"What are you doing?" Andrew cried. "I said you were to

kiss the patient man. Have you not heard I was in hospital? I'm the *patient* man here. I meant for you to kiss me!"

Everyone burst out laughing. I made good on my promise. I planted a big kiss on Andrew's cheek.

"That's better. Now, tell me, Ellie, have I come to the right place for some Christmas breakfast? I want to know that I didn't leave the disagreeable porridge of the past few days for nothing."

"Andrew, you came to the right place! I was just about to set out the Christmas buffet. Isn't it wonderful that we're all together? I couldn't be more pleased. It's a gift, isn't it? A lovely blessing. This is going to be the best Christmas ever."

Ian reached his strong arm around my shoulders and drew me close. I had the feeling he was never, ever going to let me go. He pressed his lips to my ear and whispered, "Happy Christmas, Miranda, my rose."

As he heart-meltingly rolled the *r*'s, I leaned in closer and felt my heart filling with the realization that at last I was fully engaged. Not just engaged to Ian. I was engaged to this family. I was a Whitcombe, and soon enough I would become a MacGregor.

The Father of Christmas had once again brought peace on earth. And I was home at last.

Reading Group Guide

1) In this story, the word *engage* takes on many different meanings for Miranda; the most obvious is "engaged to be married." How else is Miranda engaged throughout this story?

2) In the second chapter, Josh says, "I've found that truth has a way of rising to the surface. Sometimes you must wait for the truth to float to the top. Other times you must go to it, take it by the hand, and pull it up with all your might." What do you think he means? Do you agree with his assessment of truth? Look at the discussion between Mark and Miranda on pages 55–58 for more insight. Can you think of a time when truth was revealed in one of these ways in your own life? Briefly describe the experience.

3) Many times in *Engaging Father Christmas,* life doesn't go as planned. List some of these moments in the story. How do you see God's hand working in those moments as the story progresses? Have you ever had moments like this in your life? How was God's plan revealed as time progressed?

4) What do you think Miranda means when she says, "This is the part of Christmas when we can hear heaven and nature sing" (pg. 94)? Miranda thinks about this song phrase a little earlier in the story (pg. 82). Reread this passage. Have you ever had a moment when God seemed as big as He seems to Miranda? Please share this moment with your reading group.

5) In the passage when Mark, Ian, and Miranda stop to enjoy the moon (pgs. 81–83), what words are used to describe the moon? Why do you think the author chose those words? How is this experience a Christmas gift to Mark, Ian, Miranda, and also to God? How do you make a point at Christmastime to give the gift of your worship to God?

6) Mark and Julia's tender love toward the children in the hospital makes a difference in many young lives, including their own. What can you do this Christmas to show God's selfless love to someone in need?

7) Starting on page 99, "Princess Miranda" and "Princess Julia" enjoy breakfast together in bed. This scene reminds Miranda of her early morning Christmas "breakfasts" of chocolates with her mother. Obviously Miranda's childhood Christmas traditions were very different from Julia's. What traditions did you celebrate as a child, and what do you do to celebrate now? How have these traditions given you a sense of identity and belonging?

8) Miranda feels connected to the Forgotten Rose Cottage. How has her life compared with the story of the cottage? Read Jeremiah 29:11–12 and discuss how these verses apply.

9) Sir James was a great artist. He excelled at acting, but he was also interested in painting. On page 126 Miranda discovers her father's unfinished paintings at the Forgotten Rose Cottage. How does Miranda's evaluation of herself as one of her father's unfinished paintings apply to our relationship with Father God, the Master Artist?

10) Miranda's true identity is revealed against her will through circumstances that she has no control over. Even though she and the Whitcombe family wanted to keep the family secret hidden, what good came out of the revelation? What does this tell us about the benefit of unveiling secrets?

11) How does the Christmas story of Jesus' birth play a role in the healing that occurs between Miranda and Margaret? In what ways did this view of His birth affect you?

12) Miranda is much more capable and willing to express love in *Engaging Father Christmas* than she was in *Finding Father Christmas*. What do you think caused this change? How might this apply to your life? Read 1 John 4:7–8.

Return to Carlton Heath with Ian's cousin Anna in
Kissing Father Christmas

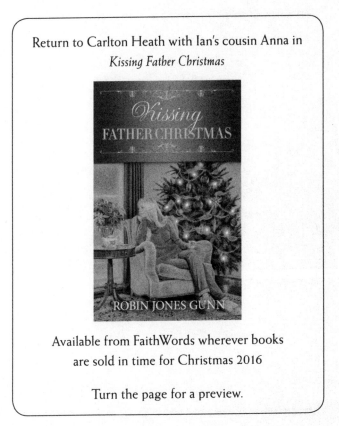

Available from FaithWords wherever books
are sold in time for Christmas 2016

Turn the page for a preview.

Chapter One

I awoke as the pale light of the December morn was finding its way into the upstairs guest room at Whitcombe Manor. The heavy drapes appeared to be etched with a silver lining that trailed like a single thread across the dark wood floor. I propped myself up in the cozy bed and folded my lily-white blond hair into a loose braid, letting it cascade over my shoulder. A contented smile rested on my lips in the hushed room.

I'm really here. I'm back in England.

This place, these people, had been in my waking dreams ever since I came to the enchanting village of Carlton Heath for my cousin's wedding last May. Ian was raised in Scotland, so I'd never met him. His mother passed away several years ago and his fiancée, Miranda, did something I'd never seen before. She included a personal note with their formal wedding invitation. The last line really got to me.

It would mean the world to Ian and me if you could be with us on our special day and represent Ian's mother's side of the family.

Somehow I convinced my mother to make the trek and honor the memory of her sister. We stayed at Whitcombe Manor, the gorgeous estate that had belonged to Miranda's family for generations. It turned into a life-altering experience for both of us. For me, Ian and Miranda's wedding day was the stuff of fairy tales. And I have long been a dreamer and a secret believer in fairy tales.

The men wore dress kilts. Miranda's shimmering white gown had the longest train I'd ever seen. The storybook couple whispered their vows inside a quaint sandstone chapel while holding hands in front of a glowing stained-glass window. Bagpipes played as they exited beneath a bower of woven forest greens dotted with dozens of fragrant, deep red roses. Their reception was held in the gardens at Whitcombe Manor. All the guests kept smiling at them as they danced until the first stars came out to watch them, to bless them.

I fell in love with love that day.

In my twenty-six years as a sheltered only child, I'd never dreamed of so much beauty and such elegantly expressed affection. My parents were practical and efficient and held to the notion that feelings should be kept to oneself and all artistic expressions were for private reflection only. They were minimalists when it came to celebrating birthdays and holidays.

That's why I had never danced before. At least not in public. But at Ian and Miranda's wedding as the stars looked on, everything changed. I knew then that one day I would return to

Carlton Heath. I would once again stay at Whitcombe Manor. Love would draw me back.

Today was that day.

The morning light now infiltrated all the open crevices around the drapes in my guest room. I tossed back the puffy down comforter and padded over to the grand picture window. With a hearty tug I pulled back the thick fabric and watched the room fill with soft light. A puff of swirling dust particles spun in midair.

The garden below that had hosted Ian and Miranda's glorious wedding reception on that pristine day last May now slumbered in a state of deep resignation. The hollyhocks, foxgloves, and vivid pink cosmos were gone. The lights and lanterns as well as the party tables that had been covered in crisp, white linen had been taken down. All that remained were rows of shorn rosebushes and mounds of waiting perennials.

I stared through the thick-paned window, narrowing my eyes and trying to remember the colors, the music, and the expression of sincere intrigue in Peter's pale blue eyes when he held out his hand to me. Every detail of that dreamy night returned to my mind's eye, starting with the moment when Uncle Andrew drew me out on the dance floor in the middle of the festivities. He spun me around with a great bellowing of Scottish pride for his son and new daughter-in-law and I laughed at the sheer boldness of his demeanor.

I felt welcomed into the clan and gladly entered in when Miranda motioned for me to join a circle of young women. We were all soon laughing and holding hands as we jigged forward into a close huddle and then hopped back to expand the circle and invite others to join in. We were like the Midsummer's Eve fairies I'd read about as a child. In my elation, I motioned for my mother to come join us, but she would not.

She watched me from a corner table as if I were someone she'd never met before.

The jig concluded and I chose to take my slice of cake and enjoy it at Uncle Andrew's table. I sat beside his new wife, Katharine, whom I liked very much. She and I sipped tea from china cups and I decided in that moment that these were my people. I had been born into the wrong branch of our family tree. I had grown up in the wrong country.

In the wake of that epiphany, I looked up and saw tall, gregarious Peter Elliott striding across the garden in his best man's kilt and dress jacket. He was coming to me, coming for me.

He held out his hand in a wordless invitation, and without hesitation I placed mine in his. In the glow of a dozen swaying lanterns, we danced. We danced and danced and I was forever changed. His short brown hair and athletic build were instantly fixed in my memory.

As we danced I thought I saw a touch of sadness in the corner of his eyes, and that hint of vulnerability endeared him to me. I hadn't seen it the night before at the rehearsal dinner. At the restaurant he had been the rowdy life of the party with great stories to tell about Ian since the two of them had been friends so long. The camaraderie between Peter and my cousin was impressive. Ian and Miranda trusted Peter and I did, too, when I let him lead me to the dance floor.

Even now I closed my eyes and swayed in front of the guest room window as I remembered how warm his hand felt as he rested it on the small of my back and our eyes did their own sort of dance, connecting for a shy, momentary gaze and then pulling away. We slow danced with our lips drawn up in thin, half-moon slivers.

One dance, then two, then a third and a fourth. We conversed in sparse paragraphs, asking each other about jobs and family and both saying what a beautiful night it was.

The last dance began and Peter asked how long I was staying in Carlton Heath. I said we were leaving in two days.

"Two days? That's not much of a visit," he murmured. "You really should stay on."

"I'd love to stay longer but I can't."

He held me a little tighter. We danced until the music came to a lingering finish, and then it happened.

Peter kissed me.

About the Author

The much loved author of the popular Christy Miller series for teens, Sisterchicks® novels, Father Christmas trilogy, and non-fiction favorites such as *Victim of Grace* and *Spoken For*, Robin's 90 books have sold nearly 5 million copies worldwide. She is also a frequent speaker at local and international events. Robin and her husband live in Hawaii where she continues to write her little heart out. She invites you to visit her website at www.robingunn.com.